Engagement

by Ka

From the desk of E
and CEO of Emera

To: My personal assistant, Luther Freemont
Re: My newly discovered grandsons, Caleb Walker, Nick Daniels and Hunter O'Banyon

The time has come to implement the plans I have for my grandsons. You are to take the corporate jet to collect them for a meeting here in Wichita a week from today. Needless to say, I will not tolerate refusals or excuses of any kind. Once I tell my grandsons who they are and what I expect of them, Caleb will be the first to receive his assignment. I already have a man in place at the financial consulting firm to report back to me on his progress. If Caleb is as intelligent and resourceful as I suspect, he should have no trouble taking over the reins of Skerritt and Crowe and turning it into a profitable venture.

As always, I am relying on your complete discretion in this matter.

Emerald Larson

Tycoon Takes Revenge

by Anna DePalo

Noah's plan was outrageous. So why was she tempted?

Kayla considered him a moment. "What would be the terms of our dating?"

She saw the flare of gratification in his eyes, but he quickly banked it. "Terms?"

"There has to be a time limit," she said firmly.

"Make your best offer," he countered.

"Two weeks."

He shook his head. "Six. These things take time."

"Let's split the difference," she countered. "Four. It shouldn't take long to repair the damage of having to be seen with you in public."

"A pleasure doing business with you." He closed the space between them and held out his hand.

Relief, followed by panic, washed through her. She took his hand, felt her own engulfed in his, and experienced a surge of sensation. She started to draw away, but he pulled her closer. He lifted her chin with his free hand and she had just a moment to lower her eyelids before he brushed her lips with his.

Available in February 2007 from Silhouette Desire

Engagement Between Enemies
by Kathie DeNosky
(The Illegitimate Heirs)
&
Tycoon Takes Revenge
by Anna DePalo

The Man Means Business
by Annette Broadrick
&
Devlin and the Deep Blue Sea
by Merline Lovelace
(Code Name: Danger)

Baby, I'm Yours
by Catherine Mann
&
Her High-Stakes Affair
by Katherine Garbera
(What Happens in Vegas...)

Engagement Between Enemies
KATHIE DeNOSKY

Tycoon Takes Revenge
ANNA DePALO

SILHOUETTE®
Desire™

All the characters in this book have no existence outside the imagination of the author, and have no relation whatsoever to anyone bearing the same name or names. They are not even distantly inspired by any individual known or unknown to the author, and all the incidents are pure invention.

First published in Great Britain 2007
Silhouette Books, Eton House, 18-24 Paradise Road, Richmond, Surrey TW9 1SR

ISBN-13: 978 0 373 40227 4
ISBN-10: 0 373 40227 9

51-0207

Printed and bound in Spain
by Litografia Rosés S.A., Barcelona

ENGAGEMENT BETWEEN ENEMIES

by
Kathie DeNosky

KATHIE DeNOSKY

lives in her native southern Illinois with her husband and one very spoiled Jack Russell terrier. She writes highly sensual stories with a generous amount of humour. Kathie's books have appeared on the Waldenbooks bestseller list and received the Write Touch Readers' Award from WisRWA and the National Readers' Choice Award. She enjoys going to rodeos, travelling to research settings for her books and listening to country music. Readers may contact Kathie at: PO Box 2064, Herrin, Illinois 62948-5264, USA or e-mail her at kathie@kathiedenosky.com.

This book is dedicated with deepest appreciation
to Kristi Gold, Roxann Delaney, Mary Gardner
and my editor, Tina Colombo. Without their
encouragement and unwavering support,
this book would not have been possible.

Prologue

Caleb Walker sat at the small round table in the corner of a downtown Wichita, Kansas, hotel bar, staring at the two men seated across from him. Not even the blond waitress giving him an interested smile and the fact that he hadn't had sex in a month of Sundays diverted his attention from the matter at hand.

All of his life, he'd been a man without siblings and with no idea who his father was. But not more than an hour ago, in a plush executive office at the corporate headquarters of Emerald, Inc., all that had changed. Caleb had learned that his father was none other than globe-trotting playboy and heir apparent to the Emerald, Inc. empire, Owen Larson. The late Owen Larson.

Now Caleb was having to come to terms with the fact not only that he knew who his father was, but that the man had gone and gotten himself killed in a boating accident off the coast of France before Caleb had had the chance to confront him for making Caleb's mother pregnant and leaving her without so much as a by-your-leave. He'd also learned that his grandmother was the indomitable Emerald Larson and that the two men sitting across from him were his half brothers.

"I can't believe we've been under that old bat's surveillance all of our lives." A muscle jerked along Hunter O'Banyon's tanned jaw. "She knew everything there was to know about us and didn't do a damned thing to fill us in on the big mystery until now."

"That 'old bat' is our grandmother. And I'd say she's done plenty." Nick Daniels took a swig from the long-necked bottle in his hand, then set it on the table with a thump. "Hiring P.I.s to report our every move from the time we were out of diapers while keeping us in the dark about it takes balls."

"The size of watermelons," Caleb added. His gut still churned with anger that Emerald Larson, founder and CEO of one of the nation's most successful female-owned and operated conglomerates, had denied them all the right to know who they were for so long. "I'm having a problem with her blackmailing our mothers with the threat of cutting us out of inheriting any part of Emerald, Inc. just to keep them silent about her worthless son being the jerk who got them pregnant." He shook his head in disbelief. "I'll give her this much, the old gal's a master at manipulation."

Nick nodded. "I can understand why our moms went along with her. They were hoping to ensure a better life for us. But they paid a hell of a price for it."

"I don't give a damn about inheriting any part of Emerald Larson's little self-made empire." Hunter shook his head. "Hell will freeze over before I dance to her tune."

"So you're going to turn down her offer?" Caleb asked.

If they accepted Emerald's conditions, they'd each be given one of her companies. She'd assured them there were no strings attached and she wouldn't interfere with the way they ran the businesses. But Caleb wasn't fool enough to believe it. It looked like his brothers weren't either.

"I haven't flown a chopper in the past five years." Hunter's mouth thinned to a menacing line. "What business would I have trying to run an air medevac service?"

"Well, it makes more sense than sending a desk jockey to run a cattle ranch in Wyoming." Nick's scowl deepened. "I've lived in a condo in St. Louis for the past twelve years. The closest I get to any kind of livestock these days is the Clydesdales when they pull a beer wagon down Market Street during a parade."

Caleb had to agree that what Emerald Larson was asking them to do was ludicrous. He'd excelled in the business courses he'd taken in high school, but that had been a good number of years ago. He didn't particularly like the idea of making a fool of himself when it became apparent he was in way over his head.

"Well, how do you think I feel?" He shook his head at the thought of what the old gal had in mind for him. "I'm a Tennessee farmer with nothing more than a high-school education. Emerald couldn't have come up with anything more ridiculous than me taking over a financial consulting firm."

Hunter reached for a pretzel from the bowl in the middle of the table. "You can bet that old girl has more up her sleeve than giving us part of Emerald, Inc. out of the goodness of her heart."

"No doubt about it," Nick said, nodding.

Caleb wasn't sure exactly what Emerald Larson had in mind, but he knew just as surely as the sun rose in the east each morning that whatever it was, she'd purposely chosen the business she wanted each of them to run. "It's my guess she wants us to prove something."

Nick looked surprised. "Like what? That we don't know what we're doing?"

"Beats me. But you can bet Emerald Larson has a reason for everything she does." Caleb shrugged as he swallowed the last of his beer. "The way I see it, we have two options. We can either turn the old gal down and walk away, making the sacrifices our mothers made to ensure our futures a total waste of time. Or, we can accept Emerald's offer and show her that she doesn't know beans from buckshot about who we are and where our talents lie."

Hunter looked thoughtful. "I kind of like the idea of showing up the high-and-mighty Mrs. Larson."

"It would serve her right when we all fall on our faces," Nick said, still looking reluctant.

"But if we're going to do this, we at least have to give it our best shot." Caleb stood up and tossed a couple of dollar bills on the table. "It's not in me to do anything half-assed."

"Me neither," the other two said in unison as they rose to their feet and added money to pay for their drinks.

"Then I guess all we have left to do is give Emerald our answer." Caleb suddenly felt as if he was about to step out onto a tightrope without a safety net.

But as he led the way out of the bar and down the street toward the corporate offices of Emerald, Inc., he couldn't help but feel a bit of nervous anticipation begin to build. He'd always enjoyed a challenge. And as unbelievable as it was, he was actually looking forward to taking over Skerritt and Crowe Financial Consultants. His only regret was that he didn't have the education or the slightest idea of how to go about doing the job right.

One

Approaching the reception desk outside the executive offices of Skerritt and Crowe Financial Consultants, Caleb plastered on the professional smile he'd been practicing for the past week. "I'm here to see A. J. Merrick."

"Do you have an appointment, sir?" the older, gray-haired receptionist asked as he started toward the doors behind her desk.

"I'm Caleb Walker." He gave her a conspiratorial wink. "I believe Merrick is expecting me."

"Hold it right there, Mr. Walton," she said, rising to block his way.

"Walker." He frowned. Hadn't Merrick let the other

employees know about his taking over as president of the firm?

The woman shrugged. "Walker, Walton, it doesn't matter what your name is. You're not going in there without an appointment."

Apparently, no one had bothered to inform this woman. "Tell you what—" he glanced at the nameplate on her desk "—Geneva. After I talk with your boss, I promise I'll come back and introduce myself."

"My *boss* is busy and doesn't want to be disturbed." Geneva pointed to a row of chairs lining the wall across the room. "If you'll have a seat, I'll see if I can work you in."

At six feet four inches tall, he towered over the woman by at least a foot, but she wasn't acting the least bit intimidated by it. From the look on her face, she was just as determined to keep him out of the office as he was determined he was going inside.

It was all he could do to keep a straight face. Geneva reminded him of a little banty hen his grandpa used to own—all bluff and ruffled feathers. And if her defiant expression was any indication, he had no doubt that he'd be sitting in the reception area until hell froze over before she picked up the phone and announced his arrival.

"There's no need to go to all that trouble, Geneva." Chuckling, he sidestepped the woman as he reached for the polished knob on the mahogany door with A. J.

Merrick engraved on a brass plaque. "Take my word for it, Merrick is going to want to meet with me right away."

"I'll call security," Geneva threatened, rushing over to the phone.

"You do that," Caleb said, nodding. "I'd like to meet with them, too."

"Oh, you will, buster," she promised, stabbing her finger at the phone's keypad.

Without waiting to see if Geneva reached the security desk, Caleb opened the door and stepped into the spacious office. His gaze immediately zeroed in on the young woman seated behind a huge walnut desk in front of a wall of floor-to-ceiling windows.

With her dark auburn hair pulled back in a bun tight enough to make his grandma Walker proud and a pair of oversize black plastic-framed glasses, she looked more like a headmistress at one of those hoity-toity private all-girl schools in Nashville than a modern corporate secretary. And if her disapproving expression was any indication, she was just as unyielding and strict about rules and protocol as one of those overly uptight teachers, too.

But as he sauntered over to stand in front of the desk, he thought he saw a hint of uncertainty about her—a vulnerability that, considering the image she was obviously trying to project, he hadn't expected. "Excuse me. I'm looking for A. J. Merrick."

"Do you have business here?" she asked, her voice cool enough to freeze ice.

Rising to her feet, she pushed her glasses up her pert little nose with a delicate hand, inadvertently drawing attention to her brilliant blue eyes—eyes that sent him a look that would have probably stopped a lesser man dead in his tracks. It didn't faze Caleb one damned bit. On the contrary. He wasn't sure why, but for some reason he found something quite intriguing about her intense blue gaze.

"I'm—"

"If you're looking for personnel, it's down the hall," she said, cutting him off before he had a chance to introduce himself. Pausing, she arched one perfectly shaped eyebrow. "Was Mrs. Wallace at her desk?"

The woman's no-nonsense tone couldn't quite mask the soft, melodic quality of her voice and had Caleb wondering why the sound seemed to bring every one of his male hormones to full alert. Wondering what the hell had gotten into him, he decided it had to be the fact that he hadn't been with a woman in the better part of a year. That alone was enough to make any normal, healthy adult male feel as though he was about to jump out of his own skin. It also made him overly conscious of every move a woman—any woman—made.

Satisfied that he'd come up with an explanation for his interest in the less-than-friendly secretary, he jerked his thumb over his shoulder. "As far as I know, Geneva's still out there." He chuckled. "Although I'm not real sure she didn't break one of her fingers punching in the number for security."

"Good."

"Good that she might have broken a finger? Or good that she was calling security?" he asked, grinning.

"I didn't mean—" Frowning, she stopped short and it was clear that for a split second, he'd thrown her off guard. "Good that she's summoning security, of course."

"Hey, lighten up. Life is too short to be so uptight."

The woman rounded the end of the desk, her expression anything but welcoming. "I don't know who you think you are or why you're here, but you can't just walk in and—"

The sound of the door crashing against the wall stopped the young woman in midsentence.

"That's him."

Caleb glanced over his shoulder to see the receptionist charge into the office with a defiant glare. Two middle-aged, potbellied uniformed men followed close behind.

"I see you got hold of the security guards, Geneva." He glanced at his watch, then nodded his approval. "Their response time wasn't bad, but I think we could work on improving it, don't you?"

Geneva managed to look down her nose at him despite the difference in their heights, then turned her attention to the woman with the remarkable baby blues. "I'm sorry, Ms. Merrick." She eyed Caleb like she didn't think his elevator went all the way to the top floor. "*He* wouldn't take no for an answer."

Caleb raised an eyebrow. This was A. J. Merrick?

Interesting. She definitely wasn't what he'd expected. Emerald had led him to believe that Merrick was a stodgy old gent, not a twentysomething woman with incredible blue eyes.

As they stared at each other like opponents in a boxing ring, his neglected libido noticed that A. J. Merrick wasn't dressed like most women her age. Instead of her black suit caressing her body and showing off her assets, it hung from her small frame like an empty tow sack. But if her delicate hands, slender neck and what he could see of her long, perfectly shaped legs were any indication, he'd bet his grandpa's best coonhound she was hiding some pretty incredible curves inside all that baggy black linen.

"It's all right, Mrs. Wallace." Ms. Merrick treated Caleb to a triumphant smile that did strange things to his insides and made him feel as if the temperature in the room had suddenly gone up ten degrees. "I'm sure you'll understand that applying for a job now would be a waste of time for both of us." To the guards coming to stand on either side of him, she added, "Please show this gentleman to the parking lot."

"That's mighty unfriendly of you," Caleb said, shaking his head.

Allowing the men to demonstrate how they would

handle the situation if he'd been a real threat, Caleb almost laughed out loud when they clumsily grabbed his arms and attempted to pull them behind his back. He immediately decided that they not only needed to work on their response time to a situation, but could both benefit from a refresher course in methods of restraint. If he'd been of a mind to, he could have broken their hold without doing much more than flexing his biceps.

"I'm not here to apply for a job." He smiled. "I already work here."

"Oh, really?" Ms. Merrick tilted her head curiously. "Since I do the final interviews for all new employees, would you care to refresh my memory and tell me what your name is, when we hired you and just which area of Skerritt and Crowe you think you work in?"

"I got the job a week ago and I intend to work in the office next to yours." Chuckling, he decided he was going to enjoy sparring with A. J. Merrick. "The name is Walker. Caleb Walker."

He could tell from the widening of her baby blues behind those ridiculous glasses that his answers were *not* what she'd expected. But she quickly recovered her composure and motioned toward the two guards. "Mr. Norton, Mr. Clay, please release Mr. Walker immediately."

"But Ms. Merrick—"

"I said, let him go," she repeated. She lifted her stubborn little chin a notch. "Mr. Walker is the new president of Skerritt and Crowe."

From somewhere behind him, he heard Geneva gasp at the same time as the two guards dropped their hold on him.

"Sorry about that, Mr. Walker," one of the men said, clumsily trying to straighten Caleb's shirtsleeve.

Silence reigned for several tense seconds as Caleb and the woman in front of him stared at each other. In a lot of ways she reminded him of another woman and another time.

He took a deep breath. That had been a while back and he'd learned a lot in the few years since. He was no longer a naive farm boy with lofty dreams and a trusting heart. He was a grown man who'd learned his lessons well.

"If you'd give Ms. Merrick and me a few minutes, I'd surely appreciate it," he finally said as he continued to meet her intense gaze. When he heard the quiet click of the door being pulled shut behind the three, Caleb smiled. "What do you say we start over?" He stuck out his hand. "I'm Caleb Walker. It's nice to meet you, Ms. Merrick."

When she hesitantly placed her hand in his, the feel of her soft palm against his sent a shock wave all the way to his toes. She apparently felt the same jolt of electric current because she dropped his hand faster than the high-school football captain's pants hit the floor on prom night. He barely managed to keep from laughing out loud.

"I know I'm earlier than you all expected, but don't you think it would have been a good idea to inform the employees about me? After all, Emerald Larson called you several days ago to tell you I'd be here at the end of this week."

"Mrs. Larson indicated that you'd be here on Friday."

"I'm only a day early," he said, breathing a bit easier when A.J. didn't refer to Emerald as his grandmother.

He'd purposely asked Emerald not to mention their relationship when she called Skerritt and Crowe, and it appeared that she'd respected his wishes. He didn't want or need the added prejudices of being the owner's grandson when he took over.

"It was my intention to introduce you to everyone tomorrow at the directors' meeting," she said, sounding extremely efficient.

"Well, I can guarantee you the cat's out of the bag now," he said, grinning. "I'll bet Geneva and her two sidekicks are spreading the word like fire through a hay field."

To his amazement, she didn't even crack a smile. "I'm sure they are."

Her calm demeanor had Caleb wondering if A. J. Merrick ever let herself lose control. Something told him that it didn't happen often. But he also sensed that when she did let go, it would be a hell of a sight. What he couldn't figure out was why he'd like to be there to see it when she did.

She waved her hand at one of the burgundy leather armchairs in front of her desk. "Please have a seat, Mr. Walker."

Sitting down, he watched her walk around the desk to lower herself into the high-backed executive chair. "Since we're going to be working together, why don't we ditch the formalities?" he asked, wondering what made A. J. Merrick tick. "Call me Caleb."

"I'd rather not, Mr. Walker," she said, straightening some papers on her desk.

"Why not?" He wasn't at all surprised by her insistence on formalities. However, he was dismayed by his own persistence in getting her to let down her guard.

She stopped fussing with the documents to give him a pointed look. "It will only complicate things when the time comes for you to let me go."

Now where had that come from? To his knowledge, he hadn't given her any reason to feel threatened or to believe he'd be firing her, or anyone else for that matter. But she was acting like it was a done deal.

He sat forward. "Where did you get the harebrained idea that I'd be letting you go?"

"Any time there's a change in upper management, the result is always the same. The new president or CEO brings in his or her own people for the top positions and the old regime is history." She shrugged one slender shoulder as she met his gaze head-on. "Since I'm the operations manager over all the departments here at

Skerritt and Crowe, mine will be one of the first heads to roll."

He wasn't sure, but he thought he detected a slight tremor in her voice. But as she continued to stare at him like he was lower than the stuff he scraped off his boots after a trip through the barnyard, he decided he'd imagined the sound. A. J. Merrick was way too professional to show the slightest bit of emotion. What shocked him more than her steely control was his sudden desire to see what lay beneath that cool facade, to discover what she was so obviously trying to hide.

"Let me put your fears to rest right here and now. I'm not getting rid of you or anyone else," he said, forcing his mind back to the matter at hand. She had no way of knowing, and he wasn't about to tell her that he didn't have a clue about running a firm of financial consultants or that he'd have to rely heavily on her and others' experience in order to keep from falling on his face. "Your job is just as safe today as it was before Emerald, Inc. bought this firm."

She pushed her glasses back up her nose with a brush of her hand. "You say that now, but it's a well-known fact that within six months of any takeover there's always a shake-up."

"That might happen with a hostile buyout, but Emerald Larson bought this company with Frank Skerritt and Martin Crowe's blessings. They both wanted to retire, but neither of them had family members who wanted to take the reins of the firm."

As he watched her nibble on her lower lip while she considered his words, he found himself wondering if her perfectly shaped lips were as soft and sweet as they looked. Swallowing hard, he decided that he'd better keep his mind on business and off the fact that Ms. Merrick had the most kissable mouth he'd seen in a very long time.

"I'll be—" he stopped to clear the rust from his throat before he continued "—making a few small changes here and there. But as far as I'm concerned, the only way any of the employees will lose their job is if they up and quit."

"We'll see," she said softly.

Her expression was completely neutral and gave no indication of what she was thinking. But Caleb knew she wasn't buying his assurances for a minute.

Deciding that he'd probably have more luck convincing a pack of wolves to become vegetarians than he would getting A. J. Merrick to believe her job was secure, Caleb took a deep breath and stood up. "I think I'll mosey on out of here and introduce myself to a few of our people."

"But what about the meeting I have set up for tomorrow morning at ten, Mr. Walker?" she asked as she rose from her chair.

Was that a hint of panic he detected in her wide blue eyes?

Interesting. It appeared that any break with tradition threw A. J. Merrick for a loop. He'd have to remember that.

"The name's Caleb." He shrugged. "The meeting is still on. I'll just use it to outline a few of the policy changes I intend to make and explain my plan of action."

He noticed the white-knuckled grip she had on her ink pen and, without thinking, reached across the desk to place his hand on hers in a reassuring manner. But the moment his palm touched her satiny skin, a charge of electricity zinged up his arm and quickly spread throughout his chest. Her startled gasp told him that she felt it, too.

Quickly moving his hand, he tried to appear nonchalant about the gesture. But considering his insides were still tingling like he'd grabbed hold of a 220-volt wire, that was mighty damned hard.

"Relax, Ms. Merrick," he said, wondering what the hell had gotten into him. Surely he didn't need to get laid so badly that he'd started getting turned on by merely touching a woman's hand. "Not only do you have my word that your job's safe, I promise that what I have in mind will improve employee morale and increase productivity."

At least, that's what he hoped to accomplish. Considering he didn't know beans from buckshot about running this or any other company, he'd just have to operate on the trial-and-error system, refer to the management manual he'd picked up at a bookstore and hope for the best.

She defensively folded her arms beneath her breasts and simply stared at him. "I suppose I'll have to take your word on that."

"I guess you will," he said, walking toward the door. He needed to put some distance between them in order to regain his perspective. He was here to take over the consulting firm, not try to figure out why this woman's reluctance to believe him bothered the hell out of him. Or why he was starting to get turned on by staring into her pretty blue eyes. "I'll see you tomorrow morning, Ms. Merrick."

"C-Caleb?" She stumbled over his name, but the sound of it on her soft voice did a real number on his neglected hormones.

His hand on the doorknob, he turned back to face her. "Yes, Ms. Merrick?"

"I suppose since you insist that I use your first name, you might as well call me A.J."

"Okay, A.J." He smiled. Maybe they were making progress after all. "I'll see you first thing in the morning."

A.J. watched the door close behind Caleb Walker a moment before her trembling legs folded and she collapsed into her leather executive chair. Why was her heart racing? And why did her skin still tingle from his touch?

She removed her glasses and buried her face in her hands. What on earth had come over her? She never had been, nor would ever be the type of woman who let a handsome man divert her attention from what was important. At least not since the fiasco with Wesley Pennington III. He'd taught her a valuable lesson, and one that she couldn't afford to forget—mixing business with pleasure was a fool's game, one that ultimately led to disaster.

Normally, it wasn't even an issue. Since losing her heart, her virginity and her first job due to her naiveté, she'd made it a point to do everything she could to appear as professional as possible. It kept things simple and helped to reinforce her strict policy of keeping coworkers at arm's length. And it had worked well.

Most people, and especially men, were put off by her all-business demeanor and didn't bother taking a second glance at her. And that suited her just fine. But Caleb Walker had not only looked twice, he'd focused his disturbing hazel gaze on her from the moment he'd walked into her office.

A tiny tremor coursed through her. He had a way of looking at her that made her more aware of her femininity than she'd ever been in her life. And that was what made him dangerous.

Shaking her head, she tried not to think about the wild fluttering in her lower stomach that she'd experienced when Caleb had smiled at her, and concentrated on the fact that he was her new boss. He was here to take over Skerritt and Crowe and eventually replace her with one of his own people. And even though he'd assured her that wasn't the case, she knew better. Everything she'd worked to achieve in the past five years was about to go down the drain and she was powerless to stop it.

She put her glasses back on and swiveled the chair

around to stare out the plate-glass windows. Blindly watching the late-June sun bathe downtown Albuquerque with its warm afternoon rays, she fought the urge to cry. She had a feeling that Caleb Walker was going to turn her structured, well-ordered world upside down. And there wasn't a thing she could do to stop him.

There was no telling what kinds of changes he intended to implement or just how quickly he'd decide she was dispensable. And the most upsetting aspect of all was the fact that all she could think about was how intense his hazel eyes were, how his light brown hair hanging low on his forehead made him look more like a rebel than a businessman. And how the combination of his deep baritone and sexy Southern accent made her insides hum.

"Don't be a fool," she muttered, turning back to her desk.

She wasn't interested in Caleb Walker any more than he was interested in her. But as she stared at the documents on her desk, she couldn't stop thinking about how broad his shoulders looked in his chambray shirt, how his jeans fit him like a second skin or how her hand still tingled where he'd touched her.

When a tiny moan of frustration escaped, she quickly stuffed the pile of accounting reports she'd been reviewing into her briefcase, grabbed her purse from the bottom drawer of the desk and headed for the door. "I'll be out of the office for the rest of the day," she told Geneva as she rushed past her.

A.J. didn't wait for the startled receptionist's reaction to her atypical behavior. She didn't have time to worry about that now. She needed to get to her apartment before the cool persona she'd perfected over the years slipped away and she revealed what only her parakeet, Sidney, knew about her.

Alyssa Jane Merrick wasn't the cold, emotionless automaton everyone at Skerritt and Crowe thought her to be. She was a living, breathing woman who collected whimsical figurines, shed buckets of tears over sentimental or touching moments, and feared failure more than anything else.

As she walked across the parking lot, she quickened her steps and trotted the distance to her sensible black sedan. She was less than a split second away from doing one of two things. She was going to either let loose with a scream loud enough to wake the dead or start crying like a baby. Neither one was acceptable behavior for her professional image.

Unlocking the driver's door, she threw her briefcase inside, slid behind the steering wheel and closed her eyes. She counted to ten, then twenty as she struggled with her emotions. For the first time in five years, she was close to losing the tight grip she had always held on herself whenever she was at work. And that was something she simply couldn't afford to let happen.

She had never, nor would she ever allow any of these people to see her lose control. Not only would it be a serious breach of her professionalism, but her late father would come back to haunt her for doing something so typically female.

From the time she'd been old enough to listen, her career-military father had stressed how important it was not to let her enemies see any sign of weakness. And there was no doubt about it, Caleb Walker posed a serious threat to her professional demeanor. But he was also the best-looking enemy she'd ever seen.

Two

"The first thing I want to do this morning is assure all of you that your jobs are secure," Caleb said, addressing the directors and department managers. He made it a point to look directly at A. J. Merrick. "Contrary to standard corporate practice, I have no intention of letting anyone go in favor of bringing in my own people. The only way you're going to lose your job is if *you* make the decision to quit."

The doubt he detected in her blue gaze stated quite clearly that she still didn't believe him. What he couldn't figure out was why it mattered to him that she trust him. If their collective sigh of relief was any indication, the rest of the occupants in the room did. What made her opinion of him so damned important?

Deciding not to dwell on the mystery of why her doubts bothered him, Caleb turned his attention back to outlining his plans for the company. "I've reviewed the quarterly reports for the last fiscal year and although growth is slow, it has been steady." He grinned. "And as my grandpa Walker always said, 'If it ain't broke, don't fix it.' That's why I won't be making changes in the daily operations of the company." *At least not until I can take a few business courses and figure out what the hell I'm doing.*

"I like the way your grandpa thinks," Malcolm Fuller said, nodding.

Caleb chuckled. "I'm glad that meets with your approval, Malcolm." He'd met the older man the day before and they'd instantly hit it off. Malcolm reminded Caleb of Henry Walker, his late grandpa—filled with country wisdom and more than willing to speak his mind.

When Caleb noticed several raised eyebrows and the exchange of curious glances between the other department heads seated at the big oval conference table, he frowned. Apparently all of the employees at Skerritt and Crowe were as unaccustomed to the laid-back, informal approach to management as A. J. Merrick was.

Taking a deep breath, he figured there was no time like the present to shake things up and see how receptive the management team was to the changes he did have planned. "Although I don't intend to adjust the operating procedures, I do plan to make a few improvements to the work atmosphere around here."

"What did you have in mind, Mr. Walker?" Ed Bentley asked, looking more than a little nervous.

"The first thing we're going to do is drop the formalities." Caleb gave them all a smile he hoped would put their minds at ease. "Don't you think it's pretty silly to work with someone eight hours a day, day in and day out and not use their given name?" Before they could react, he went on. "We'll naturally continue to give our clients the respect they deserve and address them in a formal manner. But I want you all to feel free to be on a first-name basis with me, as well as each other."

The men and women at the table began to smile. Everyone, except A.J. Her clasped hands resting on the table in front of her had tightened into a white-knuckled knot, indicating that she strongly disagreed with his decision.

Why would she object to doing away with an outdated tradition? Hadn't she learned in college that a more relaxed environment encouraged teamwork and raised productivity? Hell, he'd found that little tidbit of information on the Internet, so it couldn't be that big a secret.

"You want us to call you Caleb?" Maria Santos asked hesitantly.

Grinning, he turned his attention to the director of the payroll department. "That's my name, Maria."

"What other changes do you have planned…Caleb?" one of the other men asked.

"Effective immediately, there's an open-door policy

between upper management and the workers on the floor." He paused to let them digest his statement. "I want every employee we have, no matter what their position, to feel comfortable with bringing problems and complaints to our attention, as well as sharing ways to improve morale and bring in new clients."

"You've got a lot of good ideas," Joel McIntyre, the head of the billing department, said, nodding his approval. "Is there anything else?"

"As a matter of fact there is, Joel." Caleb smiled. He was sure the last couple of changes he was about to announce would be welcomed by everyone, including A. J. Merrick. "Since most of our business is conducted over the phone and through the Internet, I don't see any reason why we can't relax the dress code around here. I'll still expect you to dress accordingly when you meet with one of our clients, but from now on you're all free to wear whatever you like." He chuckled. "That is, as long as it's decent and doesn't look like something you'd put on to clean out the barn."

He laughed out loud when several of the men immediately reached up to remove their ties and unfasten the top button of their shirts. "I guess this means everyone is in favor of doing away with the dress code."

When he glanced at A.J. his smile faded. *Well, almost everyone.*

"Is that all?" she asked tightly. She stared straight at him and it was as clear as a cloudless sky that she wasn't happy.

None of the other department heads seemed to notice that the operations manager was even in the same room with them, let alone less than enthusiastic about his ideas. But Caleb had been aware of her presence from the moment she'd sat down in the chair at the far end of the conference table. He'd hoped that once she heard what he had planned she'd find his ideas to be innovative or at least be open to giving them a chance.

Unfortunately, she looked even more unhappy than she had yesterday afternoon when he'd walked into her office and announced who he was. But more troubling than her lack of enthusiasm was his reaction to her reluctance. He had an almost uncontrollable urge to walk over to her, take her in his arms and reassure her that the changes he planned to make would be of benefit to everyone.

He shook his head, as much to dispel his disturbing thoughts as to let her know he had more plans in the works. "I have one more announcement before I let you all get back to work." Tearing his gaze from A.J., he forced his attention to the others seated around the table. "On Monday, there will be a seminar for all managers to learn team-building techniques. Then, once a month, the firm will pick up the tab for you and all of the people in your department to take a Friday off and put what you've learned into action."

"This is where we go on picnics, play golf and things like that to build communication skills and encourage interaction with our coworkers, isn't it?" Joel asked, sounding excited by the possibilities.

"That's the plan," Caleb said, nodding. At least others could see his objective, even if A.J. couldn't. "There's no reason we can't have fun while we develop a tight, efficient team." Smiling, he pushed his chair back and rose to his feet. He'd given them enough to digest for one day. In the next week or so, he'd shake things up a little more. "Now, what do you say we all get back to work and make some money."

As the meeting broke up and her coworkers surrounded Caleb to express their enthusiasm for the changes he'd be making, A.J. escaped to the sanctuary of her office. Closing the door behind her, she leaned up against it as she struggled to breathe. She felt as if she were about to suffocate on the myriad of emotions racing through her. In less than an hour, Caleb Walker had single-handedly destroyed every reason she had for working at Skerritt and Crowe. And he didn't even realize it.

He thought he was doing everyone a favor by improving the quality of their work atmosphere. And she had to admit that what he planned would probably motivate the employees and breathe new life into the firm.

But she'd purposely chosen to accept the position

with Skerritt and Crowe, instead of at a more modern financial group, because of the formalities and old-fashioned approach to management. It enabled her to focus all of her attention on her job and kept the people she worked with at a safe distance.

Pushing away from the door, she walked around her desk and sank into the high-backed leather chair. Although she wasn't antisocial by nature, she'd learned the hard way to keep her coworkers at arm's length. It was the only sure way to guard herself against betrayal and the emotional pain that accompanied it.

But what frustrated and confused her more than anything else was her reaction to Caleb. The entire time he'd been outlining the ways he intended to destroy her safety net, all she'd been able to think about was how handsome he was and how his deep Southern drawl made her insides hum.

Barely resisting the urge to let loose with a scream that was sure to send Geneva Wallace into cardiac arrest, A.J. turned to her computer screen and opened the file containing her résumé. There was no longer any question about it. Her days as operations manager at Skerritt and Crowe were numbered and she'd do well to start looking for another job.

"A.J., could you come in here?" Caleb's voice invading her office through the intercom caused her stomach to flutter wildly. "I have something I need to talk over with you."

What could he possibly want now? Hadn't he done enough in the past hour to turn her world upside down?

Sighing, she depressed the talk button. "I'm working on something at the moment. Could we postpone the discussion until this afternoon?" He didn't need to know that she was updating her résumé or that she planned on finding another job. When silence reigned, she pushed the button again. "Mr. Walker? Caleb?"

She gasped when the door connecting their offices opened and he strolled into the room.

"Sorry if I startled you, but I'm a face-to-face kind of guy," he said, grinning. "I like to look a person in the eye when I'm talking to them."

The sound of his voice and his sexy grin sent a shiver streaking up her spine and had her wondering what else he liked to do face-to-face. Her breath caught and she did her best to hide her shock at the direction her wayward thoughts had taken.

"What did you want to discuss, Mr.—"

He raised one dark eyebrow at the same time he cleared his throat.

Resigned, she closed the computer file containing her résumé. "What did you want to discuss…Caleb?"

He smiled his approval. "I think I've come across another way to improve employee morale."

Just what she wanted to hear, she thought disgustedly, another cockamamy idea that would no doubt increase her anxiety level.

She trained her gaze on his forehead to keep from looking directly into his startling hazel eyes. "What did you have in mind?"

"I'm thinking about turning the break room into a 'family room.'"

A.J.'s mouth dropped open and her gaze flew to his. "Excuse me?"

"Better watch that." He chuckled. "You might catch a fly."

She snapped her mouth shut. Didn't he take anything seriously?

"Would you care to explain what you mean when you use the term *family room?*" she asked, rubbing at the sudden pounding in her temples.

"I'm thinking couches, coffee tables and a big-screen TV," he said, looking thoughtful. "When our employees take their breaks, they should be able to relax and enjoy the few minutes they have away from the job."

"If you make it too comfortable, they'll go to sleep," A.J. said before she could stop herself.

She hadn't meant to be so blunt. But facts were facts and he might as well be aware of them right up front.

He grinned. "Nothing wrong with a little power nap now and then. Studies have shown that it gives most people a second wind."

She'd seen the research and couldn't argue with the findings, but that didn't mean she agreed with them.

"Are you wanting to know what I think of the idea?" she asked cautiously.

"Not really." He gave her a smile that warmed her all the way to her toes. "But I would like your help putting the project into action."

Her first inclination was to refuse his request. But to her amazement, she found herself asking, "What do you want me to do?"

"I'd really appreciate your input on what colors and style of furniture to use." His expression turned sheepish. "I'm not real up on this decorating stuff."

Oh, he was good. He knew just when to turn up the wattage on that smile and use his boyish charm to get exactly what he wanted. Fortunately, she was immune to such tactics.

"What makes you think I'm any better?"

"I don't." He shrugged. "But I need a woman's perspective. The room needs to be comfortable for both men and women. If I try to do it entirely on my own, it'll end up looking like a sports bar."

"Why don't you get Mrs. Wallace to help you?" A.J. hedged. "I've heard her say she never misses that television show where friends redecorate each other's rooms."

"I have Geneva busy heading up another project," he said, grinning.

"You do?" Good Lord, what on earth had he charmed their stodgy sixty-year-old secretary into doing?

"I've given her a five-thousand-dollar budget for uniforms and equipment and put her in charge of organizing our sports teams."

A.J. couldn't believe what she was hearing. "You've got to be joking."

"Nope." His smile intensified. "Depending on the amount of interest among the employees, we're going to have bowling and volleyball teams this winter and a softball team next summer."

"You do realize this consulting firm is comprised of accountants and financial analysts, don't you?" She shook her head in disbelief. "That's not exactly the material jocks are made of."

He shook his head. "I don't care if we have winning teams. I'm more interested in creating an overall sense of unity among the employees." Rising to his feet, he stretched and started walking toward the door to his office. "You've got the weekend to give some thought to what we can do to the break room, then we'll go over your ideas next week."

As she watched him close the door behind himself, A.J. groaned. From the time she'd been old enough to understand, her father had preached the military mantra of structure and order. He'd said they were essential for a successful life. Captain John T. Merrick had believed it, had lived by it and had insisted that his daughter adhere to it. He'd even chosen the boarding school she'd attended after the death of her mother because of its strict code of conduct and rigid set of rules. And the one and only time she'd deviated from the path her father had set her on, she'd ended up in the middle of a humiliating workplace scandal.

But she'd survived because that's what her late father would have expected her to do. It had been extremely difficult, but she'd picked up the pieces of her shattered pride, became a born-again virgin and found her present job at Skerritt and Crowe. And she'd been—if not happy—content for the past five years.

Unfortunately, it seemed that contentment had come to an end with the arrival of Caleb Walker. When he'd strolled into her office yesterday afternoon with his good-old-boy attitude and devastating good looks to announce he was taking over the firm, she felt as if she'd been tossed into a vortex. He represented everything in life she'd been taught to approach with caution, if not avoid altogether. He was innovative in the way he approached management and his ideas were unorthodox and, unless she'd missed her guess, for the most part spontaneous.

So why did her pulse pound and air feel as if it were in short supply whenever they were in the same room? Why did his sexy Southern drawl send sparks of electric current over every nerve in her body? And why did the sight of his wide shoulders and slender hips cause her body to hum with a restlessness like she'd never known before?

Biting her lower lip to stop its trembling, she hastily reopened the computer file containing her résumé. There was absolutely no question about the matter. She had to find another job as soon as possible or risk losing what little sense she had left.

The following Tuesday afternoon, Caleb sat at his desk, wondering what on God's green earth Emerald Larson had gotten him into. He didn't have the vaguest idea of how he was supposed to deal with one of Skerritt and Crowe's best clients. His night classes at the University of New Mexico weren't scheduled to start until the end of next month. He somehow doubted the business administration courses he'd signed up for would start out covering the interaction with clientele, anyway.

He drummed his fingertips on the desk's polished surface. He hadn't been able to find anything on conducting meetings with clients in the management manual, either. The damned thing only covered supervising employees and ways to improve their work environment. It was completely useless for learning how to deal with clients.

But whether Caleb knew what he was doing or not, it didn't change the fact that Raul Ortiz wanted to meet with him. Caleb had taken over running the financial consulting firm that had helped Ortiz Industries create one of the best employee investment plans in the state, and he suspected that Ortiz wanted to make sure Caleb passed muster.

When he heard A.J.'s voice through the door connecting their offices, Caleb's spirits lifted. The woman might be driving him crazy trying to figure out what made her tick, but he'd read her personnel file. She really knew her stuff when it came to financial planning and marketing analysis. He'd also discovered that she'd graduated from high school at the age of fifteen and had acquired her master's degree in investment banking and business administration by the time she was twenty.

If he took her with him when he drove down to Roswell, surely the meeting with Ortiz would work out. He was good with people and A.J. was a whiz at anything to do with accounting and financial planning. Together they should make a hell of a team.

Caleb took a deep breath and rose to his feet. He hated feeling inadequate at anything. But he had decided up front that he was going to have to rely on the people working for him until he took courses and got a basic understanding of the business Emerald had given him. It looked as though that reliance was going to have to start sooner than later.

Opening the door between their offices, he smiled when A.J. glanced at him over the top of her computer screen. "I just got a call from a man down in Roswell," he said, walking over to slump into the chair in front of her desk. "He claims to be our most satisfied client."

"That would be Mr. Ortiz," she answered, nodding. "He's one of our most valued patrons."

"That's what he said." Caleb chuckled. "I get the idea he's also one of our most outspoken clients."

"I've never known him to mince words," she said, pushing her glasses up her pert little nose. The action drew attention to her remarkable eyes and Caleb had to remind himself that he'd entered her office for a reason other than staring into her baby blues.

"So you've dealt with him before?"

She nodded. "Mr. Skerritt took care of Ortiz Industries' employee investment program, but he assigned me to advise Mr. Ortiz on his own personal retirement package. Why do you ask?"

"He wants me to drive down to Roswell tomorrow for a get-acquainted meeting." Trying to sound nonchalant, Caleb added, "I've decided I'll take you with me."

"Me?" Her eyes widened behind her oversize glasses and the panic he saw in their depths reminded him of a deer caught in the headlights of a car. Was the thought of spending time with him that upsetting?

"Is there a problem, A.J.?"

"Why? I mean, I can't possibly—" She suddenly closed her mouth and simply stared at him.

As he returned her gaze, Caleb did his best to keep his attention on the issue at hand and off her perfectly shaped lips. "I realize this is on the spur of the moment, but I don't see that we have any other choice. Since I've just taken over here, I don't know diddly-squat about Ortiz or our business with him. And until I'm up to speed on the individual accounts of our clients, I'd rather not run the risk of losing them."

His argument made sense to him. He just hoped it sounded reasonable to her.

Watching her nibble on her lower lip as she mulled over what he'd said, it was all he could do to keep from groaning. Why did he suddenly find her mouth so damned fascinating? Hadn't he learned a damn thing about professional, career-minded women?

"What time is the meeting?" she asked.

Was it his imagination or was there a slight tremor in her voice?

"Ortiz wants to give me a tour of the manufacturing plant tomorrow afternoon, then have dinner around six or seven."

"It would be too late for us to drive back tomorrow evening and I have two phone meetings early the next morning." She sounded extremely relieved when she added, "I'm sorry, but I really think my going with you would be impossible. We've been courting these potential clients for several months and there's the possibility of losing them if I reschedule the calls."

He wasn't about to give up that easily. "Where are they located?"

"Mr. Sanchez is in Las Cruces and Mrs. Bailey is in Truth or Consequences." Her eyes narrowed. "Why?"

"If I remember my high-school geography, those two places aren't that far from Roswell," he said, thinking fast. "Call and tell them we'll be in their area day after tomorrow and that we'd like to meet with them in person. It'll show that we'd really like to work for them, as well as free you up to go to Roswell with me. Then we'll drive back after dinner Thursday evening." Deciding to beat a hasty retreat before she could find another excuse, he headed for the door. "I'll come by your place around ten in the morning."

"Th-that won't be necessary," she said, stopping him. When he turned back, she added, "I have to come in tomorrow morning to tie up a few loose ends. We can leave from here."

Caleb could tell she wasn't happy, but that couldn't be helped. He wasn't particularly proud of having to rely on her expertise to keep from looking like a fool in front of a client.

"Fair enough," he said, nodding. "I'll have Geneva make a reservation for tomorrow night in Roswell."

"That should be reservations—plural—as in two rooms."

"Of course."

Heading out the door to speak with their secretary, Caleb couldn't help but grin. He clearly made A. J. Merrick as nervous as the parents of a four-year-old talking to the preacher after Sunday services.

The next two days had the potential to prove extremely interesting and in a way he hadn't counted on. Not only would he get to see how A.J. dealt with clients, he had a feeling he just might see that cool self-control of hers slip, as well.

Three

After an uneventful drive down to Roswell, a tour of Ortiz Industries and a highly successful dinner meeting with Mr. Ortiz, all A.J. wanted was the solitude of her motel room and a nice, hot, relaxing bath. Thoroughly exhausted from tossing and turning the night before, she'd spent the entire day in Caleb's disturbing presence and she was more than ready to put a bit of distance between them.

"Why don't you check in for us while I get the bags from the back of the truck?" he asked as he stopped the pickup in front of the motel entrance.

She opened the passenger side door. "I assume the rooms are under the firm's name?"

"Yep. Geneva said she reserved the last two rooms

in Ros—" He stopped abruptly when a family of glow-in-the-dark aliens with oval-shaped heads and big, unblinking eyes walked past the front of the truck and got into a blue minivan.

"This is festival week," A.J. explained. She couldn't help but laugh at the incredulous expression on his handsome face. "You'll probably see a lot of that sort of thing."

"I saw the banners when we drove through town." He shook his head. "But I didn't realize they went to extremes with the alien thing."

Getting out of the truck, she nodded. "It's the anniversary of the Roswell Incident. People from all over the world converge on the town the first part of July to attend seminars, share the experiences they've had with extraterrestrials and participate in a variety of activities, including a costume contest."

Caleb chuckled when another alien, this one with tentacles and silver eyes, waved as he drove past in a yellow Volkswagen Beetle. "Sounds like we're lucky Geneva found rooms for us."

"I'm really surprised she did on such short notice."

A.J. closed the truck door and, breathing a sigh of relief that she'd soon have a little time to herself, entered the motel lobby and approached the desk clerk. "I'm with Skerritt and Crowe Financial Consultants. I believe you have a couple of rooms for us."

The smiling teenage girl behind the counter snapped her gum, then blew a bubble as she checked her computer screen. "Actually, we have you down for one room with a couple of beds."

"There must be a mistake," A.J. said, shaking her head. She knew Geneva Wallace was far too capable to make that big of an error. "Could you please double-check the reservations?"

Shrugging, the girl keyed in the information again. A moment later, she looked up, shaking her head. "It shows only one room reserved for the Skerritt and Crowe folks. But like I said, it does have two beds."

A.J.'s temples began to throb. "Do you have another room available?"

The girl smiled apologetically. "Sorry. This week's been booked solid for months. In fact, if we hadn't had a late cancellation, we wouldn't have had this room for you." Snapping her gum, she looked thoughtful. "I'd say the closest motel with rooms available would probably be down in Artesia. And that's real iffy."

"Is there a problem?" Caleb asked, walking up to stand beside A.J.

"Apparently there's been a mix-up and they only have one room for us." She suddenly knew how Dorothy must have felt when the tornado picked her up and she came over the rainbow, crashing down in the land of Oz. "With the festival going on there aren't any rooms available for miles. It looks like we'll have to drive on to Las Cruces tonight."

To her astonishment, Caleb shook his head. "It's already dark, we're both tired and some of the roads between here and there are two-lanes. Driving in unfamiliar territory under those conditions wouldn't be a good idea."

Desperation began to claw at her insides. Had he lost his mind?

"We can't stay in the same room."

"You can have the bed and I'll sleep on the floor." He made it sound so logical.

"The room has two double beds," the teenage girl spoke up helpfully.

"We'll take it," he said, setting their overnight cases down to reach for his wallet.

If she thought she'd felt desperate before, A.J. was a hairbreadth away from an all-out panic attack. Tugging on his arm, she led him over to the seating area of the lobby for a private discussion.

"You can't be serious."

"We don't have a choice."

"What happens when the employees at the firm find out that we spent the night in the same room?"

He shook his head. "Unless one of us tells them, they'll never know."

"Don't fool yourself. What do you think is going to happen when you turn in the receipt to accounts payable?" she asked, knowing that once word got out there was only one room on the bill, the gossip and speculation would run rampant.

"I'll put it on my credit card instead of Skerritt and Crowe's." He sounded so darned reasonable, she wanted to stomp.

"But—"

He reached out and put his hands on her shoulders. "I agree, it's a major pain in the butt that we can't have our own rooms. But we're both adults, A.J. We can handle this." Before she could stop him, he removed his wallet from his hip pocket and handed a credit card to the girl behind the counter.

Her heart did a backflip. Maybe he could deal with the situation, but she wasn't so sure about herself. Spending the entire day with him, first in the close confines of his pickup truck, then in the meeting with Mr. Ortiz, had more than taken its toll.

From the moment they'd left the Skerritt and Crowe offices that morning, her senses had been assaulted by the man. The scent of his woodsy aftershave, the timbre of his deep voice and the occasional brush of his arm against hers when he opened doors for her had charged every cell in her being with a restlessness she refused to define. If she had to spend an entire night in the same room with Caleb only a few feet away, there was a very real possibility she'd be a raving lunatic by morning.

As he sat on the side of the motel bed, Caleb took off his boots, then picked up the television's remote control and absently flipped through the channels. He had to get his mind off the woman changing clothes in the bathroom.

Glancing at the closed door, he shook his head. He'd put in a hell of a day listening to her soft voice and watching her move with a catlike grace that he found absolutely fascinating. But it was the few times they'd brushed against each other that had him feeling like he was about to jump out of his own skin. What was there about A.J. that sent his hormones racing through his blood like the steel balls in an pinball machine?

She was the consummate professional and gave every indication that she was totally immersed in her career. And he'd learned the hard way to avoid her type like a bachelor avoids a widows' convention. So why was she all he'd been able to think about from the moment he'd laid eyes on her? What was there about her that he found so damned compelling?

Her clothes certainly weren't provocative or meant to entice a man. And although she was far from homely, A.J. sure didn't wear makeup or style her hair in a way to make herself look anything but plain.

He frowned. It was as if she was doing everything she possibly could to keep from attracting attention to herself.

That's what he was having the devil of a time trying to figure out. A.J. didn't look or act like an executive. Leslie Ann Turner, the woman he'd been involved with a few years back, had been the perfect example of a corporate climber and taken great pains to look attractive at work, as well as when they'd gone out on the town. They'd met by accident when he'd attended a farm symposium at one of the downtown Nashville hotels and she'd stopped by the lounge after work for drinks with her girlfriends. He'd asked her out and that had started their two-year affair. She'd been a junior executive then and hadn't yet developed a thirst for power and position, nor had she looked down on him because he'd had nothing more than a high-school education.

But as time had gone on and she'd gotten a few promotions under her belt, that had changed. She'd stopped asking him to attend corporate parties with her and had adopted the attitude that the measure of a man was determined by the number of diplomas he held. And it really hadn't come as a big surprise when she'd dumped him like a blind date on a Saturday night.

However, as hard as it had been to face the fact that she apparently thought he wasn't good enough for her, he did have her to thank for a lesson well learned. A career woman wasn't anyone he wanted to become involved with, no matter how compelling her baby blues were.

But A.J. didn't seem to possess the same barracuda instincts, the same do-whatever-it-takes-to-get-ahead attitude that Leslie Ann had. Hell, there were a couple of times when he'd been outlining the policy changes, then later when he'd asked her to help with the break room renovations, that A.J. had almost looked unsure and vulnerable.

As he sat there pondering his uncharacteristic fascination with A.J., the bathroom door opened. Looking up, Caleb's jaw dropped and he felt like he'd been blindsided by a steamroller. With her owlish glasses off and her long, auburn hair down around her shoulders, A. J. Merrick was a knockout.

He swallowed hard as she walked past him to the other bed. Her emerald silk pajamas and robe enhanced the red highlights in her hair and were the perfect contrast to her flawless porcelain complexion and baby-blue eyes.

"The bathroom's all yours," she said with a wave of her delicate hand.

She still hadn't looked his way and he was damned glad. He'd been staring at her like a teenage boy stared at his first glimpse of a *Playboy* centerfold and there was no doubt in his mind that she'd think she was sharing a room with some kind of nutcase.

Suddenly feeling as if the walls were closing in on him, Caleb stood up. "I'm not all that tired," he lied. "I think I'll go down to the restaurant and get a cup of coffee." Edging toward the door, he asked, "Do you want me to bring something back for you?"

"No, thank you."

"Will you be okay here alone?"

She turned her incredible baby blues on him. "Sure. Why do you ask?"

He wasn't about to tell her that she looked prettier

and more feminine than he'd ever imagined. Nor did he want to admit that he felt like a prize jackass for running like a tail-tucked dog.

"Just checking."

She hid a huge yawn with one delicate hand. "I'll probably be asleep before you make it downstairs."

The thought of what she might look like with her long silky hair spread across the pillow, her dark lashes resting on her creamy cheeks like tiny feathers, made his body tighten and had him reaching for the doorknob in less than two seconds.

"Night," she called.

"Uh, yeah, night," he muttered, closing the door behind him. He was halfway down the hall before he realized his boots were still sitting on the floor beside the bed in their room.

He stopped dead in his tracks. "Well, hell."

"Flashback?"

Turning, Caleb found a tall, skinny man, with what looked like a piece of tinfoil molded to his bald head, standing behind him. "Excuse me?"

"I asked if you were having a flashback from your last encounter with *them,*" the man said, pointing toward the ceiling. "Some of us have flashbacks from time to time. Especially if the encounter was a really close one."

When Caleb caught on that the gentleman was referring to E.T., he shook his head. "No. This was more like a first-time sighting."

"I can totally relate. It can be a pretty disconcerting experience the first time you see *them*." Grinning, the man reached up to adjust his foil skullcap. "But as time goes on you'll find yourself looking forward to it and even hoping for an encounter of the third kind."

Caleb nodded. He was already anticipating how soft and feminine A.J. would look when she woke up tomorrow morning. And just the idea of a close encounter with her of any kind made him hard as hell.

When the man continued on down the hall, Caleb turned and walked back toward the room. "You have no idea, buddy. No earthly idea at all."

The moment the door closed behind Caleb, A.J. collapsed onto the side of the motel bed. She'd felt his gaze follow her across the room when she'd walked out of the bathroom and her knees still felt as if they were made of rubber. How on earth would she be able to close her eyes, let alone get a wink of sleep?

All she could think about was what he'd wear to bed and how he'd look first thing in the morning when he woke up. And just knowing that he'd be sleeping a few feet away sent shivers up her spine and made breathing all but impossible.

A.J. glanced around the room in near panic. She needed to get her mind off her disturbing boss. In desperation, she picked up the remote control and switched the television to a classic film channel. It would definitely be in her best interest to try losing herself in the plot of an old movie. Maybe then she'd be able to forget that she was about to spend the night in the same room as the sexiest man she'd ever known.

When she realized the film was *An Affair to Remember,* she took off her robe, pulled back the covers and crawled into bed. Even though she'd seen the movie at least twenty times and always ended up sobbing her heart out, it was one of her all-time favorites.

Settling back against the pillows, she managed to forget about her current situation as she braced herself for the movie's ending. And sure enough, when the hero discovered why the heroine had failed to meet him at the top of the Empire State Building, A.J.'s tears began to fall.

Unfortunately, Caleb chose that very moment to return to the room. "I forgot my—" He stopped abruptly. "Are you crying?"

Mortified that he'd caught her in a less-than-professional moment, she stared at the television screen. "N-no."

To her horror, he walked over to the side of her bed and sat down. "Yes, you are." He took her hands in his. "What's wrong, A.J.?"

"N-nothing." She'd known he'd be returning in a short time. Why on earth had she chosen to watch a movie that never failed to make her cry buckets?

"Look at me, sweetheart." The gentle tone of his voice caused her tears to fall faster. Why wouldn't he just go away and leave her alone?

"I…can't." Dear God, could the day get any worse?

It had been years since she'd allowed anyone to see her shed a tear. But here she was crying like a baby. And in front of her new boss, no less. She'd never been more humiliated in her entire life.

Why couldn't he find what he'd forgotten and leave? At least, long enough for her to pull herself together.

He cupped her cheek and turned her head until their gazes met. "I'm sorry, sweetheart. I didn't realize you were this upset by the situation. Please don't cry. I'll sleep in my truck if it will make you feel better."

His sincerity touched her deeply and for reasons she didn't care to analyze, she couldn't allow him to think her emotional display was because they'd be spending the night in the same room. "It's…the movie."

Glancing over his shoulder, he turned back to smile at her a moment before he reached out and took her into his arms. "That one always does a number on my mom, too."

"W-what are you doing?"

"It's all right, Alyssa."

The sound of his deep voice saying her name with such tenderness sent a shock wave straight to her core and she didn't even think to push away from him. "How did you…know my name?"

"It's in your personnel file." He pulled her to him, then smoothed his hands down her back in a comforting manner. "And don't go getting any ideas about me replacing you. I reviewed all of the managers' files."

"Why?" God help her, but with his strong arms wrapped around her and her cheek pressed to his wide chest, she wasn't sure she cared why he was going through hers or anyone else's file.

"I was trying to decide what team-building activities would best serve each manager and their department." His warm breath stirred her hair and sent shivers streaking up her spine. He hugged her close. "Cold?"

Unable to form a coherent sentence, she nodded. Even if she could have found her voice, she wasn't about to tell him the real reason she trembled.

But when he pulled back to look down at her, she knew he wasn't buying her excuse for a minute. "Are you sure?"

With his intense hazel gaze holding her captive, she wasn't sure of her own name, let alone what he'd asked her. "W-what was the question?"

"It doesn't matter, Alyssa." His sexy drawl caused her insides to feel as if they'd been turned to warm pudding and as he slowly lowered his head, she couldn't for the life of her remember why it should.

As his mouth brushed over hers, her heart skipped several beats. She should call a halt to this insanity and send him outside to spend the night in his truck. But for reasons she couldn't begin to explain, she wanted Caleb's kiss, wanted to feel his hard body pressed to her. And when he settled his lips more fully over hers, she threw caution to the wind and melted against him.

As he explored her with a tenderness that stole her breath, tiny electrical impulses skipped over every nerve in her body and she couldn't have stopped him if her life depended on it. Didn't even want to.

His kiss was slow and thoughtful and warm tingles filled her when he traced the seam of her mouth with his tongue. He was asking permission to deepen the kiss and without so much as a thought to the consequences, she parted to give him access to her tender inner recesses.

A heady warmth began to swirl through her veins when he slipped inside to caress and coax her into a response. She knew she was playing with fire, but as he teased her with featherlight strokes, temptation never tasted as good as Caleb's masterful kiss.

When he lowered her to the mattress, her stomach fluttered with the first stirrings of need and her nipples tightened in anticipation at the feel of his hand cupping her breast through the fabric of her silk pajamas. She wanted his hands on her body, wanted to feel his hair-roughened flesh pressed to her sensitive skin.

Tugging at the collar of his shirt, she was startled out of the sensual haze in her addled brain by a feminine moan of frustration. Had that sound really come from her? Dear heavens, what was she doing?

Embarrassed beyond belief, Alyssa pushed against him. "I can't. Please stop."

Caleb looked as dazed as she felt. "It's…all right,

sweetheart." He cleared his throat and sat up. "It stops right here." Rising to his feet, he smiled. "I think I'll go get that cup of coffee. Are you sure I can't bring something back for you?"

It appeared that he was going to act as if nothing had happened between them. Unsure whether she was disappointed or relieved, she decided to take his lead and ignore the fact that they'd been making out like a couple of hormone-crazed teenagers.

She shook her head. "N-no, thank you. I think I'll turn in for the night."

He stared at her for several seconds before he reached down and lifted her chin with his forefinger. "I'll try not to disturb you when I return."

"I sleep pretty sound." His touch was doing strange things to her insides and she sounded as if she'd run a marathon. "I doubt that you'll make enough noise to wake me."

"I didn't say anything about making noise, sweetheart." His deep chuckle and mischievous grin sent her pulse racing. "There's a big difference."

Alyssa felt as if her heart suddenly dropped to her stomach, then bounced back up to pound at her ribs when she realized what he meant. Before she could find her voice, Caleb gave her a quick kiss on the forehead, then picked up his boots and walked across the room and out the door without a backward glance.

Staring at the closed door, she had to force herself to

breathe. Now she knew for certain that she'd landed on the other side of the rainbow. Either that, or she and Caleb had both been taken over by aliens. After all, they were in Roswell, where the unexplained was not only accepted, it was expected.

But as she reached up to turn off the bedside lamp, she shook her head. She knew what had gotten into her and it had nothing whatsoever to do with friends from a faraway galaxy. From the moment Caleb Walker had strolled into her office, she'd fought it, tried to ignore it and even denied its existence. But the truth was, she was attracted to her new boss.

She burrowed deeper into the bed and pulled the covers up to her chin. What on earth was she going to do now?

In the past few minutes, she'd abandoned the two most important rules she'd set for herself. She'd allowed one of her coworkers to witness her emotional side and she'd practically thrown herself at him when he'd offered her comfort.

She sighed heavily. There was no way around it now. Her departure from Skerritt and Crowe was not only inevitable, it was imminent.

Closing her eyes, she tried not to think of the damage she'd done to her professional reputation and willed herself to relax. She probably wouldn't be able to sleep, but at least she wouldn't be sobbing like a baby when Caleb returned this time.

What seemed like only a few minutes later, the ringing phone roused her. Who on earth could be calling at this time of night?

She grumbled about wanting to hurt whoever was on the other end of the line as she switched on the light and snatched up the receiver before it could ring again. "Hello?"

Dead silence greeted her.

"Is someone there?" she asked impatiently.

"Who is it?" Caleb asked, sounding groggy.

She sucked in a sharp breath as she glanced over at the other bed. Apparently she'd been asleep longer than she'd realized. He'd not only returned to their room, but he'd been sleeping as soundly as she'd been.

"Ms. Merrick?"

"Yes." She looked at the digital alarm clock on the nightstand. "Who is this and why are you calling at two in the morning?"

"This is Clarence Norton, A.J.…Ms. Merrick. I'm sorry to wake you," the security guard from Skerritt and Crowe said apologetically. "The motel operator was supposed to connect me with Mr. Walker's room."

"Is there a problem?"

"The firm's silent alarm went off at the police station about an hour ago," he explained. "They called me to come down and let them in so they could do a thorough search of the building."

Fully awake, she asked, "Was there a break-in?"

"No," Clarence assured her. "But the alarm system shorted out and—"

"What's going on?" Caleb threw back the sheet and sat up on the side of the bed. "Give me the phone."

Alyssa held up her finger to silence him, but it was too late. Clarence had already heard Caleb's voice.

"I-Is that Mr. Walker?" From the tone of his voice, the security guard was shocked right down to his big flat feet.

With Caleb reaching for the receiver and Clarence stammering on the other end of the line, she surrendered the phone without another word.

Her worst nightmare had just been realized. Clarence Norton was the biggest gossip in Albuquerque. By the time she and Caleb returned to the office the day after tomorrow, everyone at Skerritt and Crowe would know that they'd spent the night together.

Four

Caleb set the cruise control, then glanced over at the silent woman seated on the passenger side of the truck cab. Other than answering direct questions, Alyssa hadn't said more than a handful of words to him since the kiss they'd shared the night before. She'd been congenial and outgoing enough when she'd discussed financial options and outlined plans for the two potential clients they'd met with in Las Cruces and Truth or Consequences. But whenever they found themselves alone, she clammed up.

"I'm pretty sure we've picked up Mr. Sanchez and Mrs. Bailey as clients," he said, trying once more to draw her out.

She nodded. "It looks that way."

"Are you going to handle their accounts personally or turn them over to someone else?"

"I'll probably turn them over to Richard Henshaw or Marla Davis."

When she let the discussion drop once again, he released a frustrated breath. "Talk to me, Alyssa. Tell me why I'm getting the silent treatment. Is it because of what happened last night?"

Nodding, she stared straight ahead. "I can't stop thinking about Clarence's phone call and the rumors that I'm sure were being passed around the office today."

"You're worried about what's being said at the office?" he asked incredulously. He hadn't given much, if any, thought to the phone call. His mind had been occupied with that kiss. To say she'd damned near knocked his socks off was an understatement.

"Aren't you concerned?" She looked at him like he'd sprouted horns and a tail. "Clarence Norton is the biggest gossip this side of the Mississippi and he's not going to let something like my being in your room at two in the morning go by without putting his spin on it. By now, I'm sure he's told everyone who will listen that we slept together last night."

"Technically, we did sleep together," Caleb said, grinning. "Just not in the same bed." The cab of the truck was dark, but he'd bet every last dime he had that her cheeks had colored a pretty pink. He wished like hell he could see them.

"I suppose that's true. But do you honestly think anyone will believe that?" she asked.

"Maybe." He shrugged. "But the way I see it, our only option is to tell the truth. After we explain things, it'll be up to everyone else to draw their own conclusions."

"You know what that will be." She glared at him like she thought he might be a little simpleminded.

"We can't control what others think or say about us, Alyssa." He gave her what he hoped was an encouraging smile. "But even if they are talking about us now, this time next week someone else will be the topic of conversation around the water cooler."

"I hope you're right."

"I'm sure—"

He stopped short when he noticed steam rolling out from under the truck's hood. Glancing at the temperature gauge on the dash, he said a word that would have had his mother washing his mouth out with soap if she'd heard. It was a dark, moonless night and they were miles away from the last gas station.

"Why is your truck smoking?" she asked, clearly alarmed.

"It's my guess we have radiator problems."

"That's not good." She pushed her owlish glasses up her nose with a brush of her hand—a gesture he'd come to recognize as a sign of her nervousness. "What are you going to do?"

"I'll have to find a place to pull over so I can check

it out." He'd no sooner gotten the words out than they passed a sign indicating a rest area less than a mile ahead. "Looks like we're in luck. At least it will be well lit and I can see what I'm doing."

Ten minutes later, Caleb stood in the parking lot of the rest area with Alyssa peering around his arm at the truck's steaming engine. "The radiator hose is busted," he said when he noticed her questioning expression.

"Do you think you can fix it?"

He shook his head, stepped back and slammed the hood. "I'll have to call roadside assistance." Pulling his cell phone from the clip on his belt, he asked, "Is there another town between here and Socorro?"

She looked anything but happy. "No. This rest area is about halfway between Socorro and Truth or Consequences. And I'm sure that everything in either direction is closed by now."

Pushing the button with the auto club's preprogrammed number, Caleb gave their location and the nature of the problem, then waited for the customer-service representative, identifying himself as Jason, to contact the nearest associate. When the man came back on the line, the news wasn't what Caleb wanted to hear.

"What do you mean they can't get to us until tomorrow morning?" he demanded.

Alyssa cringed. "They won't be here until morning?"

"I'm sorry for the inconvenience, sir. We have only

one associate garage in that area and the mechanic is out on a call," Jason apologized. "After that he has three more to take care of before he can get to you."

Thinking fast, Caleb asked, "Could you send someone with a rental car?"

"Just a moment, please."

"What did he say?" she asked anxiously.

"He's checking." Caleb smiled. "I'm sure we'll have a car here in no time." At least, he hoped they would.

"Sir, your rental car will be delivered to your location by four in the morning," Jason said, sounding as if he'd accomplished something wonderful.

"Four!" Caleb checked his watch, then shook his head. "Five hours is unacceptable, Jason. Even if the car is coming from Albuquerque, it shouldn't take more than a couple of hours."

"I'm sorry, sir," Jason said, beginning to sound like a broken record. "The agencies in both Truth or Consequences and Socorro are closed, the one in Las Cruces has all of its cars rented right now and the one in Albuquerque is having to call someone in to drive the car down to you."

Caleb glanced over at Alyssa. She looked fit to be tied.

"So that's the best you can do?" he asked the young man.

"I'm afraid so, sir," Jason answered. "If there's anything else we can do for you, please let us know."

Caleb snapped the phone shut as he turned to Alyssa.

"I guess you've figured out by now that we aren't going anywhere until around four tomorrow morning."

Looking more pale than she had a few minutes ago, she nodded and started for the passenger door. "I think one of us must be related to Murphy."

"Who the hell's Murphy?"

"I'm not sure, but his law has plagued us throughout this trip."

"Ah, yes. Anything that can go wrong, will go wrong, and at the worst possible moment." He helped her into the truck. "Well, things could be worse."

She looked at him like he had spit for brains. "How on earth could things be any worse?"

He grinned. "We could have broken down before or after we got to the rest area."

"Small consolation," she said, settling herself on the bench seat. "We're still stranded."

"Yes, but at least we're stuck at a rest area with vending machines." He hooked his thumb over his shoulder. "I'm going to see if they have bottled water. Do you want one?"

She nodded. "Thank you."

As Caleb walked the short distance to the row of vending machines, Alyssa took one deep breath, then another. How much anxiety could one woman handle before she lost her mind?

She'd been stressed enough over her behavior when he'd kissed her. Then, after the phone call from the security guard, she'd spent the rest of the night tossing and turning as she'd thought of the office gossip that would surely be spreading like wildfire. Now, she was having to spend another night in Caleb's disturbing presence.

Watching him get bottles of water from the machine, then start back toward the truck, she shivered. He looked darned good in his sports jacket, dress shirt and jeans. On some men, the combination just wouldn't work. But on Caleb, it was sexy beyond words. And she had to admit that spending more time with him wasn't an unpleasant thought. He wasn't just devastatingly handsome, he was intelligent, easy to talk to and had a nice sense of humor. And boy, oh boy, could he kiss.

Her cheeks heated and she had to force herself to breathe. The more time she spent with him, the more she wanted to know about him, the more she wanted him to kiss her again. And therein lay the problem.

For heaven's sake, they worked together. She shouldn't want to spend more time getting to know him. And she definitely shouldn't want his kiss. She knew all too well from past experience that becoming friendly with a coworker spelled disaster with a great big capital *D*.

But the choice had been taken out of her hands. Fate had stepped in and taken over—first with the room mix-up and now with a broken radiator hose.

When he opened the driver's door, he handed her two bottles of water and a package of cookies before removing his sports jacket. Tossing it on the seat between them, he rolled up the sleeves of his white dress shirt, then slid in behind the steering wheel.

Her breath caught and she decided she was in real trouble if all it took to make her insides hum was the sight of his bare forearms. But as he turned up his shirt sleeves, the movement drew attention to the play of muscles and sent her pulse into overdrive.

"I thought you might get hungry while we're waiting on the rental car," he said.

She glanced down at the package of cookies. It was only a stale vending-machine snack, but his thoughtfulness touched her more than she could have imagined. No one, including her father, had ever shown her a lot of consideration. She'd always been the bookish nerd who blended into the background, no matter where she went or who she was with. There had even been times after her mother had died that she'd suspected her father had forgotten she existed.

"Thank you," she said, barely able to get the words past the lump clogging her throat.

"Are you all right?" He reached out to put his arm around her, then, moving his jacket out of the way, pulled her to the middle of the seat. "I know being stuck here is upsetting, but—"

"I'm fine. Really." Wanting to change the subject before she made a complete fool of herself, she asked, "Do you really think going on picnics and getting closer with the employees is going to make Skerritt and Crowe a more efficient consulting firm?"

He nodded. "Let me ask you this. How much do you know about the people who work under you?"

Thinking hard, she shook her head. "Not much."

"Exactly." Twisting in the seat to face her, he leaned back against the driver's door. "Would you say Geena Phillips has been working up to her potential lately?"

She didn't have to think twice about the matter. The woman had been late several times in the past couple of weeks. "No. Lately, she's seemed distracted and I've been meaning to talk to her about it."

"Don't," he said, shaking his head. "A disciplinary talk will only add to the problem."

"I take it you know something I don't."

His mouth flattened into a grim line. "She's battling a case of morning sickness. It's her first pregnancy, she doesn't know where the father of her baby disappeared to and she's scared witless that she won't be able to handle things by herself."

Alyssa was shocked. "I had no idea Geena was going through anything like that."

"That's because in the past it's been company policy to check your private life at the door when you come to work." He shook his head. "Geena's a good accountant who's hit a rough patch in her life. She needs our support and assurance that she's not going to lose the job she'll need to support herself and the baby. That kind of encouragement from an employer can go a long way to instill loyalty in an employee, as well as inspire them to work harder for the company."

She could see where a change was definitely in order in that area. "I'll talk to her about coming in a couple of hours later until she starts feeling better."

Yawning he nodded his approval. "Now you have the right idea." It seemed that he'd no sooner gotten the words out than he was sound asleep.

As she leaned her head back against the seat and tried to get comfortable, she had to admit that Caleb's approach to management made a lot of sense. *By the book* wasn't necessarily the best way to handle employees.

But the idea of letting her employees know her better still made her extremely nervous. The more someone knew about you, the more they could use against you. At least, that was the philosophy her father had preached to her for as long as she could remember.

She sighed. If she stayed at Skerritt and Crowe, becoming friendly with those around her was definitely going to take some getting used to.

Reluctant to open her eyes and end the dream of having two strong arms holding her securely to a wide masculine chest, Alyssa burrowed deeper into her dream lover's embrace. It felt wonderful to be held while she slept and she wanted to enjoy it for as long as she could, even if it was just a dream.

"Good morning."

Her eyes flew open and she started to pull away. Dear heavens, she wasn't dreaming. She was lying on a very real Caleb Walker, who, at the moment, seemed intent on keeping her right where she was.

"I—I'm sorry," she stammered, trying once again to extricate herself from his hold.

He tightened his arms around her and his deep chuckle beneath her ear vibrated all the way to her soul. "Don't be sorry. I'm not. You were comfortable and I thought I'd let you sleep."

Her heart did a funny little flip. "It was nice of you to think of me," she said, straightening her glasses. She managed to put a little space between them to look up into his twinkling hazel eyes. "But—"

"Sweetheart, I think about you more than you realize." He gave her the sexy grin that never failed to curl her toes as he drew her closer, then rested his forehead on hers. "In fact, you're about all I've been able to think of since night before last."

Shivers skittered up and down her spine from the mere memory, but the only way she'd been able to face him had been to tell herself that she'd dreamed it. "Nothing happened," she insisted.

He chuckled. "Then I must have a real vivid imagination, because after that kiss, I walked out of the motel room hotter than a two-dollar pistol at a skid-row pawnshop."

Alyssa felt as if her heart had stopped completely and even if her vocal cords hadn't suddenly become temporarily paralyzed, she couldn't think of a thing to say.

Leaning back, he gazed at her for several long seconds. "You want to know something else?"

"I—I'm not sure," she said, feeling extremely short of breath.

"I want to do it again." He removed her glasses, then placed them on the dash. "Do you want me to kiss you, Alyssa?"

Mesmerized by his remarkable gaze and promising smile, she didn't even hesitate. "Yes."

He removed first one, then another of the pins holding her hair up. "You have beautiful hair. You should wear it down more often."

"I've always hated my hair," she said honestly.

"Why?" Running his fingers through it, he cupped the back of her head and started to draw her forward. "It feels like strands of silk."

Unable to breathe, much less think, Alyssa's eyes drifted shut as she allowed Caleb to nibble at her lips, then cover them with a kiss so tender it made her feel as if she were the most cherished woman on earth. What was there about this man that she couldn't resist?

She'd never had trouble rejecting advances from other men. But when Caleb touched her, rational thought seemed beyond her capabilities. All she wanted was to feel his big, hard body pressed to hers, to taste the desire on his lips and hear his sexy Southern drawl as he said her name.

When he used the tip of his tongue to coax her to open for him, she decided it didn't matter that she had no will of her own where he was concerned. The truth was, she liked the way he made her feel when he kissed her and the last thing she wanted him to do was stop.

As Caleb slipped his tongue inside, Alyssa met him halfway in a sensuous game of advance and retreat and he felt like his heart would pound a hole right through his rib cage. He'd tried to tell himself to leave well enough alone, that Alyssa Jane Merrick was off-limits.

For one thing, she was a career woman and, considering his history with them, he should be running as hard and fast as his legs would carry him in the opposite direction. And for another, he was having to rely on hers and the other managers' experience at Skerritt and Crowe to keep the firm running until he could get some business courses under his belt. He didn't need an emotional involvement added to the mix. It would only complicate things and increase the possibility of one of them getting hurt.

But whether it was wise or not, he hadn't been able to resist the temptation of holding her soft body against his, of once again savoring her perfect lips. He'd spent a hell of a day yesterday and an even worse night reliving that kiss and he needed to know if she was as fantastic as he remembered.

When she lightly stroked his tongue with hers, the sweet, shy response aroused him so fast it made him light-headed and he immediately decided that if anything, his memory had been more than a little faulty. He'd never in all of his thirty years been this turned on by simply kissing a woman.

Slowly tugging her blouse from the waistband of her skirt, he slipped his hand under the beige silk. Her smooth skin felt like satin beneath his palm as he slid it over her ribs to the underside of her breast. Cupping the soft mound, he gently caressed her as he nibbled his way from her lips down the slender column of her throat.

Her tiny moan of pleasure sent a fresh wave of heat straight to his groin. But when he realized that she'd unbuttoned the first few buttons on his shirt and was doing a little exploring of her own, his body tightened with an intensity that quickly had him shifting to relieve the pressure in his suddenly too-tight jeans. Just knowing she was as turned on as he was sent his blood pressure skyrocketing.

At that moment, he wanted her more than he wanted to draw his next breath. He wanted to lay her down and discover all of her secrets. And he wanted to share all of his with her.

"Hey man, get a room."

Glancing through the windshield, Caleb noticed a group of grinning teenage boys walking past the truck on their way to the information center.

Damn! His timing couldn't have been worse. The front seat of his truck in a rest area with God and everybody strolling past wasn't exactly the place for the pleasurable kind of exploring he had in mind.

He took in some much-needed oxygen as he rearranged Alyssa's blouse. "Sweetheart, there's nothing I'd like more than to continue kissing you and a hell of a lot more. But if we keep this up, somebody's going to call the cops. And I'm not real keen on the idea of our being arrested for lewd conduct in a public place."

She made no comment as she stared at him, but the heightened color on her cheeks indicated that she'd forgotten where they were, the same as he had.

"It's daylight," she said, looking around. "What time is it?"

Checking his watch, he shook his head to clear it. "It's a little past eight."

"Where's the rental car?" She slid over to the passenger side of the seat. "I thought it was supposed to be here by four."

Caleb shrugged. "They're late."

"No kidding." She tucked her blouse back into the waistband of her skirt. "Have you called them?"

"The driver thought we were in the rest area north of Socorro," he said, nodding. "When he didn't find us there, he turned around and went back to Albuquerque instead of calling roadside assistance to get a verification on our location."

He didn't add that he wasn't all that sorry the guy was incompetent. Whether it was smart or not, he'd enjoyed holding her while she'd slept.

"Are they sending another car?"

He shook his head. "I told them not to bother."

"You did what?" If looks could kill, he'd be dead in about two seconds flat.

"The mechanic from Truth or Consequences should be here any time with a new radiator hose." He stretched to relieve a few of the kinks in his muscles. "I didn't see the need for a car when he'll have the truck fixed in less than fifteen minutes."

"I suppose that makes sense." She frowned. "But I was hoping we'd be back at the office well before everyone arrived for work. I wanted to run home for a quick shower and to change clothes." She glanced down at her wrinkled suit. "I'm a mess."

"Don't worry about it. We won't get there until midmorning." He gave her his most reassuring smile. "Everyone will be busy and you can get your car without anyone being the wiser."

She looked more than a little doubtful. "I hope you're right."

He didn't tell her, but he hoped like hell he was, too.

Five

When Caleb steered the truck into his reserved parking space, Alyssa immediately noticed that something was wrong with her car. Instead of sitting level, it was tilted to one side. So much for making a quick getaway before someone in the office saw her disheveled appearance.

"Looks like you have a flat tire," Caleb commented when he got out of the truck and came around to open the passenger door for her.

"Great. Just what I wanted to do before I go home," she said, wondering what else could go wrong. "I get to change a tire."

He frowned. "You're going to do it yourself?"

She nodded. "I've been changing my own tires since I learned to drive. My father insisted on it."

"You don't have an auto service plan?"

"No."

He held out his hand. "Give me the keys."

"Thanks, but I'll take care of it," she said, removing her suit jacket.

"Not while I'm around." He took the keys from her, then motioned toward the building. "Why don't you go inside and get out of this heat?"

She nibbled on her lower lip. The temperature was rising, but so was her apprehension that someone would see her.

"I'd rather not."

She could just imagine the stares if she walked into her office looking the way she did. Her clothing couldn't have been more wrinkled from spending the night in the truck and her hair was hanging down her back like a limp mop because Caleb had lost most of the pins when he'd taken it out of her usual chignon.

"Don't be silly." He opened the trunk of her sedan. "It's already in the nineties and—"

"No need for you gettin' all hot and dirty, Caleb," Ernie Clay called as he hurried out of the building toward them. The security guard stopped in front of them, then, grinning like a Cheshire cat, he nodded at her car. "Clarence noticed Ms. Merrick's tire was flat and had me call my brother-in-law. He owns a garage and tow-ing service and should be here in a few minutes to take care of it."

"Thanks, Ernie." Caleb placed his hand at the small of her back and started urging her toward the entrance. "We'll be in our offices. Let us know when your brother-in-law has the tire changed."

The last thing Alyssa wanted to do was walk into the office looking the way she did. But before she had a chance to protest, Caleb ushered her through the building entrance and over to the elevators.

When the elevator door slid shut, she looked down at her clothes. "I'm a complete mess."

He frowned. "You look fine to me."

She shook her head. "My hair is down, my pantyhose has a huge run and I look like a raccoon from the mascara smudges under my eyes."

Removing her glasses for a closer look, he shook his head. "Just one little place under your left eye."

Her jacket fell to the floor as she was thrown off guard by his unexpected touch, and she braced her hands on his chest to keep from falling when the elevator came to a halt on their floor. "I'll take care of—"

The doors opened at that very moment and to Alyssa's horror, Malcolm Fuller and the entire public-relations department observed her clinging to Caleb as he used his thumb to wipe gently at the tender skin below her eye. From the looks on their faces, she could tell exactly what they were thinking.

"Well, hello there," Malcolm said, not even bothering to hide his ear-to-ear grin. "We're headed out to our first team-building picnic. Would you two like to join us?"

"No, thank you," she said before Caleb could get them into something else that would no doubt cause her further humiliation. "But have a good time."

Her cheeks burned with embarrassment as she picked up her jacket, then brushed past the group and headed straight for her office. She didn't wait to see if Caleb followed, nor did she care that he still had her glasses. She'd spent two and a half nerve-racking days with him and she needed some space.

Although her father would strongly disapprove and probably come back to haunt her for being such a coward, all she wanted to do was hide out in her office until her car was fixed. After that, she had every intention of going home, climbing into bed and sleeping the entire weekend. Hopefully, when she woke up Monday morning, she would escape the nightmare she'd been trapped in for the past week.

But even as she mourned the loss of her well-ordered work environment, she couldn't deny that her body still hummed from Caleb's touch. And just the memory of his steamy kisses was enough to leave her aching for things she had no business wanting.

As she walked down the hall toward the conference room to meet with a client, Alyssa finally began to relax.

It had been a week since she and Caleb had returned from the Roswell trip and it appeared that he'd been right about the gossip dying down once they'd told the whole story. To her immense relief, she hadn't heard a single word about them spending the night together or being caught in a compromising position in the elevator. Other than a few smug smiles and knowing looks from a couple of her male coworkers, it had been business as usual around the office.

"Has anyone seen them together since Friday?" Alyssa overheard someone ask as she approached the door to the break room.

The hushed voice stopped her dead in her tracks.

"No. I think they're probably trying to be a little more discreet about their affair." The woman laughed. "I mean really, getting caught in the elevator like that, then trying to convince us that he was looking at her eye. How dumb do they think we are? I heard that half of her clothes were on the elevator floor and she was tearing at his shirt when the doors opened."

A chill raced through her and it felt as if ice water had replaced the blood in her veins. She wanted to scream that they were wrong in their assumptions, that it really was just as Caleb had told them. But she knew it was useless.

"You know there's a door connecting their offices," she heard a third voice chime in. "There's no telling how many times during the day they get together for a little tête-à-tête."

The laughter that followed the erroneous statement made Alyssa nauseous. Feeling as if her world had just caved in on her, she retraced her steps and headed back to her office. She'd heard enough to know that her professional reputation at Skerritt and Crowe had gone down in a blaze of glory—and that there was nothing left but cinders.

"Please call Geena Phillips and have her meet with Mr. Holt in the conference room," she said, placing the client file on Geneva's desk.

"Is something wrong?" the older woman asked, her obvious concern reflected in the tone of her voice. "You don't look like you feel well."

"I don't." That was the understatement of the year, Alyssa thought as she walked into her office and closed the door.

She'd been a naive fool to think that people weren't talking about her and Caleb. How could she have been so stupid? The employees weren't going to discuss their thoughts on the issue in front of the two people involved.

Walking straight to her desk, she sat down at her computer and began drafting her resignation. She'd hoped to have another job lined up before she quit, but the choice had been taken out of her hands. There was no way she could stay at Skerritt and Crowe now. By close of business this afternoon, she'd be unemployed.

"Geneva told me you're sick," Caleb said, walking

into her office without so much as a tap on the connecting door. "Do you need to see a doctor?"

"No." Alyssa should have known their secretary would run to him with her concerns. Geneva, the traitor, had embraced every one of Caleb's ideas and took it upon herself to keep him informed of everything that went on in the office as soon as it happened.

"Are you sure you're all right?" He frowned. "You do look pale. I'll drive you—"

"I'm fine." She glared at him as she keyed in the command to print her resignation. "Now, will you please leave?"

"You don't feel well and you're cranky as hell. But you're fine?" An understanding smile suddenly turned up the corners of his mouth. "That time of month, huh?"

Exasperated, she threw up her hands and sat back in her desk chair. "Why do men automatically think of PMS when a woman wants to be left alone? Did it ever occur to you that I might be tired and just want a little peace and quiet?"

Instead of going back into his office as she requested, he sat down in one of the chairs in front of her desk. "You were on your way to outline a retirement plan that you've been working on for the past week, then all of a sudden you turn the file over to Geena. If you aren't sick, what's the problem?" Before she could answer, he shook his head. "And don't feed me that line about peace and quiet. What's going on?"

Suddenly feeling much too tired to argue, she removed her letter of resignation from the printer, signed it and handed it to him. "I think this is self-explanatory."

He scanned the letter, then shook his head. "You can't resign."

She laughed humorlessly. "I just did."

"I'm not going to accept it." He ripped the paper in half, rose to his feet, then rounded the desk to turn her chair to face him. Placing a hand on each of the chair arms, he had her trapped and she had no alternative but to listen to him. "Talk to me, Alyssa. Tell me what's brought on this sudden decision to bail out of a job I happen to know you love."

His face was only inches from hers and it took every ounce of her concentration to remember what he'd said. "You were wrong," she finally blurted out before she could stop herself.

He frowned. "About what?"

Defeated, she fought to keep her voice even. "The gossip hasn't died down about us. If anything, it's led to more speculation among the employees."

"That's it?"

"Isn't that enough?"

"No."

Caleb's gut churned with a mixture of anger and desperation. He'd known they were still the favorite topic of idle conversation around the office and although he wasn't happy about it, he'd done his best to ignore it. Trying to set the record straight once again would only make matters worse and add more grist to the rumor mill.

Unfortunately, that was only the tip of the iceberg. The possibility of Alyssa leaving the firm was what had him tied in knots. He wasn't proud of having to rely on her without her knowing it, but he needed her expertise to keep things running smoothly until he got a grasp on what he was supposed to be doing.

But as important as her business acumen was to him, the real reason his stomach churned like a cement mixer whenever he thought about her leaving Skerritt and Crowe was far simpler. He'd hated to admit it, even to himself, but he just plain didn't want to face coming to the office without her being there.

Noticing a tear at the corner of her big blue eyes, he removed her glasses and gently wiped it away. "Did you overhear something, sweetheart?"

She nodded. "According to some, you and I are having a grand old time in here." She rolled her eyes. "Several times a day."

He chuckled. "I'm good, but I wasn't aware that I'm *that* good."

Her cheeks turned a pretty pink. "I wouldn't know anything about that. But I do know that I can't effectively supervise when everyone thinks I'm sleeping with the boss."

Lifting her chin with his index finger, he stared at her for several long seconds. God, she was pretty and it tore him up to see her upset like this.

"It's going to be all right, Alyssa. I promise."

"I don't know how."

She looked so dejected, it was all he could do to keep from taking her into his arms. But that would only add fuel to the fire if someone walked into her office and caught them.

As he continued to stare at her, a germ of an idea began to form. It was crazy enough that it just might work.

"I think I have a solution that will stop the tongues from wagging and allow you to keep your job here," he said, smiling.

She looked doubtful. "I'm listening."

"Let's go along with the rumors."

He laughed when she looked at him like he might not be playing with a full deck. "Have you lost your mind?"

"Probably." He took her hands in his, then pulling her to her feet, took her in his arms. "My grandpa used to say that sometimes the only way to put out a fire is to throw kerosene on it."

"In other words, insanity runs in your family?"

Caleb grinned. "Grandpa did have his share of peculiarities, but most of the time his logic made a hell of a lot of sense. Toss a little fuel on a fire and it burns itself out real quick and that's the end of it. Leave it alone and it can smolder for a while, then flare up again and again."

"Would you care to explain how that relates to our current problem?" To his satisfaction, she'd wrapped her arms around his waist and seemed genuinely interested in hearing him out.

"If we come out in the open and tell everyone that we are romantically involved, there won't be anything left to speculate about." He paused as something else came to mind. "In fact, as of right now, we're engaged. Then, in a few weeks, we'll announce that we've changed our minds and decided to just be friends."

"Now I'm sure you've gone over the edge." Pulling away from him, she stepped back and shook her head. "It would never work."

"Sure it will. And the sooner we announce our big news the sooner we'll be back to business as usual." Giving her a quick kiss, he reached over to press the button on her intercom. He wasn't waiting for her to come up with any more arguments why his plan was faulty. "Geneva, call a mandatory meeting of all employees for two this afternoon in the lobby downstairs."

"Consider it done," the secretary answered. "Is there anything else?"

"Nope. That's it. Thanks, Geneva." Turning back to Alyssa, he smiled. She had that deer-in-the-headlights look again. "Relax. In about an hour, we'll make our big announcement and the problem will be over."

She sank into her chair as if her knees would no longer support her. "Or just beginning."

"Trust me, sweetheart. An engagement is just what the doctor ordered to take care of this little problem."

She sighed. "Which doctor would that be? Kevorkian?"

Laughing, he headed back into his office. "Hang on to your sense of humor and everything will work out great. You'll see."

When he closed the door behind him, Caleb walked over to stare out the window behind his desk. A fake engagement? What the hell had he been thinking?

But when Alyssa had shoved her resignation at him, he'd felt like his stomach had dropped to his shoe tops. And it hadn't been entirely due to the fact that he needed her to stay at the firm and keep things running while he took his classes.

The simple fact of the matter was he didn't want Alyssa to leave because he had a case of the hots for her and there didn't seem to be any way he could stop it. Not even reminding himself of his miserable track record with a career woman had lessened her appeal. Since their trip to Roswell last week, all he'd been able to think about was how soft and sweet she'd looked when she slept and how good it had felt to hold her.

He took a deep breath and shook his head in an effort to clear it. If they were going to convince the Skerritt and Crowe employees they were wild about each other, it was going to take some planning.

A slow grin spread across his face. They had an entire weekend to get their act together and he knew the perfect place to hold their strategy session. Now all he had to do was convince Alyssa to go with him.

* * *

"This is never going to work, Caleb," Alyssa said as they walked out of her office into the deserted hall.

"Just follow my lead and act happier than you've ever been in your life." He waited for her to step onto the elevator. "I'll take care of the rest. Did you get your purse?"

She nodded. "Although I can't understand why you think I need it."

"You'll see."

His grin told her that he had something up his sleeve, but she didn't have time to think about what it could be. What was about to take place was foremost in her thoughts and had her wondering if they'd both lost their minds. In just a few short seconds, the elevator doors were going to open and they'd tell the entire Skerritt and Crowe staff they were engaged.

When the elevator came to a halt on the ground floor, Caleb grinned and took her hand in his. "Ready?"

"No."

"Smile," he whispered as the doors swished open.

Stepping off the elevator, instead of looking deliriously happy, she'd bet everything she owned that she looked more like she was about to throw up. The sick feeling intensified when she watched several of her colleagues exchange knowing glances.

"Since our trip to Roswell last week, there's been a lot of speculation about the nature of the relationship between me and A.J.," Caleb said, getting right to the heart of the matter. "That's why we've called you all here this afternoon. We want to end the speculation and set the record straight, once and for all."

There was no turning back now. She took a deep breath and trained her unwavering gaze on Caleb. She wasn't certain she'd be able to get through the next few minutes if she had to look at anyone else.

"Yes, there's something going on between me and A. J. Merrick." Her heart skipped several beats when he looked down at her and smiled. "I'd like to announce that as of this afternoon, Alyssa and I are engaged."

Stunned silence reigned for several seconds before the crowd suddenly broke out in a round of enthusiastic applause. But when Caleb pulled her to him and kissed her like a soldier returning from war, the cheers were so loud it was almost deafening.

When he raised his head, he announced, "Alyssa and I are leaving town for the weekend, so don't try calling us. We'll be busy making…" His pause and suggestive grin caused several knowing smiles. "Wedding plans," he finished. He pointed to Malcolm. "You're in charge until we return on Monday."

The kiss and Caleb's announcement that they were going away together had taken her by surprise, but he shocked her beyond words when he swept her up into his arms and carried her from the building to the uproarious cheers and applause of the Skerritt and Crowe employees. Unable to find her voice and not knowing what else to do, she threw her arms around his shoulders and hung on for dear life.

"What in the name…of all that's holy…do you think you're doing?" she finally managed to squeak out as he walked across the parking lot toward his truck.

He laughed. "I'm whisking you away like any white knight worth his weight in beans would do when he's won the hand of his fair maiden."

"Don't you think you're taking this farce just a bit far?" she asked when he opened his truck door and deposited her on the bench seat.

When she started to scoot over to the passenger side, he slid behind the steering wheel and pulled her up against him. "If this is going to work, we have to look like we're wild about each other, right?"

"Yes, but—"

"Don't you think everyone would expect us to spend time together away from the office?" he asked, starting the truck, then backing it from the parking space. "And especially right after we got engaged?"

She sighed. "All right, you've made your point."

He gave her a grin that curled her toes inside her black pumps. "We'll drop by your apartment for you to get some clothes together, then head up to my place to hide out for the weekend."

Feeling as if her life was spinning out of control with no hope of recovery, she gasped. "I beg your pardon.

When did this fiasco escalate to me actually going away with you?"

As he drove the truck out onto the street and headed in the direction of her apartment, he shook his head. "Think about it, Alyssa. Ed Bentley lives in the same complex you do. In fact, he and his wife live in the building across the street from yours. Even if you stayed in for the entire weekend, he'd notice your lights going on and off and know you were home." He gave her a pointed look. "The success of our plan hinges on this, sweetheart."

Her temples began to throb and her stomach felt as if it had been filled with rocks. "Why did I ever let you talk me into this?"

"Because the rumors and gossip were getting to you." He took her hand in his to give it a gentle squeeze. "Besides, we need to map out a game plan for how we'll play our engagement and eventual breakup."

Everything he said made perfect sense, but that did little to lessen the apprehension building inside her as he steered the truck into her apartment complex. She didn't even have a clue where he lived.

As if he'd read her mind, he smiled. "Be sure to bring a jacket. It gets chilly at night."

"You live in the mountains?" Somehow, she wasn't surprised.

"Yep. About twenty miles from here, in the East Mountain area," he said, parking in front of her building. He shrugged. "I never have been much of a city boy."

She took a deep breath and reached for the door handle. "I'll pack accordingly." When he started to get out of the truck, she shook her head. "If you don't mind, I'd like a few minutes alone to collect my thoughts."

He stared at her for a moment before he nodded. "Don't forget to pack your swimsuit. I have a hot tub and pool."

As she entered her small apartment to begin packing a few things for her weekend away with Caleb, Alyssa wasn't sure whether to laugh or cry. Why on earth had she allowed him to talk her into such a ridiculous scheme?

But as she finished folding clothes into her small bag, then made arrangements with Mrs. Rogers to take care of her parakeet, Alyssa knew exactly why she'd gone along with Caleb's plan. She simply didn't want to leave Skerritt and Crowe to find a position elsewhere. Other financial firms might offer the same opportunities to do the work she loved, but there was one thing they didn't have—a handsome CEO with hazel eyes, a sexy as sin grin and kisses that turned her into melted butter.

Six

Opening the wrought-iron gate, Caleb wondered what was going through Alyssa's pretty little head as he led her across the courtyard to the front door. The farther out of the city they'd driven, the more silent and speculative she'd become.

"If you're worried about the sleeping arrangements, don't," he said when they entered the house. He set her small case down to punch the deactivation code into the security system. "There are three extra bedrooms. You can take your pick."

"I really hadn't given where I'd be sleeping much thought." When he turned to face her, she gave him a sheepish grin. "I've been mentally calculating how much stucco homes cost and what the investment potential in real estate is on this side of the Sandia Mountains. I would think that the equity would build quickly since this area seems to be growing pretty fast."

He chuckled as he picked up her overnight case. "Once an accountant, always an accountant, huh?"

"Something like that." She gave him an odd look. "With your background in business, wasn't it something you considered when you moved here?"

"Not really." He wasn't about to tell her that the house had been given to him when he'd accepted Emerald's offer to take over the firm or that his background in business started two weeks ago when he'd walked through Skerritt and Crowe's front doors. "I was more interested in the fact that it's fairly secluded and has several acres of land."

She seemed to accept his explanation and, breathing a little easier, he followed her into the great room. But his heart damned near hammered a hole clean through his rib cage when she stopped to stare at a portrait of a middle-aged Emerald Larson and her infamous playboy son, Owen—Caleb's late father.

"Are they your relatives?" she asked, smiling.

The picture was at least twenty-five years old and it was apparent that Alyssa hadn't recognized the pair. Hopefully, she wouldn't.

"That's my grandmother and father," he said cautiously.

Gazing at him a moment, she nodded. "There's a strong family resemblance."

He placed his hand at the small of her back to usher her toward the bedrooms before she had a chance to study the picture closer and figure out who they all were. He hadn't lied to her thus far and he wasn't about to start now. If she'd recognized the Larsons, he'd have admitted to being one of the heirs to the Emerald, Inc. conglomerate. But she hadn't. And although omission of the facts was something he wasn't proud of and continued to struggle with, being outright dishonest was out of the question. It just wasn't his style.

"Feel free to check out the other two bedrooms, then decide which one you want," he said, opening the door to the room closest to his. The room had been done in yellow and green and looked a little more feminine than the other two bedrooms. "They all have their own private bathroom, but this one is the only one besides the master suite that has a sitting area."

"This is fine," she said, glancing around. She walked over to the French doors on the opposite side of the room to look out at the patio and pool. "It's a lovely area and your home is beautiful, Caleb. You must love living up here."

"Thanks." He set her bag on the end of the bed, then walked over to stand behind her. "The terrain is a lot different here than in Tennessee, but I'm getting used to it." He didn't tell her that it was a far cry from the humble farmhouse he'd grown up in or that he was having a hard time thinking of it as his, even though it had been signed over to him when he'd accepted Emerald's offer.

"I'd like to hear about where you used to live," she said, sounding wistful. "I've never been east of the Mississippi, but I've heard the southern states are quite beautiful."

"They are. Back home when I look at the mountains, I'm used to seeing them covered with trees, and everything is green. Here it's just as pretty, but in a different way. There aren't as many trees and everything is shades of tan, brown or orange." Without thinking, he slipped his arms around her waist and drew her back against him. "I'll have to take you to see the eastern mountains sometime."

He heard her soft intake of breath a moment before she turned to face him. "Caleb, what are we doing?"

Staring down at her, he wondered the same thing. She was the type of woman he'd vowed to steer clear of, yet there was something about Alyssa Jane Merrick that he couldn't resist. He wanted to show her where he'd grown up, wanted her to know who he was and what had molded him into the man he'd become, and he wanted to know all about her. And that scared the living hell out of him.

Suddenly needing to put a little space between them in order to figure out what the hell had gotten into him, he kissed her forehead then, releasing her, started for the door. "While you get your things put away and freshen up, I'll go see what I can scare up for supper."

As Alyssa watched him leave the room, she sighed

heavily. It hadn't been lost on her that he'd avoided answering her question. Could he be as confused about what was going on between them as she was? What *was* happening between them?

She certainly wasn't an expert at affairs of the heart, but it was evident there was something drawing them together. They couldn't be in the same room for longer than five minutes without being in each other's arms.

What was there about Caleb Walker that made her forget the lesson she'd learned five years ago at the hands of a man just like him? Hadn't she suffered enough humiliation when she'd learned that men weren't above using women to achieve their own goals or advance their careers?

Sitting on the side of the bed, she thought about Wesley Pennington III, the man who'd taught her just how cutthroat the business world could truly be and the lengths that some men were willing to go to in order to get ahead. Handsome and charming, Wesley had swept her off her feet about a year after they'd both started working at the prestigious financial group of Carson, Gottlieb and Howell. And right up until the end of their six-week affair, she hadn't had a clue that he'd been using her to gain information about a potential client.

But as she mentally compared Caleb to Wesley the weasel, she had to admit there were very few, if any, similarities. Wesley wouldn't have been caught dead in a pair of jeans and boots, nor would he have chosen to live in a secluded house in a quiet rural area over his ultramodern uptown condo. And that was just scratching the surface of how the two men differed.

Wesley had been a polished sophisticate and tended to act superiorly with anyone below him on the corporate ladder. But Caleb wasn't anything like that. His casual, down-to-earth personality immediately put everyone at ease and he not only treated those who worked for him as his equals, he seemed to genuinely care about them as well.

That was something she knew firsthand to be beyond Wesley's capabilities. He didn't care about anyone but himself and he wasn't above stepping on those who posed a threat to, or got in the way of, his lofty ambitions. He hadn't thought twice about using her affections for him to gain information that had led to his obtaining a coveted corporate account and ultimately the promotion that rightly should have been hers. When she'd confronted him about it, he'd readily admitted that he'd only started dating her for the purpose of getting ahead. But the most devastating blow had come when she'd overheard her coworkers gossiping about the whole sordid mess. That's when she'd decided she had no alternative but to look for another job and had found her present position at Skerritt and Crowe.

But she was certain Caleb would never stoop to that level, would never take credit for her or anyone else's accomplishments, even if he wasn't already the head of

Skerritt and Crowe. Nor would he publicly humiliate her. On the contrary. He'd come up with the pretend engagement and had her spending the weekend with him because he was trying to squelch the rumors and gossip that she found hurtful.

Sighing, she put the last of her clothes in the dresser drawer, then changed into a pair of baggy camp shorts and a T-shirt. She'd tried every way in the world not to like Caleb. But the truth of the matter was, she trusted him more than she had anyone in a very long time. And whether it was smart or not, she might as well admit it—if she hadn't already fallen for him, she was well on her way.

"Thank you for a delicious dinner. You're a very good cook."

"Not really." Caleb grinned. "Throwing something on the grill and fire roasting a few vegetables is about the only thing I know how to fix, besides frying bacon and scrambling eggs."

"Well, I thought it was scrumptious." Her sweet smile did a real number on his insides. "And I'm glad you suggested we eat out here on the patio." He watched her look past the pool at the valley below. "The view is absolutely gorgeous."

He couldn't agree more; the view was beautiful. But he wasn't looking at the cedar trees or the valley. The woman seated at the table with him was far prettier than anything he'd ever seen.

Rising to his feet before he did something stupid like take her in his arms and kiss her senseless, he gathered their plates. "I like sitting out here after the sun goes down. Other than an occasional coyote howling, it's pretty quiet."

"Let me help with those," she said, standing up.

He shook his head. "I'll take care of the cleanup."

"That's not fair," she protested. "You cooked. I should clear the table."

He started toward the house with the dishes. "While I'm doing this, why don't you change? I don't know about you, but I could use some time in the hot tub before I turn in for the night."

"That does sound wonderful, but are you sure I can't help you first?"

Damned if she didn't follow him into the kitchen. Taking a deep breath, he shook his head. He was about two seconds away from kissing her until they both needed CPR or carrying her to his bedroom to make love to her for the rest of the night. But he couldn't tell her that. She'd probably belt him a good one, then run as hard and fast as she could back to Albuquerque.

"I'll just put these plates in the dishwasher, then meet you in the hot tub in ten minutes," he said, surprised that his voice sounded fairly steady. Considering his state of mind and the changes his body was going through at that very moment, he figured it was nothing short of a miracle he could talk at all.

"Okay." She gave him a smile that caused his blood

pressure to shoot up a good fifty points. "But I'm cooking breakfast tomorrow morning."

"You've got yourself a deal, sweetheart." He'd agree to just about anything as long as she left the room and let him get a grip on his runaway libido.

But as he watched her walk away, his heart stalled and his body tightened so fast it left him feeling lightheaded. Even though her khaki shorts and pink T-shirt looked to be a couple of sizes too big, it couldn't disguise the sexy sway of her shapely hips or the fact that her long, slender legs looked like they could wrap around a man and take him to heaven.

Caleb closed his eyes and forced himself to breathe. What the hell had he been thinking when he'd suggested they get in the hot tub? If just watching her walk made him hard, what would happen when he saw her in a swimsuit?

The mental image his overactive imagination conjured up made his knees wobble and sweat pop out on his forehead and upper lip. Leaning against the kitchen counter for support, he groaned. How on God's green earth was he going to keep his hands to himself for the next two days?

When the phone rang, he was grateful to whoever was on the other end of the line for interrupting his disturbing thoughts. "Thank you."

"You're welcome. Now, do you want to tell me what I did?"

"Hey, Hunter." Once he and his brothers had learned

about each other, they'd all, by unspoken agreement, stayed in touch. And Caleb was happy with the bond they were forming.

"What's up with answering the phone the way you did?"

"Just thinking out loud," Caleb said, hoping his oldest brother forgot about his slip of the tongue.

"How's the financial world? Any new advice on how I can turn my savings account into a fortune?"

"If you want to build your money, the best advice I can give you at this point is to leave it where it's at," Caleb said dryly.

Hunter snorted. "You sound about as sure of yourself at this financial stuff as I feel about running an air-ambulance service."

Caleb smiled. "How's the EMT course going?"

There was a pause before Hunter finally answered. "I've been in that damned class for almost two weeks and I still get light-headed whenever I see a needle."

"At least you've stopped passing out at the sight of them," Caleb said, laughing.

"Just barely." Obviously wanting to change the subject, Hunter asked, "Are you going to attend Emerald's birthday party at the end of the month?"

It was Caleb's turn to snort. "I don't think we've been given a lot of choice about going. The invitation read more like a summons than a request to help her celebrate her seventy-sixth birthday."

"It sounds like the one I got." Hunter laughed humorlessly. "I knew that old gal was going to yank our chains every chance she got."

"Have you talked to Nick lately?" Caleb asked.

"He called me last night and suggested we all meet for a beer before we attend Emerald's party."

"That's a good idea." Caleb chuckled. "Maybe if we have a buzz going, it'll make the evening more tolerable."

"I like the way you think."

Finalizing plans to meet before the party, Caleb hung up and headed for his bedroom to change. He was looking forward to seeing Nick and Hunter again. And his only regret about finding out that he had two brothers was that he hadn't learned of their existence sooner.

But he really had no room to complain. He'd had a great childhood with the love and guidance of his maternal grandparents and a mother who had been totally devoted to raising him the right way. He'd asked who his father was a few times, but his mother would only smile and tell him to be patient—that one day he'd learn all about the man. After a while he'd given up asking, and if he'd missed having a father, Caleb couldn't ever remember it. His grandfather had taught him everything he'd needed to know, from how to tie a fishing lure to what it meant to be a good, honest man.

But as he pulled on a pair of gym shorts, he decided he couldn't say he'd missed knowing his manipulative paternal grandmother. No matter what she said about not meddling in their lives back then or the way they ran the businesses she'd given them now, he had a feeling she still had their every move under surveillance and would have no problem stepping in to take over if she felt it was warranted.

But when Caleb opened the French doors to step out onto the patio and spotted Alyssa standing by the hot tub, his grievances with Emerald Larson were quickly forgotten. Damn, but Alyssa looked good. Her black one-piece bathing suit clung to her body and enhanced all the curves that he'd been fantasizing about ever since walking into her office the day he'd arrived to take over the financial firm.

He swallowed hard. He'd been right about her legs, too. They were long, sleek and perfect for holding a man close while he made love to her.

"I'm sorry." Walking over to her, he had to clear his suddenly dry throat. "It took longer than I planned. One of my brothers called."

"I heard the phone ring." She smiled wistfully. "It must be nice to have siblings."

"You're an only child?" He wasn't ready to tell her that a little less than a month ago, he hadn't even known his brothers existed.

Nodding, she took off her glasses and, laying them on a nearby chair, started to climb the steps to get into the hot tub. "I always wanted a brother or sister to share memories with, but it wasn't meant to be."

Caleb took hold of her arm to help steady her as she stepped into the bubbling water, but the second his fingers touched her satiny skin, a jolt of electric current zinged straight up his arm and exploded in the pit of his belly. Climbing into the hot tub on shaky legs, he sat down beside her and tried to think of what they'd been talking about.

"I, uh, haven't always been close with my two brothers."

"Is there a big age difference between you?" she asked, sounding genuinely interested.

"No, we're all about the same age." He knew he was walking a fine line, but he wanted to be as truthful with her as possible. "We had the same father, but different mothers." Deciding it was time to change the subject before he revealed more than he intended, he smiled. "Could you tell me something, Alyssa?"

"It depends on the question and whether or not I know the answer," she said, looking a little apprehensive.

"Why do you go by your initials at work, instead of your given name?" He'd wanted to know the answer since reviewing her personnel file. "It's very pretty." *Like you.*

She shrugged one slender shoulder. "That's what my father always called me. I think it was his way of pretending I was the son he always wanted, but never had."

Reaching out, Caleb traced his index finger along her porcelain cheek. No matter what kind of hell he'd have to go through, he couldn't seem to stop touching her. "I'm sure he loves you more than you realize, sweetheart."

She remained silent for several long moments before nodding. "I suppose it was possible that he cared for me, but it's something I'll never know. He died on a mission in the Middle East during my junior year in college."

Caleb felt like a complete jerk for bringing up an obviously painful subject. Without thinking twice, he lifted her onto his lap and did his best to ignore how her shapely bottom felt pressed to his rapidly hardening body.

She stared at him for several long seconds. "Caleb, this isn't a good idea."

"Hush." Cradling her to his chest, he held her close as the water bubbled around them. He tried to tell himself that he was offering her comfort, but the truth was she felt so right in his arms, he couldn't bring himself to let her go. "I'm sorry, Alyssa. I didn't mean to pry."

"It's all right." He felt her begin to relax against him. "I've never had any illusions about it. My father and I didn't have a great relationship."

He kissed her temple. "What about your mom? Are you close to her?"

"Mother passed away when I was eight." She sighed. "That's when I started attending school at the Marsden Academy for Girls."

"Your dad sent you to a boarding school?" Anger burned at his gut. How could Merrick have done that to his only child? Caleb could only imagine how lonely and scared she must have been. At that moment, he despised the man for abandoning her when she'd obviously needed him most.

"Actually, Dad didn't have a lot of choice about sending me to Marsden," she said softly. "He was a navy SEAL and never knew when his team would be called out on a mission."

"Couldn't you have stayed with a relative?"

He wondered why her grandparents hadn't stepped forward to take her in. There was no way in hell his grandparents would have ever turned their grandchild away. They'd stood by his mother when she'd found herself pregnant and alone, and had helped her raise him, even though it hadn't been as socially acceptable then as it was now for a single woman to have a child.

Alyssa shook her head. "I've never even met my grandparents. My dad was raised in the foster-care system and my maternal grandparents didn't think he was good enough for their only child. When my mom eloped with him on graduation night, her parents more or less disowned her."

Alyssa had no idea why she was telling Caleb about her family or, more accurately, her lack of one. Normally, she didn't share any details about herself with anyone. But he was easy to talk to and his compassion made her feel at ease and free to discuss it for the first time in years.

"What about you?" she asked, enjoying the feel of

his wide bare chest against her arm. "What was your childhood like?"

"It was pretty average," he said, shrugging. "I grew up on a farm in central Tennessee—"

"If you hadn't told me before that you were from the South, I'd have never known," she said dryly.

He chuckled. "You can take the boy out of the South, but you can't take the Southern accent out of the boy."

"Something like that," she said, laughing. Wanting to hear more about his childhood, she asked, "What was it like growing up on a farm?"

"I guess it was pretty much like growing up anywhere else," he said, thoughtfully. "I did most of the things other kids my age did—played Little League baseball, helped Grandpa around the farm and went skinny-dipping in the creek every chance I got." His mischievous grin curled her toes. "Still do."

Her insides fluttered. "You swim in the nude?"

He nodded. "I don't even own a pair of swim trunks. The only reason I'm wearing gym shorts now is to protect your tender sensibilities."

She suddenly felt a warmth course through her that had nothing to do with being in the hot tub. "I've never gone swimming without a suit."

His grin caused her to feel as if the water temperature rose a good ten degrees. "You should give it a try sometime."

She'd never been good at sexy banter and, unable to

think of a suitable comeback, she asked, "Where did you go to school?"

His muscles tensed slightly before he answered. "No private academies for me. I went to public schools."

"University, too?"

"There's no other team like the University of Tennessee Vols."

"Vols?"

"Short for Volunteers," he said, smiling. He pulled her closer. "But I don't want to discuss schools or sports teams right now." He brushed his lips over hers as he slid his finger under one of the straps of her swimsuit. "Do you have any idea how great you look in this little black number?"

She'd purposely ignored the fact that she was still sitting on his lap, but suddenly several things became quite apparent. They were alone in the semidarkness; their water-slick bodies were pressed together and his muscular thighs under her bottom weren't the only things that were hard.

Her eyes widened and a breathtaking charge of need filled every cell in her being. "I think…I'll move over to the seat."

"I like you right where you are." With one arm around her waist, he held her in place as he slid his hand from her shoulder down her upper arm, taking her swimsuit strap with him. "Your skin feels like silk, Alyssa."

Desire so hot she felt scorched by its intensity washed over her and, closing her eyes, she sighed. "This is insanity."

"Do you want me to stop?" he asked, his voice so low and intimate it caused goose bumps to shimmer over her skin.

God help her, but she didn't want him to stop. She wanted him to kiss and hold her. She wanted to feel his strong hands caressing her body. And if she was really honest with herself, that's what she'd wanted since their trip to Roswell.

She shook her head as she opened her eyes to meet his questioning gaze. "That's what's insane. I don't want you to stop. I should. But I don't. And that's what's so confusing. I've never been the type of person to throw caution to the wind." A shiver streaked up her spine when he cupped her cheek with his palm and she had to take in some much-needed air before she could finish. "But being with you, I find that I don't want to analyze every move I make. I don't want to be sensible. And living for the moment suddenly sounds so very tempting."

"It's up to you, Alyssa. All you have to do is tell me what you want and I promise to respect your wishes." He smiled. "But if it's left up to me, I'll take this suit off of you and show you just what temptation is all about."

His sexy drawl made her insides hum and all of her

secret places pulse with a hunger stronger than anything she'd ever experienced. "I want you to make me feel alive. I want you to touch me and…" She took a deep breath. "More."

Seven

As he gazed at her, Caleb wondered if he'd lost every ounce of sense he'd ever possessed. He had an incredibly desirable woman sitting on his lap, telling him that she wanted him. And what he was about to say could very well end things before they ever got started.

But his sense of honor wouldn't allow him to proceed without giving her the chance to call a halt to it right here and now. He had a feeling it was going to be one of the most meaningful nights of his life and he didn't want her regretting one minute of what they would share.

"Alyssa, I'm going to tell you something and I want you to think about it very carefully."

She looked apprehensive. "Okay."

He took a deep breath and went on before he had a chance to change his mind. “If I continue, I’m not going to stop. I’m going to take this bathing suit off and kiss every inch of your beautiful body. I’m going to touch you in places that will make you moan with pleasure. I’m going to do things to you that will drive you crazy and have you calling my name when you find your release. And then, when you think I’m finished, I’m going to start all over again.”

To his immense relief, instead of the small spark of desire in her luminous blue eyes dimming, it grew to a hunger that matched his own. But he needed to hear her say the words, needed for her to tell him that she wanted him to make love to her.

“Is that what you want, Alyssa?”

“Yes.” There wasn’t a moment’s hesitation in her simple answer, nor a hint of reservations in her steady gaze.

Groaning, Caleb covered her mouth with his, then traced her perfect lips with his tongue. If she’d told him no, he’d have had a hell of a time finding the strength to walk away. But she hadn’t. And just knowing she wanted him enough to let down her guard made him hot in ways he’d never imagined.

Her contented sigh encouraged him and he took advantage of her acceptance to slip inside and once again explore her sweetness. As he tasted and coaxed her with strokes that mimicked a more intimate union, he decided that kissing Alyssa was quickly becoming as addictive to him as any drug.

The way she held on to him, the way she responded to his kiss was all any man could dream of and proved what he'd thought from the moment they'd met. She wasn't the emotionless woman she tried to lead her coworkers to believe. She was warm, affectionate and, if her enthusiastic response to his kiss was any indication, passionate as hell when she let herself go. He just thanked the good Lord above that he was going to be the man holding her when that happened.

As he worshipped her with his mouth, he moved his hands over her shoulders and down her arms to slide the top of her swimsuit out of the way. He wanted to feel her soft body melting into the hard contours of his. But when he pulled her more fully against him, nothing could have prepared him for the reality of having her firm breasts pressing into his chest, their pebbled nipples scoring his skin.

"You feel so damned good," he rasped as he kissed his way from her mouth to the tender skin just below her ear.

Shuddering against him, she whispered close to his ear, "Please…don't stop."

Turning her to face him, he lifted her until her breasts cleared the surface of the warm water. "Sweetheart, there's not a chance in hell of that happening."

Slowly moving his lips over her creamy skin, he made his way from her shoulder down the slope of her breast to the hardened tip. Taking the tight bud into his mouth, Caleb sipped the water droplets from her puckered flesh, savored the sweetness that was uniquely Alyssa.

As he sucked and teased her nipples, a moan of pleasure escaped her parted lips and, raising his head, he asked, "Does that feel good?"

"Mmm." Threading her fingers through his hair, she held him close. "It's wonderful."

Suddenly needing to feel all of her against him, Caleb quickly shoved her swimsuit down her hips and legs, then tossed the wet black spandex over the side of the hot tub. His gym shorts quickly followed.

Reaching for her, he pulled her to him and the feel of smooth female skin against his hair-roughened flesh sent a flash fire to every nerve in his being. He wanted to take things slowly, to do all the things he'd promised, but his body was urging him to stake his claim and make her his.

"Alyssa, I want you so damned bad I can taste it," he said through gritted teeth. "I think we'd better get out of here and—"

"Please, Caleb," she said, wrapping her arms around his shoulders. Her eyes were glazed with hungry need when she added, "I need you inside. Now."

At her throaty plea, a shaft of longing rushed through him at the speed of light and white-hot desire enveloped him. With his mind clouded to anything but the need to possess her, he sank to his knees and lifted her to him.

Determined to enter her slowly, he clenched his back teeth together so hard it would probably require surgery to separate them. But as he guided himself to her, she proved his other theory about her when she wrapped her long, slender legs around his waist and her body consumed his in one smooth motion. He definitely felt like he was in heaven.

But her quiet gasp, the tightness surrounding him, penetrated the haze of passion. If he'd caused her any discomfort at all, he'd never forgive himself.

"Did I hurt you? You're really tight, sweetheart."

"It's been a…while." She nibbled at his neck and damned near caused him to have a coronary when she whispered, "You feel absolutely wonderful right where you are."

Crushing her coral lips beneath his, he kissed her until they both gasped for breath. "I'm so hot right now…" He closed his eyes in an attempt to slow down. "I think I might just spontaneously combust."

She touched his cheek with one wet finger as she moved her lower body. "Make love to me, Caleb."

Her request and the motion of her body unleashed the hungry need he'd been trying to hold in check and, groaning, he began to thrust into her. He'd never had a woman hold his body quite so perfectly or respond to him in ways that, until tonight, he'd only imagined in his wildest fantasies.

But as ideal as the moment was, the warm water bubbling around them enhanced the spirals of fiery passion binding them together and he could feel her body straining for the same mind-shattering release that he'd been trying to forestall from the moment they'd become one. All too soon her feminine inner muscles held him captive, then quivered as he felt the tight coil inside her let go. The sound of her whispering his name and the amazing sensation of her pleasure triggered his own release from the tension gripping him. Groaning, he thrust into her one final time and held her to him as he emptied himself deep inside of her.

With their energy completely spent, they clung together for several long moments before reality began to clear his passion-fogged brain. Saying a word that he usually reserved for smashed thumbs and drivers who cut him off in traffic, he eased away from her.

"What's wrong?" she asked, clearly alarmed by his harsh curse.

He ran an unsteady hand across the tension gathering at the back of his neck. "Tell me you're on the pill or patch or some kind of birth control."

"N-no. It hasn't been an issue for several years." As she stared at him, her eyes suddenly grew wide. "We didn't—"

He shook his head. "I'm sorry. There's no excuse for me not taking precautions."

She nibbled on her lower lip for a moment. "I probably don't have anything to worry about."

"We," he said, placing his hands on her shoulders. "I want you to know that we're in this together, Alyssa. If you do become pregnant, I'll be right there with you every step of the way."

"I'm tired," she said suddenly. "I think I'll take a shower and turn in."

Caleb didn't try to stop her when she climbed out of the water, wrapped herself in one of the towels and, grabbing her glasses, hurriedly disappeared through the doors into her room. They both needed time to come to terms with what they'd shared and the possible consequences of his carelessness.

He couldn't believe he'd been so thoughtless. Where the hell had his mind been, anyway?

In the past, he'd never failed to use protection. Even before knowing who his irresponsible father was, Caleb had been determined not to be anything like the man who had impregnated Caleb's mother, then left her to face things on her own. He'd always made it a point never to get so carried away that he lost sight of what an unexpected pregnancy could mean for him or his partner.

But he'd been so turned on, so mind-numbingly hot for Alyssa, the thought of protection hadn't even crossed his mind. All he'd been able to think about was how perfectly she fit within his arms, how soft her body was and how her sweet kisses warmed him to the depths of his soul. His body hardened at the very thought of how amazing their lovemaking had been and had him wanting nothing more than to go inside and make love to her for the rest of the night.

Cursing a blue streak, he splashed out of the hot tub and made a beeline for the pool. When he dove into the much cooler water and started swimming laps, his muscles protested, but he didn't care. He had to get himself under control.

When he reached the end of the pool on his tenth lap, he stopped to catch his breath and, glancing toward the French doors, shook his head. His body still throbbed with a need that left him dizzy and he had a feeling he could swim from now until his dying day and not even come close to easing the burning ache to make Alyssa his once again.

Climbing out of the pool, he wrapped a towel around his waist and, picking up his gym shorts and her swimsuit, headed for his room. He had a feeling one of two things was going to happen this weekend. Either they were going to make love again or, first thing Monday morning, he was going to be seeking medical attention for a perpetual erection.

Alyssa stared at the ceiling as she thought about what had happened in the hot tub. She still couldn't believe what had taken place when Caleb had touched her, nor did she understand it. It was as if she'd been taken over by a shamelessly uninhibited wanton who not only lived for the moment, but threw caution to the wind and didn't even consider the possibility of the consequences.

She'd never in all of her twenty-six years acted that way before. Not even when she and Wesley had been seeing each other and she'd thought she was in love had she experienced a total loss of control. And that scared her as little else could.

But all it took was one kiss, one touch of Caleb's hands and she lost all sense of herself. It was as if she became part of something larger than either of them, emotionally as well as physically. If his reaction was any indication, he'd experienced it, too.

The best thing she could do for her own well-being and peace of mind would be to have him take her back to Albuquerque tonight. Then, first thing Monday morning, insist that he accept her resignation, effective immediately.

She knew their coworkers would question why their "engagement" was off and why she no longer worked at Skerritt and Crowe. But that couldn't be helped. Caleb could tell them whatever he liked about the matter. She wouldn't be there to hear their comments and speculation on what might have happened between them.

Tossing the sheet aside, she climbed out of bed and pulled on her robe. The sooner she got back to the safety of her apartment, the better. Not only could she finish updating her résumé, she needed to check her personal calendar. Until she did that, she really wasn't certain whether she needed to worry about an unplanned pregnancy.

"Caleb?" She tapped on his bedroom door. "Are you still awake?"

When there was no response, she turned to go back to her room. She'd only gone a couple of steps when the door opened.

"Did you need something?"

The sight of him standing in the doorway in nothing but a pair of white cotton briefs rendered her temporarily speechless and all she could do was nod.

When they'd gotten into the hot tub there hadn't been enough daylight left to see the details of his body, then, when he'd removed his gym shorts, they'd been in the water. But the light from his bedside lamp cast just enough light now to enhance the ridges and ripples of his well-defined muscles and drew attention to the fact that Caleb Walker was perfection and then some.

His heavily padded pectoral muscles, bulging biceps and sculpted shoulders were proof that he'd spent years doing a lot more on that farm than just going skinny-dipping. Her gaze drifted lower and her pulse sped up.

Caleb's stomach had so many ripples it resembled a washboard. But it was everything below the waistband of his white briefs that had her gulping for air. The stretchy cotton hugged him like a second skin and outlined the size and heaviness of his sex. The lack of a tan line on his long, muscular legs was confirmation that he did, in fact, swim in the nude.

"You look a little shook up."

Why wouldn't she be? He was standing there practically naked and didn't seem the least bit self-conscious about it.

Taking a step toward her, he placed his hand on her shoulder. "Are you all right?"

Nodding, she tried to remember why she'd knocked on his door, but the feel of his warm palm touching her through her thin robe made it extremely difficult to breathe, let alone think.

He stared at her for several long seconds before he smiled and lightly touched her cheek with his index finger. "We need to talk, sweetheart."

Her insides fluttered wildly and she couldn't seem to catch her breath. "I…agree. I have something I need to ask you."

He stepped back and motioned toward his open door. "Let's go into my room and sit down."

She shook her head. "I'm not sure that's a good idea."

"I think it is." Before she could stop him, he grabbed her hand and tugged her into his bedroom. "I have something I need to do."

"Caleb—"

"It's all right, Alyssa." Leading her past the bed to the sitting area by the French doors, he sank into one of the armchairs, then pulled her onto his lap. "I want you to listen to me before you say anything. Will you do that?"

"Y-yes."

Why was she allowing him to take command of the situation? Why wasn't she demanding that he immediately take her back to Albuquerque before something else happened? But with all of the bare male skin surrounding her, she found she was too distracted to do much of anything but go along with what he wanted.

"Good." He gently stroked her hair as his hazel gaze held hers captive. "I want to apologize for the way I acted earlier and set the record straight. I wasn't upset with you, Alyssa. I was mad as hell at myself for letting you down. I know that's no excuse. But the truth of the matter is, I failed you, then acted like a real bastard about it. And I'm sorry, sweetheart."

Her conscience wouldn't let him shoulder all of the responsibility. "You weren't in that hot tub alone. I'm just as much to blame as you. I should have thought—"

He stubbornly shook his head. "It's a man's place to protect a woman."

"I beg to differ. Both partners should share the responsibilities of prevention." When he looked like he was going to protest, she reached up to place her finger to his lips. "But I'm not going to argue that with you now. I think it's safe to say we both got a bit carried away."

"You're right about that, sweetheart." His sexy grin sent waves of heat coursing through her. "I was so hot for you, I'm surprised we didn't cause the water in the hot tub to boil."

His candor and the sound of his low drawl caused her to feel as if the blood in her veins had been replaced with warm honey. Deciding it would definitely be in her best interest to move before she lost sight of what she needed to ask him, she started to stand up.

"Hey, where are you going?" he asked, holding her in place. He brushed his lips over hers in the gentlest of kisses. When he raised his head, he asked, "Didn't you say you had something you wanted to ask me?"

With every cell in her body tingling and her heart skipping every other beat, how was she supposed to think? Why had she knocked on his door? For the life of her, she couldn't remember.

But Caleb didn't seem to mind that she had temporary amnesia. Giving her a promising smile, he lowered his head again to kiss her with such tenderness it brought tears to her eyes. As he used his tongue to trace her lips, spirals of desire slowly swirled to every part of her and a shiver of excitement skipped up her spine. All he had to do was touch her and her will to resist melted away like mist under an early summer sun.

As he teased her to open for him, then dipped his tongue inside to explore her inner recesses, she was shocked at her own eager response. Boldly stroking him, she wrapped her arms around his shoulders and pressed closer.

His groan of pleasure rumbled up from deep in his chest and the vibration against her breasts sent a flash of heat streaking through her at the speed of light. When he broke the kiss, his lips seared a path from her neck to her collarbone, making her feel as if she were about to go up in flames.

He pushed her gown and robe aside to continue a blazing trail of nibbling kisses to the valley between her breasts and Alyssa was certain she'd been branded by the intensity of it. The ribbons of need flowing through her began to wind their way to the pit of her stomach, forming a coil of hungry desire deep in the most feminine part of her.

Seated on his lap, she knew immediately when his body began to change, to grow hard with the same passion that was overtaking her. Right or wrong, wise or not, she wanted to be warmed by the heat of his desire, to once again have him claim her body and soul.

"Please, Caleb."

"I want you again, sweetheart." His drawl sounded rough and impassioned. He raised his head to give her a look that seared her all the way to her soul. "Do you remember what I told you in the hot tub?"

"I—I'm not sure." She was about to burn to a cinder and he wanted her to recall something he'd said earlier?

The wicked grin he gave her sent a wave of goose bumps shimmering across her skin. "I promised you that I was going to kiss you all over. That I was going to touch you in all of your secret places and make you cry out with pleasure. Then, when you think I'm finished, I'm going to start all over again."

His suggestive words caused the coil in her stomach to tightened to an empty ache that robbed her of breath.

"And I have every intention of keeping that promise." His intense hazel gaze made her feel as if she'd melt right then and there when he added, "I'm going to love you the way you deserve to be loved. Right here. Right now."

Alyssa's pulse pounded in her ears and without a moment's hesitation, she nodded that she wanted that, too.

It fleetingly crossed her mind that she was playing with fire and there was a very real possibility that she'd end up being burned. But she didn't want to think about that now. She wanted to be held and touched and loved by the man who had stolen her heart.

Eight

If Caleb had given her time, Alyssa might have panicked at the realization that she'd fallen in love with him. But he was already taking matters into his own hands. Lifting her as if she weighed nothing at all, he stood up with her in his arms and walked over to his king-size bed.

Setting her on her feet, he held her gaze with his as he slowly untied her robe and slid it from her shoulders. "This time we're going to take things slow and easy. I want to savor every inch of you and by the time I'm through, there won't be a doubt in your mind about how special I think you are."

With every word he spoke, her limbs felt a bit weaker

and the restlessness deep inside her grew stronger. "I'm going to hold you to that," she said, wondering if that sultry female voice was really hers.

He slid his palms along her arms, then, taking her hands in his, he lifted them to kiss each one of her fingertips before placing them on his shoulders. "I'd rather you hold *me* to you."

She threaded her fingers through the hair at his nape, then, drawing his head down for her kiss, she pressed herself to his hard frame. "There are a few things that I want to do to you, too. Holding you against me is just one of them."

If she'd thought about it, she might have been appalled at her shamelessness. But it was as if she shed every one of her inhibitions when Caleb took her in his arms. And, for the first time in her life, she felt free to explore her own sexuality.

His smile increased the humming in the very core of her as he gathered her nightgown in his hands and slowly pulled it up over her head. "Let's get the rest of these clothes off."

Tossing the peacock-blue silk to join her robe on the floor, he ran his hands along her sides to her hips, then, hooking his thumbs in the elastic waistband of her panties, slowly pushed them over her hips and down her thighs. Once she kicked them aside, he stepped back to strip himself of his briefs. Her breath caught and an ache of pure need filled her at the sight of him.

She'd been right. Caleb's body was sheer perfection. Hard and lean, there wasn't a spare ounce of flesh anywhere on him.

But it was the sight of his strong arousal that caused her heart to skid to a stop, then take off at a gallop. He was above average in height and it appeared that other things about him were above average as well. If she hadn't already experienced the power of his lovemaking, she might have been a bit apprehensive. But she trusted Caleb implicitly. Although he'd been as excited for her as she'd been for him, he'd taken great care not to hurt her when they'd made love in the hot tub.

"You're beautiful." His voice was so reverent, so filled with awe that she had no doubt that he meant what he said.

"I was thinking the same thing about you," she said softly. "You're perfect."

As he took a step toward her, his deep chuckle made her feel as if the temperature in the room had suddenly risen several degrees. "I'm not perfect, sweetheart, but you know what they say about practice."

She felt color flood her cheeks. "I didn't mean—"

"I know. But I intend to spend the rest of the night making sure our lovemaking is perfect for *you,*" he said, reaching for her.

If his words hadn't sent her into total meltdown, the feel of his hard male flesh against her softer female skin would have. A shudder ran through his big body and she knew he felt the same scorching heat she did.

Closing her eyes, she reveled in the differences between a man and woman—the contrast of hard ridges to soft curves. "I love the way your body feels pressed to mine."

As he lowered his head, his slow grin held a wealth of promise. "I like the way I feel inside you more."

Her knees wobbled and, feeling as if she'd melt into a puddle at his feet, she sagged against him. Opening her eyes to gaze up at him, she whispered, "I do, too."

Without warning, he swung her up into his arms, placed her in the middle of his bed, then stretched out beside her and pulled her to him. "Keep talking like that, sweetheart, and I'll go off like a Roman candle on the Fourth of July."

Before she could respond, he captured her lips with a desperate hunger that sent a flash fire streaking all the way to her soul. But when he broke the kiss to nibble his way from her collarbone down the slope of her breast, then took the tight bud into his mouth, she felt as if she'd burn to a crisp. His gentle sucking, the feel of his tongue on her sensitized nipple caused the spiraling heat to increase the tension building deep in her womb.

A moan escaped as she held his head to her. The delicious sensations Caleb created with his erotic teasing were driving her absolutely wild.

"Do you like that?" he asked, kissing her abdomen.

Nodding, she shivered from the exquisite feeling of his warm breath whispering over her. "Please…"

He dipped his tongue in the indention of her navel as he ran his calloused hands along her sides. "Tell me what you want, Alyssa."

"M-more."

"Are you sure?"

There was an underlying tone, a warning of sorts in his quiet question. He was asking for her trust, asking for permission to take her places that no man had taken her before.

"Yes!" If he didn't do something soon she was going to die from wanting.

Without another word, he raised his head and the blazing passion she saw in his hazel eyes stole her breath. Sliding his hands over her hips, then down her legs, he held her captive with his heated gaze as he caressed the insides of her thighs. Her heart pounded hard beneath her breast as inch by slow inch he came closer to the nest of curls at the apex of her thighs. When he finally reached his goal, pleasure radiated throughout her body at his featherlight touch.

"Oh, my!"

"Does that feel good?" he asked as he continued to drive her mad.

"Yes."

"More?" His deep drawl was as seductive as the feel of his hands on her.

"P-please!"

His kiss on the inside of her thigh sent a tingling excitement straight to her core. Clenching her eyes shut, she gripped the sheet with both hands. "I feel like…I'm on fire."

"Easy, sweetheart. It's only going to get better." He'd no sooner gotten the words out than he lowered his head and gave her the most intimate kiss a man can give to a woman.

Shock waves of pure ecstasy raced through her and she couldn't stop a moan from escaping. "C-Caleb, please…I need—"

Kissing his way back up her body, he nibbled at one of her aching nipples. "What do you need, sweetheart?"

"You. Now."

"Why?" he asked, treating the other taut nub to the same sweet torture.

"I can't…take…much more."

"Open your eyes, Alyssa." When she did as he commanded, he shook his head. "Remember what I told you?"

"N-no." He expected her to think at a time like this?

His promising grin sent another wave of heat flowing through her veins. "I told you that just when you think I'm finished, I'm going to start all over again."

If she could have found her voice, she'd have told him that much more and she'd go stark-raving mad. But before she had the chance, he lowered his head and held true to his promise.

Worshipping her body with his hands and lips, Caleb took her to the crest again and again. But just when she thought she'd find the peace of sweet release, he'd pause just long enough for the tightening inside her to ease a bit, then he'd start all over again.

"I can't take…another second…of this." The tension inside her was so great that it made her feel as if she were coming apart at the seams. "Please…make love to me, Caleb. N-now."

His kiss was so tender it brought tears to her eyes. "Just a minute, sweetheart." He slid open the bedside table to remove a foil packet. "I'm not going to let you down a second time," he said, rolling the condom into place.

With their protection arranged, he took her into his arms, then, nudging her knees apart, held her gaze with his as he moved to cover her. Her pulse thundered in her ears as he slowly, carefully sank himself deep inside her welcoming body.

When he was completely immersed within her, she watched him close his eyes and she knew he was fighting for control. "I think…I've died…and gone to heaven," he said, the strain of his struggle evident in his husky voice.

Tilting her hips, she felt him sink into her a fraction more. "Take me to heaven with you, Caleb," she whispered close to his ear.

His big body shuddered and a groan rumbled up from deep in his chest a moment before he opened his eyes to stare down at her. The hungry need in the hazel depths matched her own and as he eased himself back, then forward, she wrapped her arms around him and joined him in the wondrous dance of love.

Holding her gaze with his, he set a slow pace that tightened the pit of her stomach and made her feel cherished in a way she'd only dreamed of. He must have realized the delicious sensations within her were building to a crescendo because he strengthened his thrusts and Alyssa found herself straining to reach the summit.

She was suddenly there and, as the coil inside her burst free, she cried out his name as she shattered into a million shards of brilliant light. Tightening her arms around him, she tried to absorb him into her very soul as she rode the waves of utter and complete fulfillment. No more than a second later, she felt Caleb tense, then heard him call her name as he found his own release from the storm.

When he collapsed on top of her, she held him close as her heart filled with an emotion like nothing she'd ever felt before. She'd done her best to resist. But in that moment, she knew beyond a shadow of doubt that she'd done the unthinkable. She'd fallen in love with Caleb Walker.

The following Friday afternoon, Caleb sat at his desk tapping his ink pen on the polished surface as he stared off into space. As far as work went, he hadn't been worth a damn all week. All he'd done was sit around with a sappy grin on his face and think about how fantastic the past weekend had been and how totally amazing Alyssa was.

Her response to his touch had been everything a man could ever dream of, and he'd been just as hot for her. They'd spent the entire time making love, falling asleep in each other's arms, then awakening to make love again.

When his lower body tightened, he took a deep breath and willed himself to relax. All he had to do was think about her and he got aroused so fast it made him dizzy.

But his desire to be with her wasn't just physical. Once he'd gotten to know the real woman behind those baggy suits and owlish glasses, he'd found that she was warm, compassionate and had a great sense of humor.

He grunted. How on God's green earth had he ever thought her to be anything like Leslie Ann?

Even if he hadn't checked the personnel records and found her employee evaluations, he would have figured out that Alyssa had used her brains and education to get where she was with Skerritt and Crowe. She'd worked her cute little tail off and hadn't had to step on anyone's toes to get the promotion to operations manager six months ago.

But Leslie Ann had taken the easy way to the top. She'd done anything and everything to climb the corporate ladder. Hell, he could even remember a couple of times when she'd bragged about taking credit for the hard work of those working under her. And her barracuda instincts hadn't stopped there. He had no doubt that she'd have crawled off her deathbed just for the chance to attend a party where she could schmooze with the big boys. Nor was she above kissing a few executive rear ends along the way to get what she wanted.

Disgusted with himself for wasting two years chasing after such a selfish, self-absorbed woman, he shook his head. Leslie Ann had never been, nor would she ever be half the woman Alyssa was. And somewhere between walking into her office that first day and sitting here thinking about their weekend together now, he'd fallen for her.

His heart stalled and he felt like he couldn't breathe. When had Alyssa gotten past his defenses? Why hadn't he seen it coming?

He sat for several long minutes feeling as though he'd just been run over by the Tennessee Titans' entire defensive line. His timing couldn't have been worse. He'd barely taken over running Skerritt and Crowe and he hadn't attended one of his classes at the university, let alone earned a degree.

Propping his elbows on the desk, he buried his head in his hands. Now that he'd found Alyssa, he wasn't about to let her go. But what could he do about the situation? There was no way in hell they could build a relationship unless he came clean and told her who he was and that he didn't have anything more going for him than a high-school education.

He raised his head to stare blindly out the plate-glass window at downtown Albuquerque. He'd boxed himself into one hell of a corner.

How was he going to tell her that he was a fraud, that he wasn't really qualified to run a financial consulting firm? And how would she react when she found out that he was one of Emerald's grandsons?

"Caleb, you have a call on line one." Geneva's voice coming through the intercom broke into his unsettling thoughts.

He depressed the talk button. "Take a message, Geneva."

"It's Mrs. Larson," Geneva said, as if in awe of Emerald.

Great. Just what he needed right now—a conversation with his manipulative grandmother. "Thanks, Geneva. I'll take the call."

Taking a deep breath, he picked up the phone. "Hello, Emerald."

"Caleb, darling, how are you?" Emerald Larson might be at least three-quarters of a century old, but she looked and sounded like a much younger woman.

"I'm tied up with something pretty important right now." At the moment, his newly discovered feelings for Alyssa and trying to figure out what he was going to do about them took top priority. "Could I call you back this evening?"

"Of course. You have the number at the mansion, don't you?"

"It's on speed dial at the house."

"Good. I retire around ten," she added. "I'll expect your call before that."

Before he could say another word, she hung up. "Well, goodbye to you, too," he muttered, replacing the receiver.

He briefly wondered what Emerald wanted, but he quickly dismissed the call when Geneva's voice once again came across the intercom. "Caleb, you're needed in the break room."

"Can't it wait?"

When Geneva failed to answer, he impatiently walked over to open the door to the outer office. The secretary was nowhere in sight.

"Did you just get a page from Geneva to go to the break room?" Alyssa asked, walking out of her office.

He nodded. "Did she tell you what was going on?"

"No." She looked around the deserted office. "Where is everyone?"

Shrugging, he walked over to take her in his arms. "Beats me."

As he gazed down at her, he didn't think he'd ever seen her look more beautiful. Since their weekend together, she'd started wearing her hair down and she'd replaced her baggy dark suits with pastel silk blouses and linen slacks. Today she wore pink and tan and looked so damned lovable she took his breath away.

"Have I told you how incredible you look today?" he asked, kissing the tip of her nose.

Her breathless laughter sent a shaft of longing straight to the region below his belt buckle. "I was thinking the same thing about you."

"We need to talk," he said suddenly. He wasn't sure how she'd react when he told her everything about himself and the reason he'd taken over the firm, but he knew for certain there couldn't be any secrets between them. "Come home with me for the weekend."

"I'm not sure—"

"I am," he said, nodding. "Remember, we're supposed to be planning our wedding. Don't you think we'd be expected to spend our weekends doing just that?"

"My poor parakeet will think I've abandoned him," she said, laying her head against his chest.

He wasn't about to let a bird keep him from being with the most desirable woman he'd ever known. "We'll take him with us."

"Are we going to discuss my ideas for the break room?"

"Among other things," he said, distracted by the feel of her softness.

"There you are," Geneva called from down the hall. She looked extremely flustered. "Please hurry. We need you both in the break room. It's an emergency."

"What's wrong, Geneva?" With Alyssa hot on his heels, Caleb jogged down the hall. But when he entered the room, he stopped dead in his tracks. "What the hell?"

"What's going on?" Alyssa asked, bumping into his back.

"Congratulations!" the entire Skerritt and Crowe staff shouted in unison.

Shocked to see all of the firm's employees crammed into the break room, it took a moment for Caleb to figure out what was going on. He and Alyssa were the guests of honor at a surprise engagement party.

"Oh, my dear heavens." Alyssa's cheeks colored a deep rose and her baby-blue eyes were round with disbelief.

"We wanted you two to know how happy we are for you," Geneva said, dabbing at her eyes with a lacy handkerchief.

Caleb put his arm around Alyssa's shoulders to draw her to his side. "I think I speak for both of us when I say we really didn't expect you all to do this."

"I…we truly don't know what to say," Alyssa added, leaning against him as if her knees were about to buckle.

"Well, I do." Grinning from ear to ear, Malcolm Fuller stepped forward and handed them each a champagne flute. "Since I'm the oldest employee here at Skerritt and Crowe, I have the honor of being the first to toast the happy couple." Clearing his throat, he held his own glass high. "It's with great pleasure that I have the opportunity to celebrate Caleb and Alyssa's happiness. May your engagement be brief and your wedding perfect, and your honeymoon go on for a lifetime." His voice grew gruff. "Congratulations, kids. You make a beautiful couple."

As they listened to several others express their good wishes, Caleb realized that was exactly what he wanted—a long and happy life with Alyssa at his side. He wanted to make love with her every night and wake up with her in his arms each morning for the rest of his life.

When she glanced up and smiled at him, he knew he'd walk through hellfire and back just to make her happy. And if she'd let him, he had every intention of making their pretend engagement real.

Nine

After a leisurely swim, Alyssa sat between Caleb's legs on a lounge chair by the pool, watching the shadows of evening fade into the dark of night. What were they going to do now? she wondered. The surprise party had been a wonderful gesture and she really appreciated their coworkers' thoughtfulness, but it had also greatly compounded an already complicated situation.

She and Caleb couldn't break off their "engagement" right away. It would look far too suspicious and without a doubt, everyone would know that it had been a sham from the beginning.

Unfortunately, continuing their pretend commitment posed an even bigger problem for her. The more time she spent playing the role of Caleb's loving fiancée, the more she found herself wishing their engagement was real.

"You're mighty silent tonight, sweetheart." Caleb's whispered drawl caused a wave of goose bumps to shimmy over her skin as he pulled her back against him to wrap his arms around her.

She sighed. She wasn't about to tell him the real reason for her pensive mood. "I like watching the shadows cover the valley as the sun goes down."

His low chuckle seemed to vibrate right through her. "Besides the scenery, is there anything else you like about being here?"

"Hmm, I really like the pool," she teased.

He nuzzled the side of her neck. "Anything else?"

She closed her eyes as a wave of need swept over her. "The hot tub…is very…nice."

"Yes, it is," he murmured against her skin. "It's very relaxing." He nibbled her earlobe. "It's really wet." He nipped her shoulder. "It's definitely hot." Slipping the top of her swimsuit down, he covered her bare breasts with his warm palms as he kissed her temple. "And it's a great place to make love."

Her heart thumped her ribs and her breathing grew shallow. "If I remember correctly, that's what you said about the pool, your bed, the sofa in the great room, the—"

He nodded. "Anywhere is a good place to make love with you, sweetheart."

"We proved that last weekend." With his hands caressing her breasts and his growing arousal pressed to her bottom, Alyssa felt as if her insides had been turned to warm pudding. Closing her eyes as her temperature rose, she added, "I think we made love in every room in the house, as well as out here by the pool and in the hot tub."

Shaking his head, he chafed her nipples with the pads of his thumbs. "There's one place we haven't made love." He kissed the nape of her neck, then set her away from him. Rising from the lounge chair, he held out his hand. "And I think it's high time we changed that, don't you?"

Without so much as a moment's hesitation, she placed her hand in his and let him pull her to her feet. As they walked through the French doors to his bedroom, she reminded herself that she should resist temptation, run as hard as she could back to her apartment and protect what was left of her heart.

But when he led her into the master bathroom and turned her to face him, she realized that she didn't have a choice in the matter. Staring up into his intense hazel eyes, she knew it was far too late to save herself. Her heart was no longer her own. It belonged to Caleb, and it had from the moment he'd swaggered into her office the day he'd arrived to take over Skerritt and Crowe.

Smiling, he peeled her damp swimsuit away, then tossed it aside. "Your body is way too beautiful to cover up with clothes."

She grinned. "Even at work?"

As he lightly slid his hands from the swell of her breasts down to her hips, the wicked gleam in his eyes stole her breath. "I don't share. Seeing you this way is for my eyes only, sweetheart."

"That street goes both ways," she said, tugging his wet gym shorts from his lean hips. "I love the way your body looks, too. But I wouldn't want any other women appreciating it the way I do."

He took her into his arms as he lowered his head. "Only for you, Alyssa. Only you."

He fused his mouth with hers then, and the promise in his gentle kiss, the feel of his muscular body surrounding hers caused her pulse to race and stars to dance behind her closed eyes. The warmth of need that she only experienced in Caleb's arms flowed through her—heating her blood, filling her with passion so strong it made her weak in the knees.

His arms tightened around her as he slipped his tongue inside to entice her with the taste of his hunger, and a fluttering swirl of desire began to form in the very core of her. But when he ran his hands down her back to cup her bottom and lift her closer, the feel of his hard arousal pressed to her lower belly caused an answering tightness deep within her and a delicious ache to commence in all of her feminine places.

Lost in the sensations he'd created inside her, she vaguely realized that he was moving them into the large tiled shower, closing the door and turning on the water. He tightened his arms around her once again to pull her to him and the feel of his wet skin against hers sent ribbons of excitement twining to the most interesting places.

Sliding his hands along her sides, then back up to cup the heaviness he'd created in her breasts, he lowered his head to sip the trickling water from her aching nipples. He teased first one hardened tip, then the other and by the time he raised his head to kiss her, she tingled all over.

Caleb's gaze held her spellbound as he reached for the soap, then ran it over her shoulders, her breasts and down her abdomen. His slick hands touched her everywhere, sliding over her skin, sending tiny sparks of electricity skipping over every nerve in her body and it took all of her concentration just to remember to breathe.

Determined to treat him to the same sensual massage, she smiled as she took the soap from him. Lathering her trembling hands, she smoothed them over his wide chest, rippling stomach and lean flanks. She wanted to give to him as he'd given to her and, taking him in her palms, she slid her fingers along his taut skin, measured his length and the strength of his need for her.

He closed his eyes and a deep groan of pleasure escaped his parted lips. "Sweetheart, if I die right now, I'll leave this world a happy man."

"But I don't want you to be just happy," she said, wondering if she had the nerve to take her exploration to the next level. "Open your eyes, Caleb." When he did as she commanded, she waited until the water had rinsed away the last traces of soap. "I want you to be fulfilled."

Caleb's heart stalled and he didn't think he'd ever breathe again as he watched Alyssa sink to her knees in front of him. "Sweetheart, you don't have to—"

At the feel of her sweet lips on his heated body, he stopped abruptly and clenched his teeth together so hard he'd probably end up with a broken jaw. Her intimate kiss was sending liquid fire streaking though his veins at the speed of light and he wasn't altogether sure how much longer his legs were going to support him.

Placing his hands on her shoulders, he lifted her to her feet. "If you keep that up much longer, fulfillment won't be an issue."

She smiled. "You don't like what I was doing?"

"I didn't say that." He drew some much-needed air into his lungs and shook his head. "The problem is, I like it too much. But I want both of us to be there for the grand finale. And I fully intend to be inside you when that happens."

He lowered his head to swirl his tongue around one beaded nipple, while he chafed the other one with his thumb. Teasing her with his teeth, then sucking the tight tip into his mouth, he slid his hand down between them to find the sensitive nub at the apex of her thighs. She trembled against him as he gently stroked her and he decided that he'd like nothing better than to spend the rest of his life bringing her pleasure.

By the time he raised his head to gaze at her beautiful face, her porcelain cheeks were painted with the rosy glow of passion and her baby-blue eyes sparkled with deep longing. Her heightened excitement fueled his own and Caleb suddenly needed to possess her body and soul.

"Do you want me, Alyssa?"

"Yes."

"Now?"

"Yes."

Somehow he found the strength to step back and momentarily leave the shower. When he returned with their protection in place, he turned her away from him, then wrapped his arms around her and pulled her back against his chest.

"Caleb?" Her uncertainty was evident in the tone of her voice.

"Do you trust me, Alyssa?" When she nodded, he kissed her shoulder. "I'm going to caress your body while I make love to you."

He supported her weight as he lifted her to him and in one smooth motion entered her from behind. Her soft moan of pleasure mingling with his deep groan sent waves of hot, urgent desire coursing from the top of his head all the way to the soles of his feet and he had to struggle to retain what little control he had left.

The feel of her holding him deep inside, her inner muscles clinging to him as she adjusted to his size almost sent him over the edge. But, determined to ensure her pleasure above his own, he covered her breasts with his hands then, kissing her shoulder and the slender column of her neck, slowly began to rock against her.

Their water-slick bodies moving in perfect unison caused the pulse in his ears to roar and, wanting her to find the same release that was rapidly overtaking him, he slid his hand down to touch her intimately. Stroking her with a rhythm that matched the movement of their bodies, he felt her inner muscles constrict, then gently caress him as she found the culmination they both sought. Her release triggered his own and, holding her to him, he shuddered as he followed her over the edge and gave up his essence to the woman he loved.

When his mind began to clear, Caleb carefully lowered Alyssa to the tiled floor, then turned her to face him. Even with her hair hanging wet and limp around her shoulders, she was the most beautiful woman he'd ever had the privilege to lay eyes on and he had every intention of making her his—permanently.

But he couldn't do that until he'd told her everything—who he was, why he'd been sent to run the financial firm and that he lacked the credentials to do the job right. He just hoped liked hell she'd forgive him for not telling her about himself from the beginning.

"We need to talk, sweetheart."

Wrapping her arms around his waist, she grinned. "Here?"

He smiled as he shook his head. Standing buck naked in the shower wasn't exactly the best place for the kind of confessions he'd be making. "Let's dry off and get in bed."

"I like the sound of that."

Taking her by the hand, he pulled her out of the shower. "I'm going to make sure you like doing it even more."

The next morning, when Alyssa woke to the sound of Caleb warbling an off-key version of a popular country song, she couldn't keep from smiling. She found his habit of singing while he showered quite endearing. But in the few short weeks they'd known each other, she'd come to realize there wasn't anything about him that she didn't find completely irresistible.

He was outgoing and compassionate and when they made love, he never failed to ensure her pleasure before finding his own. And even though she'd had serious doubts about him taking over Skerritt and Crowe, she had to admit he was an absolute genius in his approach to management. Since his arrival, employee morale had been greatly improved, productivity was on the rise and they'd signed several new clients.

But as she lay there thinking about all the reasons she'd fallen in love with him, she couldn't help but wonder what he wanted to discuss with her. He'd mentioned before the party, then again in the shower last night that they needed to talk. But when they'd toweled each other dry, their insatiable hunger had taken over and, after making love again, they'd immediately fallen asleep.

Had he decided their role-playing posed too great a threat to his peace of mind? Was he wanting to discuss how they were going to handle breaking off their pretend engagement?

Her stomach clenched painfully at the thought of never being held in his strong arms, of never tasting his need for her in his tender kiss. She'd given her heart to him, but she had no idea how he felt about her.

Deciding that she had a few questions of her own that needed to be answered, she tossed the covers aside and got out of bed. She grabbed his shirt from one of the chairs and quickly pulled it on. Sleeping with him in the nude was wonderful, but they needed to talk without being distracted again.

She got halfway across the room, but the ringing phone stopped her. Glancing at the clock, she wondered who on earth would be calling this early on a Saturday morning. She frowned when she read the words *No Data* on the caller ID.

As she stood there wondering if she should let the machine pick up the call, Caleb stopped singing. "Could you get that, Alyssa?"

"Sure." She picked up on the third ring. "Hello?"

There was a moment of silence, then a commanding female voice demanded, "Who am I speaking with?"

Alyssa frowned at the censure in the older woman's voice. "Who are you wanting?"

"My grandson, Caleb Walker. Is he there?"

"He's unavailable at the moment. Could I take a message?"

"Is this Ms. Merrick?" the woman asked, suddenly sounding much more pleasant.

"Yes, it is." How on earth had the woman known who she was?

"Emerald Larson here. I thought I recognized your voice. How have you been? I don't think we've had a chance to talk since I called to let you know Caleb would be taking over the firm."

Alyssa felt as if her stomach had dropped to her feet. Emerald Larson, one of the most successful businesswomen ever and the first female to break into the Fortune 500 top ten, was Caleb's grandmother?

"I must thank you for everything you've done for Caleb, my dear. I've heard the two of you make a great team," the woman went on. "Considering Caleb's lack of education, making the transition from simple country farm boy to running a financial firm the size of Skerritt and Crowe was a major challenge. But I'm not surprised that he's been successful. He has the Larson genes, after all."

"Of course," Alyssa said, feeling more sick inside than she'd ever felt in her life.

"I'm sure that once he gets a few college courses

under his belt, he won't have to rely so heavily on you to run things. But rest assured, my dear, I'll see that you're well compensated for your efforts."

Alyssa had to get off the phone before her fragile composure shattered into a million pieces. She'd done it again. She'd fallen for a man who only wanted to use her to accomplish his goal. The only difference this time was that she'd fallen hopelessly in love with Caleb.

"I really need to go, Mrs. Larson. I'll tell Caleb to call you."

Before the woman could respond, Alyssa broke the connection. When she looked up, Caleb was walking through the bathroom door as he secured a towel around his waist.

"Who was that?"

"Your grandmother." Walking over to place the cordless phone in his hand, she fought to keep her voice even as she looked into his incredible hazel eyes. "Emerald Larson. She wants you to call her."

When he reached for her, Alyssa successfully sidestepped his touch. "Please, don't."

His expression stoic, he took a step toward her. "Let me explain, Alyssa."

"I think your grandmother explained things quite clearly. You've been using me to keep the firm running while you played at being the successful businessman." A sudden rush of emotion threatened to choke her and she had to take a deep breath before she could finish.

"You know, I never paid much attention to the tabloid headlines about Owen Larson and his nefarious escapades." She laughed humorlessly. "I should have. Maybe I'd have recognized the same traits in his son and avoided making a fool of myself."

"Alyssa—"

Shaking her head, she impatiently wiped a tear from her cheek. "I can only imagine how pathetically desperate for a man I must have appeared to you. The frumpy numbers cruncher whose entire life revolved around her job." Straightening her shoulders, she drew on a lifetime of being taught to face the enemy with courage and grace. "But that no longer matters. Please tell your grandmother that I don't want, nor do I need, the compensation she mentioned."

His scowl deepened. "Compensation?"

"I'm certain she was unaware that you had devised your own way of appeasing me."

He shook his head as he quickly stepped forward to place his hands on her shoulders. "It's not like that, sweetheart."

"Don't call me that." Jerking from his grasp, her shaky voice rose considerably as she fought to keep her emotions in check. "Don't ever call me that again."

"Dammit, Alyssa, listen to me."

"Why should I? You haven't been honest with me thus far, why should I believe you now?"

"You have to calm down and see reason."

Struggling to keep the torrent of tears in check just a few moments longer, she glared at him. "I don't *have* to do anything but leave, Mr. Walker. And that's exactly what I intend to do."

Her legs felt as if they might not support her as she walked over to pick up the small overnight case she'd packed when they'd stopped by her apartment the evening before. Heading down the hall, she stopped at the first bedroom she came to, quickly changed out of his shirt and into her own clothes, then called a cab.

When she walked out into the hall, Caleb was waiting for her. He'd changed into a chambray shirt, worn jeans and scuffed boots.

If he thought reverting to his good-old-boy persona would make a difference, he was sadly mistaken. "Excuse me," she said, starting to walk past him. "I'll wait outside for my ride."

He stood stock still. "I'll drive you back to Albuquerque."

"No, you won't."

Folding his arms across his wide chest, he looked dubious. "Then how do you expect to get back home?"

"If I have to, I'll walk." She brushed past him. "But that's no longer any of your concern, Mr. Walker."

"Don't be so damned stubborn that you do something foolish," he said, following her down the hall to the front door.

When she turned on him, her body trembled with a

combination of anger and emotional pain. "We've already established that I cornered the market on foolishness."

Opening the door, she walked out and slammed it behind her. As she hurried down the driveway, she remembered that she'd left Sidney's cage in the family room. But she couldn't go back for the parakeet. She'd have to call later and request that Caleb bring the bird to the office.

Right now, she needed to put as much distance as she could between herself and Caleb. If she went back, he'd realize that she'd fallen hopelessly in love with him. And that was something she'd rather die than have him do.

Caleb stood watch until Alyssa got into the cab, then, turning away from the window, he walked out onto the patio. Everything inside him shouted for him to go after her, to bring her back and make her listen to reason, to convince her to hear what he had to say. But she was hurting right now and just knowing that he was the cause of it tied him in knots.

He'd had every intention of telling Alyssa about himself last night. But when they'd gone into the bedroom, he'd been so hot for her again that they'd made love until they'd both fallen asleep from complete exhaustion. Then he'd planned as soon as he finished his shower to serve her breakfast in bed, tell her everything, then ask her to make their engagement real.

But, Emerald had beaten him to it. That complicated

matters greatly, but it didn't mean he was ready to throw in the towel.

Alyssa needed time to calm down. And he needed time to make a few plans.

If there was one thing he'd inherited from his paternal grandmother, it was her determination. The old gal hadn't gotten where she was today without it and he fully intended to use her legacy to win back the only woman he'd ever love.

Ten

Alyssa sniffed back a fresh wave of tears as she sat on her couch, staring at her apartment walls. She'd expected Caleb to call on Monday after finding her resignation on his desk, along with a request that he leave Sidney in Geneva's care. But by close of business Wednesday, she realized that he didn't care about her leaving Skerritt and Crowe. And it was apparent he didn't intend to return her bird.

"The least he could have done was give Sidney back to me," she muttered miserably.

When the doorbell rang, she sighed. It was probably Mrs. Rogers again. The older woman had been sweeping her walk Saturday morning when Alyssa had gotten out of the cab and, taking one look at Alyssa's red-rimmed eyes, the woman had decided to lend moral support. She'd been over at least twice a day since, and today it appeared that she was going to make it three times.

Getting up from the couch, she walked over to open the door. "I'm fine, Mrs.—" She stopped abruptly. "You aren't Mrs. Rogers."

The red-haired, freckle-faced young man in a white courier's uniform grinned and shook his head. "Afraid not." He glanced at the clipboard in his hand. "Are you Ms. Alyssa Jane Merrick?"

"Yes."

"I have an express for you," he said, handing her an envelope marked Urgent. "Could you please sign on line twenty-four?"

Signing where the young man indicated, she started to thank him, but he was already halfway back to his delivery truck. When he squealed the tires as he pulled away from the curb, she decided that he took the company's claim of being the speediest delivery service in the world a little too seriously.

As she closed the door, she glanced at the return address. Who on earth did she know in Wichita, Kansas?

Her heart suddenly stopped, then started hammering at her throat. Emerald, Inc.'s headquarters were in Wichita.

Her hands shook as Alyssa pulled the tab to open the thin cardboard packet. If Emerald Larson had sent anything but a final paycheck, she'd get it back so fast she'd wonder if it had ever left her office.

But when Alyssa pulled the papers out of the envelope and thumbed through them, her mouth fell open. It was her letter of resignation, along with a handwritten note from Emerald Larson, herself.

Dearest Alyssa,
In order for your resignation as operations manager of Skerritt and Crowe Financial Consultants to be effective, you'll need to deliver it to me in person. I've arranged for a car to pick you up at your apartment tomorrow morning at eight. Please be prompt. The corporate jet will be waiting to fly you to Wichita, then return you to Albuquerque later in the day.
Yours truly,
Emerald Larson

Suddenly feeling as if her knees were made of jelly, Alyssa sat on the couch to stare at the letter. She'd never heard of anyone having to hand deliver their resignation. Why would the woman do that? Was it even legal for Emerald Larson to require that of her?

Alyssa wasn't sure. But she'd go to Wichita if that was what it took to divorce herself from Skerritt and Crowe, Emerald, Inc. and the fiasco with Caleb. Then she'd spend the rest of her life trying to forget the only man she would ever love.

"Who's your mole at Skerritt and Crowe, Emerald?" Caleb sat in the executive office of Emerald, Inc., staring across the French provincial desk at his indomitable grandmother. "And don't tell me you don't know what I'm talking about. You had to have someone at the firm feeding you information. Otherwise, you wouldn't have mentioned that Alyssa and I make a good team."

To her credit, she didn't even try to pretend that she didn't know what he was talking about. "Does it matter, darling?"

"Yes, it does." He wasn't about to let her get away with playing her little mind games. "You told me, Hunter and Nick that we'd have free reign in managing the companies you gave us—*without* your interference."

"I haven't interfered with the way you're running the financial firm." She smiled. "I just wanted to keep track of how you're doing, that's all."

"Did it ever occur to you to ask me?"

She patted a platinum hair back into place. "I wanted an unbiased opinion."

Caleb sat forward. "Let me assure you. If I'm about to land on my ass, I'll let you know so you can send in one of your ace managers to clean up the mess before it's too late. I'm not about to let the employees at Skerritt and Crowe pay the price for my screwups. They're good people and I don't want to see them hurt by your little experiment."

Instead of being offended by his statement, the old gal looked as pleased as punch. "All right."

"And I'll tell you something else." If she thought he was finished, she was sadly mistaken. "If I find out you're playing any more of your little games with me or the firm, I'm out. I'll go back to Tennessee and you can forget offering me any more of your sweet deals because I'll turn them down flat."

To his surprise, she grinned. "I would expect no less from a grandson of mine." She glanced at the diamond-encrusted watch on her left wrist. "Alyssa should be arriving in just a few moments. Are you sure you don't want me to stay? I might be able to clarify the facts about your father."

He shook his head. "You're getting her here was enough. I'll handle it from here on out."

She stood up and walked toward the door. "If you need me—"

"I won't." Too keyed up to remain seated, he rose to his feet. If he had any chance of a future with Alyssa, he had to be completely honest with her. And the information about himself would have to come from him, not his rich-as-sin grandmother. "I got myself into this. I'll get myself out."

Emerald nodded approvingly. "I hope your young

woman realizes what a good man you are, Caleb. Best of luck, son."

Caleb stared at her for several long moments. There was a sincerity in her voice that he hadn't expected. "Thank you…Grandmother."

When Alyssa stepped off the elevator on the sixth floor of Emerald Towers, a distinguished-looking gentleman of about fifty was waiting for her. "Ms. Merrick, please follow me. I'm Mrs. Larson's personal assistant, Luther Freemont. I've been instructed to take you directly to her private office."

As she followed the man down a long hall, Alyssa clutched the folder containing her resignation. She wasn't nervous, but she was eager to get her meeting with Emerald Larson over with. Once she'd done that, she could work on rebuilding her life.

Mr. Freemont stopped in front of a set of tall, ornately carved mahogany doors. Holding one of them open for her, he stepped back. "I hope your meeting turns out to everyone's satisfaction, Ms. Merrick."

"Thank you."

Why would the man tell her something like that? Was Mrs. Larson going to try to talk her out of resigning?

If so, the woman was in for a disappointment. There was no way Alyssa could continue working at the firm as long as Caleb was there.

But when she walked into the office, her heart felt as

if it had dropped to the floor. Instead of finding Emerald Larson in the plush executive office, she saw Caleb looking out the plate-glass window.

When he turned to face her, he looked so devastatingly handsome that her breath caught and a shaft of longing went straight to her soul. His low-slung jeans emphasized his lean waist and muscular thighs, while the knit fabric of his navy polo shirt drew attention to the well-developed muscles of his upper body, reminding her of how strong he was, how easily he'd held her when they'd made love in the shower. His light brown hair was slightly mussed as if he'd recently run his hand through it, but it only added to his appeal.

"Good morning, Alyssa."

"Where's Mrs. Larson?"

He shrugged. "I suppose she's around the offices here somewhere."

His smile and the sound of his deep Southern drawl caused a wave of emotion so strong it threatened to bend her double, to sweep through her. She turned to leave. "I can't do this," she whispered.

"Wait, Alyssa." He quickly crossed the room to take hold of her upper arms. "Please, I need for you to hear what I have to say. Then, if you still want to resign, I promise I won't try to stop you."

"Is this the only way you'll accept my resignation?" she asked, already knowing his answer.

"I'm afraid so, sweetheart." He turned her to face

him, then stepped back and motioned toward a sitting area by the doors. "Have a seat."

"I'd rather not."

"This may take a while."

She shook her head. "Caleb, I don't really think there's any point in—"

He folded his arms over his wide chest. "I do."

Suddenly feeling completely defeated, she walked over to sit down on the edge of one of the overstuffed armchairs. She stared at the folder on her lap. "Please make this quick."

He was silent for a moment and she could tell he was waiting for her to look at him. But she couldn't. If she did, she knew without question she'd fall apart.

"Everything I told you about myself is true, Alyssa," he said quietly. "I grew up on a farm in central Tennessee and I have two brothers—Hunter O'Banyon and Nick Daniels." He hesitated as if he didn't like what he had to say next. "I've never lied to you. But I am guilty of omitting a few facts."

"B-but you did lie to me," she said, hating that her voice shook with emotion. She looked at him directly. "You told me you went to the University of Tennessee."

He smiled sadly and shook his head. "I said there was no other team like the UT Vols. I never said I attended classes there."

"But you knew what I'd think."

Nodding, he ran his hand over the back of his neck.

"I'm not proud of that. But it was easier to let you draw your own conclusions than it was to admit that I have nothing more than a high-school education."

His expression grim, he sat on the end of the coffee table in front of her. When she noticed their knees were almost touching, she scooted back in the chair. If he touched her in any way, she feared she'd lose the tenuous hold she had on her feelings.

She watched him prop his forearms on his thighs and stare down at his loosely clasped hands. "I had an academic scholarship to go to UT at Knoxville, but I had to turn it down. Grandpa got sick that summer and I was needed at home to keep the farm going. Then later on, it was a matter of economics."

There was deep regret in his tone and she could tell that his lack of a postsecondary education bothered him a lot. "There's still time to get your degree."

He shrugged. "I'm enrolled in night classes for the fall semester."

She frowned. Something didn't add up. "Now, hold it. Emerald Larson is your grandmother. Why couldn't she have helped you out with school?"

"It wasn't until last month that my brothers and I learned about each other and that we're the product of the late Owen Larson sowing his wild oats." He laughed humorlessly. "Until then, we didn't have a clue who our father was or that we were related to one of the richest women in the world."

"You're kidding."

"I wish I was joking," he said, shaking his head. "But unfortunately, I'm not."

She couldn't begin to imagine what a shock that must have been for the three men. "How did you find out?"

"Luther Freemont showed up at the farm one day to tell me that I was needed in Wichita." He looked as if he still had trouble believing it himself. "When I asked him who was making the request and why, he said he wasn't at liberty to tell me. So, I told him to go to hell and went back to working on my tractor."

"I take it he didn't give up?"

Caleb shook his head. "My mom stepped in and told me that it was time to learn about my father and that she wanted me to go."

"I don't understand," Alyssa said, wondering why it had been such a big secret. All things considered, she shouldn't care. But she could see that he'd been deeply affected by what had taken place and she couldn't stop herself from asking, "Why hadn't she told you who your father was?"

"That's where it gets complicated." Taking a deep breath, he added, "Emerald Larson knew about all of us, practically from the moment we were conceived. But she didn't want us turning out like her son—our father."

"So she didn't acknowledge any of you until recently?" Alyssa couldn't understand how Emerald Larson could live in the lap of luxury while denying her grandsons the opportunities that would have made their lives easier.

He shook his head. "She told us that she knew she'd made a lot of mistakes when she gave Owen everything he wanted, instead of giving him the time and attention he needed from her. She said she also knew that we'd have a better chance of turning out to be decent men if our lifestyle was more down-to-earth and we were raised by mothers who taught us the values that she'd failed to teach Owen." He smiled. "As crazy as it sounds, Emerald was actually trying to protect us."

Alyssa thought about it for a moment. "I guess, in a strange way, that makes sense." She shook her head. "But it doesn't explain why your mother failed to tell you about your father."

His expression turned dark. "I'm still having a problem with this part of the whole sordid mess. Mom worked at one of the luxury hotels in Nashville. She was a young, naive country girl and Owen swept her off her feet. Then after he left town, Emerald contacted Mom through a private investigator while she was pregnant and arranged to support us with a modest monthly allowance. The only requirement was that Mom couldn't tell anyone—including me—who my father was. Emerald even went so far as to have Mom sign a legal agreement stating that if she divulged who had gotten her pregnant that I would be cut out of inheriting any part of Emerald, Inc. and the Larson fortune. She did the same thing with Hunter's and Nick's mothers."

Alyssa could understand Mrs. Larson's not wanting the boys to turn out like their father. No one in their right mind would want to see a child grow up to be a hedonistic, irresponsible adult, which she'd heard Owen Larson had been before the boating accident that had claimed his life six months ago. But what Caleb was describing that Emerald Larson had required of the women sounded suspiciously like blackmail.

"And in all that time, your mother never told anyone who your father was?"

His intense gaze met hers. "No. She felt that she was ensuring a better future for me than she could ever give me on her own."

Alyssa couldn't help but be a bit envious. Her mother had loved and doted on her when she'd been alive, but after her death, Alyssa hadn't felt that she'd been loved by anyone.

They remained silent for several long moments before he took a deep breath. "When we all arrived in Wichita and Emerald explained about our father and that she was going to give each of us one of her companies to run, I fully intended to turn her down because I didn't feel qualified to run a place like Skerritt and Crowe."

"What changed your mind?"

"I thought about my mom's dream of giving me a better life and I knew I had to give it a try." He shrugged.

"So I started reading books on management and went on the Internet to search for everything I could about creating a better work atmosphere and unity among the workers. Then I remembered seeing a report on one of the news shows a year or so back about companies using innovative ways to keep employees motivated. I bought a couple of books, did a little more research on the computer and the changes I've made at Skerritt and Crowe are the result."

"It worked." Her conscience wouldn't allow her to say otherwise. "Everyone at the firm is a lot happier than they were under the old management."

He shrugged. "I also figured if I made it a nice place to work, left everyone alone to do their jobs and let you make the business decisions, I'd be okay until I could take some administrative courses and get an idea of what I was really supposed to be doing."

His admission caused her chest to tighten and she wasn't sure she'd be able to draw her next breath. Thinking he'd been using her was one thing, but hearing him put it into words hurt more than she could have ever imagined.

"I—I really need…to go." She quickly stood up and shoved the file containing her resignation into his hands. If she didn't get out of there soon the floodgates were going to open. "G-good luck with…the firm."

Rising to his feet, he tossed the folder to the floor and pulled her into his arms. "I haven't told you the most important detail of all, Alyssa."

He cradled her close and the feel of his strong arms folded around her, the wide expanse of his chest pillowing her head, and the tender way he stroked her hair caused her heart to break even more. Just knowing that once she walked out the door she'd never again be held by him or know the softness of his kiss was almost more than she could bear.

"C-Caleb, p-please—"

"Don't cry, sweetheart. It tears me apart to see you cry." His chest rose and fell beneath her ear as he took a deep shuddering breath. "Do you want to know what happened when I arrived at Skerritt and Crowe?"

"N-no."

"I fell in love with a beautiful, intelligent woman who tried to hide how wonderful she is behind baggy suits and oversize glasses." Leaning back, he cupped her face with his large hands and the sincerity she saw in his incredible hazel gaze caused her heart to skip several beats. "Yes, I let you call the shots at the firm. But I never used you. I never took credit for anything."

As she stared up at him, she realized that what he'd said was true. The main reason everyone at Skerritt and Crowe was so happy was the fact that Caleb left them alone to do their jobs and didn't try to micromanage their every move.

"I—I'm sorry that I jumped to conclusions." She took a deep, steadying breath. It was suddenly important that he understand why she'd refused to listen to him that morning, how she'd let fear blind her to the facts. "Before I came to work at the firm, I made a huge mistake by getting involved with a coworker who used our relationship to gain information about a client I had been hoping to sign. He took all the credit for the research and winning the account, then got a promotion for all of *his* hard work."

"The jerk should be shot for doing that to you." Caleb shook his head. "No wonder you thought I'd been using you to make myself look good."

"I suppose in a way, I was looking for it to happen." Her voice caught. "I guess I expected for you to hurt me the same way he had."

His intense gaze held hers. "Do you still feel that way, Alyssa?"

"No." Caleb may have omitted a couple of important facts, but he had told her as much as he could about himself without revealing who his grandmother was and that he didn't have the credentials to run Skerritt and Crowe.

Caleb kissed her temple. "I love you, Alyssa Jane Merrick. Never doubt that. And I'd never do anything to hurt you, sweetheart."

"I know that now." Her eyes filled with moisture, but this time they were tears of joy. "I…love you, too, Caleb. So very much."

He crushed her to him, kissing her until they both gasped for breath. "I want to spend the rest of my life proving to you just how much you mean to me, sweetheart." Stepping back, he pulled a small velvet box from his jeans pocket and removed a diamond-and-sapphire ring from inside. Then, dropping to one knee, he took her left hand in his. "Alyssa, will you marry me?"

Her heart filled with so much love it felt as if it would burst. "Yes."

Slipping the ring on her finger, he rose to take her into his arms. "I intend to spend the rest of my life making sure you never regret becoming my wife, sweetheart."

She wrapped her arms around his waist. "I could never regret marrying the only man I'll ever love."

"God, I missed you," he said, kissing her eyes, her cheeks and the tip of her nose. "And I wasn't the only one."

"I missed you, too." She leaned back to look at him. "What do you mean you weren't the only one?"

Caleb laughed. "Sidney missed you, too."

Grinning, she asked, "Why didn't you return him?"

His sexy grin caused her stomach to flutter. "I had every intention of holding him hostage for as long as it took to get you to say yes."

"There was no way I would have said otherwise." She glanced at the ring on the third finger of her left hand. "How did you know what size of ring I wear?"

He shook his head. "I don't know how Emerald does it, but after I picked out the ring I wanted to give you, she told me she'd take care of having it sized."

"But we'd only spoken on the phone, she's never met me. How did she know?"

"I'm not sure, but she has her ways. Now, let's introduce the two of you, then head for the airport." He took her hand in his and led her to the door. "We have something waiting for us back at my house."

"And what would that be?"

Caleb's sexy grin sent waves of heat coursing through every cell in her body. "A hot tub."

"I like the way you think." Raising up on tiptoe, she kissed his lean cheek. "I love you with all my heart, Caleb Walker."

His tender smile lit the darkest corners of her soul. "I love you, too, Alyssa Jane Merrick. Now, let's go home and I'll get started on that lifetime promise of showing you just how much."

Epilogue

"How much longer?" Caleb asked, walking over to gaze out the farmhouse window.

"I swear to God if you don't stop pacing, Hunter and I are going to tie you down," Nick said, laughing.

Hunter checked his watch. "You have approximately fifteen minutes of freedom left, bro." Grinning, he slapped Caleb on the shoulder. "There's still time to make a run for it."

Caleb shook his head. "No way. Alyssa's everything I've ever wanted."

"You're one lucky son of a gun," Nick said, smiling. "She's a great girl."

"Nick and I both wish you the best," Hunter added

as they headed for the door. "When is she taking over the reins at the financial firm?"

"Right after we get back from our honeymoon in the Bahamas." Caleb led the way toward the meadow down by the creek. "Our plan is for her to keep things going until I get my business degree, then we'll run it together."

"And Emerald is okay with that?" Nick asked, looking doubtful.

"She's the one who suggested it," Caleb said, taking his place beside the preacher from the local Methodist church.

As he gazed over the small crowd seated in white folding chairs under the shade of the oak tree he'd climbed as a boy, he noticed that several of the Skerritt and Crowe employees had made the trip from New Mexico to Tennessee for the wedding. His smile widened when his gaze drifted to his mother and grandmothers. On opposite sides of the aisle, they were chatting congenially. All things considered, he'd have never believed it was possible, but his mother, his grandma Walker and Emerald had become fairly good friends.

His heart swelled with love for the women in his life. When he'd brought Alyssa home to meet his mother and grandmother, they'd immediately accepted her as the daughter and granddaughter they'd never had. Then, to his surprise, his mother had called Emerald and the four of them had had a grand old time planning the wedding together.

But when the string quartet that Emerald had insisted on hiring started playing "Here Comes the Bride" and the crowd rose to their feet, Caleb turned his attention to the woman being escorted down the aisle by Malcolm Fuller. Alyssa was dressed in a long, white, satin-and-lace wedding gown, and he'd never seen her look more beautiful. Her gaze never wavered from his and, when Malcolm put her hand in Caleb's, her radiant smile lit the darkest corners of his soul.

"I love you, sweetheart. Are you ready to become Mrs. Walker?"

"I've been waiting for this moment my entire life," she whispered.

"They make a very striking couple," Emerald murmured, watching Caleb raise Alyssa's veil.

"Quite," Luther Freemont agreed.

As she watched her handsome grandson kiss his lovely bride, Emerald smiled. She'd been right to pair Caleb with Alyssa. From the first time she'd spoken on the phone with the young woman, Emerald had been impressed with her intelligence and business acumen. Then, after a discreet check into Alyssa's background, she'd instinctively known each was exactly what the other needed. Caleb was a natural-born leader and Alyssa a sensitive intellect. They were a perfect match and together they would be a major force to contend with in the financial world, not to mention producing beautiful, intelligent heirs.

Extremely pleased with the results of her first endeavor, she turned her attention to her other two grandsons. Hunter and Nick were going to be a challenge. Both of them had pasts that would have to be overcome before they could find their happiness.

But she wasn't worried. She and Luther had done their research and had put their plans into action. In the months to come, she fully expected everything to turn out to her satisfaction with Hunter and Nick as well.

When Caleb and Alyssa walked down the aisle as husband and wife, Emerald turned to Luther with a smug smile. "One down and two to go."

* * * * *

Don't miss Reunion of Revenge, *the next book in Kathie DeNosky's mini-series* THE ILLEGITIMATE HEIRS. *Available April 2007 from Silhouette Desire.*

TYCOON TAKES REVENGE

by
Anna DePalo

ANNA DEPALO

A lifelong book lover, Anna discovered that she was a writer at heart when she realised that not everyone travels around with a full cast of characters in their head. She has lived in Italy and England, learned to speak French, graduated from Harvard, earned graduate degrees in political science and law, forgotten how to speak French and married her own dashing hero.

Anna has been an intellectual-property lawyer in New York City. She loves travelling, reading, writing, old movies, chocolate and Italian (which she hasn't forgotten how to speak, thanks to her extended Italian family). She's thrilled to be writing for Silhouette.

Readers can visit her at www.annadepalo.com.

For my sister, Pina,
and my cousin Anna Dagostino,
who've always been there for me

One

Gossip is news running ahead of itself in a red satin dress.

—*Columnist Liz Smith*

Smooth, moneyed and used to having things fall in his lap.

In short, Kayla thought disdainfully, as she watched him move toward her with a thin gloss of civility, he was everything that her family history had taught her to avoid.

Noah Whittaker. She'd spotted him instantly when she'd arrived at the cocktail party tonight at one of Boston's finer hotels to celebrate a retired Formula One race-car driver's newly published autobiography.

Her headline about Noah in that morning's *Boston*

Sentinel flashed through her mind: Caught with Fluffy, Huffy Calls It Quits. Will Buffy the Man Slayer Be Next for Noah?

She supposed he hadn't liked her story one bit. But she didn't make the news, she just reported it. And he gave her plenty of material to work with. He had, in fact, become a popular figure in her column.

And writing about him was easy. She knew his type. He acted as if the world were his cocktail, served up dry with a twist just for him, exactly as her biological father did.

She watched him approach and pushed aside the irritating twinge of nervousness. *She had nothing to be nervous about.*

She knew that, for *some* women, thoughts of sin and Noah Whittaker went hand in hand. But she'd been inoculated at birth against the players of the world—though she could dispassionately assess the attraction: Noah's hair, closely cropped but thick, looked as if he dried it with a blow-dryer set on scorch, its shade a burnished bronze. Over six feet tall, he had the honed body of an athlete. He'd had a brief but meteoric career as a race-car driver, though these days, he was better known as a vice president of Whittaker Enterprises, the family conglomerate in Carlyle, near Boston.

Noah stopped in front of her. "Kayla Jones, right?" He paused for a moment, his face all lean, hard planes of masculinity. "Or should I say," he added, his tone betraying a hint of derision, "Ms. Rumor-Has-It?"

Her chin came up. If he thought to faze her, he had

another thing coming. She'd gotten plenty of practice handling barbs from the pampered and privileged at the fancy prep school she'd attended on scholarship. "That's right. It's nice of you to remember."

One side of his mouth quirked up. "Hard to forget when you've been wielding a machete all over my social life. Or is that part of your job description as the *Boston Sentinel*'s resident gossip columnist?"

Her shoulders stiffened. They'd seen each other a few times at various social events, but this was the first time he'd deigned to speak with her personally. "I prefer the term *society columnist.* I write for the style section of the *Sentinel.*"

"Is that what they're calling the fiction part of the paper these days?"

She attempted a dismissive laugh. "If I hadn't heard that line before from more people than I can count, I'd say you were trying to insult me."

He cocked his head, seeming to consider her question. "That depends. Are you trying to spread lies about me, or is that just a nice little fringe benefit in your line of work?"

"For your information, all my columns are carefully researched and my sources checked for reliability."

"Obviously you need to work harder."

"Are we by chance discussing my column in today's paper?"

"Oh, yeah, we're discussing that all right. And last week's column. And the one before that. One guess as to what they all have in common."

"There's no need to descend into sarcasm," she said. "I'm aware of how often I've mentioned you in my column."

"Are you?" he asked silkily. "And are you also aware it's your fault that Eve Bernard—or as you've referred to her, Huffy—broke up with me?"

From what she'd heard, Eve had done more than break up with him. According to eyewitnesses with whom she'd spoken, Eve had delivered the news—along with a slap to the face—in the presence of dozens of departing guests at a glittering banquet on Saturday night. A *Sentinel* photographer had gotten a great shot of Noah, glowering at Eve and holding her by the forearms.

But what did he mean it was *her* fault?

"As a result of my column?" she asked with skepticism. "Don't you mean as a result of your cavorting with Fluffy?" At his sardonic look, she caught herself. "I mean, Cecily?"

He chuckled cynically. "Cavorting? My, my, what colorful language you society columnists use. All the better to write innuendo, I suppose?"

She tossed her head. "Whatever," she retorted, dropping all pretense of politeness. Out of the corner of her eye, she noticed other guests had begun to throw curious glances their way. "There was a photo of you and Cecily kissing outside the Kirkland Club."

"And we all know a picture is worth a thousand words, right?" he responded. "Or, in this case, a thousand lies. In fact, if you had done some inquiring instead of relying on that shot that your photographer snapped, you would have discovered that Cecily caught me by surprise with that kiss."

"How nice for you."

He ignored her. "You see, Cecily has this weird idea that making the gossip columns will bolster her fledgling acting career—and so much the better if the guy on her arm happens to be rich or famous. So she plastered herself to me the minute she spotted the *Sentinel*'s photographer."

"Perhaps then," she said sweetly, "you should reconsider the risk of dating publicity-seeking aspiring actresses. Or, for that matter, intellectually challenged models. And, hmm—" she pretended to consider for an instant, tilting her head "—I seem to recall at least one ruthless reality-show contestant as well."

"Oh?" he responded, letting his gaze rake over her from head to toe. "Considering that the field doesn't yet include any gossip columnists, I don't think my tastes can be called into question."

"From what I've been able to see, your *tastes* can best be described as blond, platinum-blond and strawberry-blond."

"Are you calling me shallow?"

"If the shoe fits," she retorted.

He shook his head. "So young and yet so bitter."

Bitter? No, she was *cautious*, but that's how a single woman budgeting to make rent payments had to be. And how the product of a fling between a slick, social-climbing financier and his young college intern knew to be. But then *Mr. Playboy Whittaker* didn't have a clue about the struggles of ordinary people.

Aloud, she countered, "We journalists have jobs that require us to *think*, and thinking doesn't appear to be high on your list of criteria for a girlfriend."

"Whether it is or not isn't anyone's business but mine," he responded.

"For your information, I didn't just rely on the photo. I called Huff—I mean, Eve—about it and she confirmed she was planning to break up with you over the, ah, incident."

"That's because Eve was thinking of her public image. She believed me when I said your column had misconstrued things because she knows Cecily is a publicity hound. But, as she put it, publicly she had to at least look like she was punishing me for being a naughty boy."

Kayla felt her lips twitch. "Well, that's not my fault, is it?"

"It *is* your fault," he disagreed. "You're printing salacious gossip and you're wreaking havoc on my social life."

"So find yourself another aspiring starlet," she retorted. "In fact, I think Buffy the Man Slayer is between men these days."

"Right, and that's another thing," he said tightly. "I don't need you trying to line up dates for me. Particularly not with someone known as a barracuda in heels."

"Now that's not nice." She spread her hands in an expansive gesture. "You should consider expanding your horizons."

He braced an arm on the wall near her head and she took an involuntary step back. He leaned in, his gaze, green and grim, boring into hers. “You know, I wonder why you consider me such a fascinating subject. Is it because you wish you were one of those women I date?”

“Don’t be absurd,” she snapped.

He gave her a slow once-over, dwelling on her ringless hand and letting his eyes linger on her chest before coming back to meet her outraged expression. “You do appear a little uptight. What’s the matter? Wish your life had a little more *zing* in it?”

“No thanks. My mother taught me to stay away from the players among men.”

“Ah,” he said. “Now we’re getting somewhere. The intrepid reporter is repressed.”

“This isn’t about me,” she said coldly. *What nerve.* He knew nothing about her life. *Nothing.*

“So, you have no problems dishing about others’ lives, but yours is off-limits, is that it?”

“There’s nothing to dish about,” she retorted. “I don’t have anything as interesting as a fatal racing accident in my past!”

The minute she blurted the rejoinder, she winced inwardly, realizing she may have gone too far. He might be a first-class jerk who believed his money and his family name would get him out of any predicament, but she didn’t need to throw a terrible tragedy in his face.

His face turned stony and he straightened. “Be glad you don’t.”

"Excuse me," she said, brushing past him and hurrying for the nearest exit.

Noah stared broodingly at Kayla's retreating back. Damn.

"Problems?"

Turning, he noticed Sybil LaBreck, gossip columnist for the *Boston World,* standing behind him.

"Yeah. A little lovers' spat," he replied sarcastically.

Sybil's eyes widened, and Noah realized she'd taken his flippant comment seriously.

Sybil was Kayla's biggest rival among local gossip columnists. In her late fifties, Sybil looked like an updated version of Mrs. Santa Claus, but she could shovel the dirt with the best of them.

Sybil looked perplexed. "But you've been seen everywhere with that model—what's her name?—Eve."

Noah was about to tell Sybil that he'd been joking, but he suddenly realized he'd been handed a golden opportunity to even the score with Kayla. "The so-called relationship with Eve was just a smoke screen, a way to throw the paparazzi off the scent. Eve got a little publicity out of the arrangement, and Kayla and I got a little privacy. It was perfect."

"But only last week Eve was seen slapping you for cheating on her!" Sybil blurted before seeming to catch herself.

"Really?" Noah said, raising an eyebrow while privately relishing the thought of the headline in Sybil's column tomorrow. "It was a great way to signal the end of our pretend relationship for the benefit of the press, wasn't it?"

Sybil opened her mouth—in all likelihood to probe for more details—but he cut her off smoothly. "Excuse me." He let his eyes focus on a spot across the room. "I just spotted someone I need to say hello to."

"Of course," Sybil said, stepping aside.

He chanced a glance at her out of the corner of his eye as he moved past: she looked like the cat that had swallowed the canary.

As he headed to the bar at the far side of the room, he pondered again about his problem with Ms. Rumor-Has-It. If newspapers were printed in color, he thought to himself disgustedly, Kayla's column would be nothing but a series of hot-pink exclamation points. It had the same breathless quality as the gossip that sorority sisters shared over drying nail polish.

Of course, her column had nothing on the woman herself. Tonight she'd been wearing a clingy black cocktail dress that revealed a tantalizing bit of her full chest and a fair expanse of her shapely legs, her honey-blond hair hanging in a smooth curtain past her shoulders. Her eyes were large and wide set but balanced by lips that were lushly curved. Under other circumstances, she'd have been exactly his type—blond, busty and beautiful.

Still, even the attractive packaging couldn't obscure the fact that the woman was a menace. And he'd had enough. More than enough.

His reputation as the playboy Whittaker brother

made him a favorite of the press as well as the object of more than a little ribbing from his older brothers, Quentin and Matt, and his younger sister, Allison.

But the truth was that he worked damned hard in his position as vice president of product development for Whittaker Enterprises, the family business started by his father, James. His degree from the prestigious Massachusetts Institute of Technology was put to excellent use in his capacity as head of Whittaker's computer business.

If he liked to consort with models and actresses when he was let out of his prison cell—uh, office—well, he wasn't going to begrudge himself some fun. Besides, there was a worldwide shortage in decent-looking computer geeks like himself.

Frowning, he ordered a cocktail. Kayla had some gall taunting him with the car accident that had marked the end of his career racing Indy cars. God knew, if he could take back the accident that had killed another driver, he would. Didn't everyone understand that? Couldn't the press that had plagued him after the accident comprehend that?

His physical scars had healed but the emotional scars on his soul would never go away.

Turning away from the bar, he took a sip of his drink and thought again that it would be a shame to miss Kayla's reaction to Sybil's column in the morning.

But then again... A smile rose to his lips.

Reaching into the pocket of his pants, he pulled out his cell phone. The number he wanted was already programmed in, having been used both before and after countless dates: Bloomsville Florists.

The following morning, Kayla's first sign that something was wrong was the large bouquet of red roses parked on her desk in her cubicle at the *Boston Sentinel*'s headquarters.

At first she thought there must have been some mistake. She glanced around the office, then put her purse down and reached for the note that was tucked among the flowers.

After pulling the card from the envelope, she scanned the contents: "Kayla, thanks for a wonderful evening."

Confused, she turned the card over and then looked at the envelope, but there was no further clue as to who had sent the flowers and why—not even the name of a florist.

Hmm, interesting. Who could have sent the bouquet? She hadn't had a date in a couple of months, ever since she'd gone out with a radio-show producer before quickly deciding they had no chemistry.

Frowning, she sat down and logged onto her computer. She'd e-mail the receptionist; every visitor had to sign in at the front desk.

Out of habit, however, she first surfed to the news sites to check out the day's headlines and, more importantly, to scan the society pages. She made it a practice to read her rivals' gossip columns just to keep up with what the competition was doing.

When she got to the *Boston World*'s gossip page,

Sybil LaBreck's years-old, black-and-white photo stared back at her along with the headline Dangerous Liaisons: Noah Whittaker's Secret Relationship with Gossip Maven Kayla Jones, aka Ms. Rumor-Has-It.

She froze, blinked, and then stared.

No. But the headline was still there, staring at her, taunting her.

She scanned the rest of the article while a sickening feeling settled in the pit of her stomach.

Sybil alleged that Noah and Ms. Rumor-Has-It had been secretly involved for some time. The column went on to disclose a lovers' row that they'd had at the book-launch party last night. It ended by toying with the delicious possibility that Kayla's skewering of the millionaire playboy in her column had been a smoke screen for her own clandestine relationship with him.

Kayla's mind raced. Had Sybil witnessed her argument with Noah last night and wrongly concluded she'd been privy to a lovers' spat? Or—a more ominous thought intruded—had someone led Sybil to believe it *was* a lovers' spat?

She looked up from her computer screen and caught one of the *Sentinel*'s health columnists giving her a curious look. Had Sybil's headline already been making the rounds?

Kayla's eyes went to the flower bouquet again. Now that she'd read Sybil's headline, the flowers suddenly made sense.

Noah. The rat. Whether he'd started the flames or was just fanning them, she had a thing or two to tell him.

Using the Internet, she located the main number for Whittaker Enterprises. Once she dialed it, she was quickly transferred to Noah's secretary.

"May I ask who is calling?" the secretary intoned once Kayla had asked to speak with Noah.

"It's Kayla Jones."

"I'm sorry, Ms. Jones, but Mr. Whittaker isn't in the office yet this morning. May I take a message?"

He wasn't in the office yet? Probably due to his late-night carousing, she thought acidly. Her eyes strayed to the clock on the wall, which indicated it was just after nine.

As she looked down and started to tell Noah's secretary that she'd call back later, her gaze landed on the man striding toward her.

Noah Whittaker, smiling sunnily.

"Never mind," she said absently into the receiver. "I've found him." She couldn't believe he had the nerve to show up at her office! Planning to milk this baseless rumor for all it was worth, was he?

She hung up and straightened, rising from her chair just as Noah came to a stop in front of her.

He nodded to the impressive arrangement of red roses. "Glad to see I got my money's worth."

"You snake." She kept her voice low, not caring that her tone sounded furtive. The last thing she needed was for someone at the *Sentinel* to overhear her conversation. Fortunately, it was still early enough that a lot of the staff hadn't rolled in yet.

Noah chuckled. "Now is that any way to thank the guy who's come to apologize for our lovers' quarrel?"

"You know it was no such thing!" she exclaimed in a low tone, catching another curious look from the *Sentinel*'s health columnist.

"I suppose," he returned placidly, "you're about to express outrage and claim bloody retribution."

She looked at him. He seemed so smug, and he was so infuriating. "You planned this," she accused. "You let Sybil think we were...*involved.*" She could barely get that last word out. "You sent the flowers to make it seem as if Sybil's story held water."

"Not only did I let Sybil think we were involved," he replied, "I told her we were."

"What?" she squeaked. That was the best she could manage without drawing attention. Inside, however, she felt like screaming.

"Right after you left last night, I had an unexpected run-in with Sybil. Apparently she witnessed enough to know we'd been arguing."

Kayla closed her eyes. It was a nightmare, a complete nightmare.

"I'll say this for her," Noah continued, "that woman has a nose for gossip like a bloodhound on a scent." He regarded her blandly. "Anyway, I made some sarcastic remark about a lovers' spat, and she took it seriously. I was going to correct her when I realized it would be much more fun to make the most of the situation."

"So instead of letting her believe we were arguing, you told her that we were *involved?*" she asked incredulously.

"What's the matter?" he asked. "Uncomfortable being the subject of rumors? Not too pleasant, is it?"

"You're enjoying this, aren't you?"

He shrugged. "I'll admit to some grim satisfaction at being handed an opportunity to even the score."

She grabbed her shoulder bag and her blazer. "Let's discuss this somewhere else."

He looked mildly surprised. "If you say so."

They had to talk, she thought, but this wasn't the place to do it. She wasn't about to provide fodder for the office gossip mill. But somehow she had to convince him to call Sybil and get her to print a retraction. The alternative didn't bear thinking about. She refused to be lumped together with Huffy, Fluffy and Buffy.

As he followed her down the hall and into an elevator, she was aware of his tread behind her—and of the glances that the two of them attracted.

When they got downstairs and outside into the still-warm September sun, she sighed with relief. At least they were away from prying eyes.

Turning to Noah, her brows snapping together, she began, "Now look—"

Her planned reprimand ended with a gasp as he swept her into his arms.

Her eyes widened. "What—"

Out of the corner of her eye, she saw a man—a photographer—leap forward and snap a shot of them just before Noah's mouth closed over hers.

Two

Kayla put her hands on Noah's chest and pushed, but he held firm.

For the next few seconds, several thoughts tumbled through her mind. Who was that guy with the camera? Were any of her co-workers around? She'd be mortified! What the heck was wrong with Noah? However, those thoughts were quickly drowned out by one overwhelming sensation: the feel of Noah's lips on hers.

He kissed expertly: his lips soft but sure and his focus concentrated on making her *feel*. His big, solid body pressed against her. He smelled of soap and shaving cream and just plain *guy*, and tasted of mint and warmth and subtle sweetness. He overloaded all her senses at once, and she was intoxicated.

It was like being kissed by the captain of the football team in front of the entire school—except she was a twenty-seven-year-old woman with a job and rent payments who happened to be standing in front of her office building at exactly the time that her boss or innumerable other people might be happening by.

That last thought brought her back to reality with a *thunk!*

She pulled her mouth from Noah's and shoved him away.

Noah loosened his hold on her—the expression on his face a mixture of pleasant surprise and—*help*—male curiosity.

"What are you doing?" she demanded, then glanced around. The guy with the camera was still there, snapping away. "And, you! Who are you?"

When he lowered his camera, she recognized him as a photographer for the *Boston World.*

Suddenly she felt ill.

The photographer, who frequently worked with Sybil LaBreck, smiled and waved at her. "Hey, there, Kayla. You know, if I hadn't just seen it with my own eyes, I'd never have believed the rumor about you and Noah." He shook his head bemusedly.

She didn't have a chance to respond because just then she noticed that, striding down the sidewalk toward them, on his way to the office, was Ed O'Neill, managing editor of the *Sentinel.*

Her boss.

She whirled back to Noah.

One look at his amused face, however, and she realized she hadn't just been sunk, she'd been torpedoed—or, more precisely, set up.

The irony wasn't lost on her either: she'd just been photographed apparently kissing *him* in the same way *he'd* been snapped apparently kissing Fluffy.

She jabbed a finger into his chest. "You! This was all part of the plan, wasn't it?"

Noah caught her finger. "Sweetie—" he said, and she knew he was playing to the audience "—is it really so bad to announce our love to the world?"

She yanked her hand away from his.

"Hello, Kayla."

The two of them turned, and she came face-to-face with Ed, whose expression said he was wondering what the hell was going on.

"Er—hello, Ed." She smiled brightly.

Noah held out his hand. "Hi, Ed."

Noah knew her boss?

Ed took it and said gruffly, "Noah. What brings you here first thing in the morning?"

Noah looked amused. "Well—"

"We were just saying goodbye," Kayla interrupted, then took a step toward the *Sentinel*'s entrance. "I'll take the elevator up with you, Ed."

Ed looked from one to the other of them, then glanced at the photographer at the curb. "Anyone want to explain to me what's going on?"

She was going to die, right there in front of the *Sen-*

tinel's headquarters. She could already see the headline: Ms. Rumor-Has-It Slain by Innuendo.

Noah smiled. "Sorry, Ed. Gotta run." His eyes met hers. "I'm sure Kayla will explain everything. Won't you, honey?"

She gritted her teeth while Ed raised his eyebrows at the endearment. "*Of course,*" she said. "Say hello to Huffy, Fluffy and Buffy for me, won't you?"

His eyes laughed at her. "Sure."

To Ed, she said in a low voice, "There's a *Boston World* photographer standing at the curb. I'll explain, but once we're inside."

At Ed's nod, she turned and stalked toward the revolving doors. Later, she promised herself, she'd take some time to throw darts at Noah Whittaker's picture or burn him in effigy.

The only silver lining to this morning's catastrophe was that, since he'd now exacted his revenge, with any luck she'd never have anything to do with him again.

Unfortunately, luck happened to be vacationing in Tahiti the next day.

"Ed, you can't be serious!"

Why were they discussing having her drive over to Whittaker Enterprises to cover a press conference? A press conference at which Noah Whittaker would be presiding!

Hadn't she explained everything to Ed yesterday? Hadn't she explained that she and Noah really loathed each other? Did she not detail how the "affair" had just been a rumor generated by Noah as payback for the stories she'd printed about his bad behavior?

The fact that panic roiled through her at the thought of facing Noah Whittaker again had nothing to do with yesterday's kiss and everything to do with the fact that she couldn't stand the man. He was altogether too high-and-mighty for her taste.

She regarded Ed levelly. He was her boss but also her mentor—surely he could see that sending her to cover this press conference wasn't the best allocation of personnel.

Ed scratched his balding pate. It was the second time he'd done so since showing up at her cubicle. "Look, I thought you were gunning for a position covering hard news."

"I was! I am!" she exclaimed in dismay. She'd gotten into journalism so she could be a business reporter, not so she could write about the latest fashions at debutante balls.

"Well, here's your chance to prove yourself," Ed said. "Rob was supposed to cover this press conference at eleven o'clock, but he's off on a breaking story and everyone else has a full plate."

"I know, but Noah Whittaker hates me. He'll never field a question from me." Her opportunity to cover hard news wasn't supposed to arrive *like this*.

"So?" Ed countered. "When you get there make nice with Noah, smooth over any ruffled feathers, and everything will be fine."

Kayla wished she could be as confident as Ed that she could make nice. It was more likely she'd wind up conking Noah on the head with her purse: Sybil LaBreck's column that morning featured a picture of her and Noah kissing in front of the *Sentinel*'s offices.

"If you do nothing else, just make sure you pick up a copy of the press release that they give out," Ed said, seeming to take some pity on her. "That'll give you enough to write a where, what, how, and when article about whatever it is that Whittaker is announcing today."

She felt her shoulders slump. "Right."

"Jones," Ed said gruffly, "I've been trying to look out for you since the day you got here. You've got enough ambition to fill a football stadium. Now go and put it to good use."

She should have been grateful for Ed's little pep talk. Instead, all she could do was manage some weak waves of the cheerleading pom-poms. She smiled wanly. "Thanks, Ed."

"And," Ed continued, "if you're interested in getting a position on the business beat, Noah Whittaker is as good a person as any to start with."

"What do you mean?"

Ed shrugged. "I mean there have been rumors circulating for a while about some suspicious offshore company in the Cayman Islands linked to Noah Whittaker. It could be nothing, but you never know. If there's a story there, it would be big because Whittaker has a pristine business reputation." He added significantly, "A story like that could practically guarantee you the job you want."

Kayla didn't have to ask what kind of story Ed meant.

She knew that some offshore companies were just tax havens for the wealthy. Others, however, provided excellent cover for money laundering and other shady dealings simply because some localities required very little information to be made public about the companies created there.

Her mind skittered across the idea of Noah connected to something less than completely legal. What could his motivation be? He had all the money he needed. Yet, wasn't her own biological father proof that greed knew no bounds?

Aloud, she said, "Thanks for the tip."

Ed nodded curtly. "I'm willing to give you a chance." Then he nodded at the clock on the wall. "You better get going."

"Right!" she said with as much enthusiasm as she could muster.

As Ed walked away, she picked up her handbag and grabbed her jacket. Well, what choice did she have? The things she had to do to pay the bills!

Unlike the women Noah dated, and, for that matter, her classmates at the fancy prep school she'd attended, she didn't have a trust fund to fall back on or family connections to milk to get ahead.

Instead, she'd gotten her foot in the door of the journalism world by getting an entry-level job straight out of college with the *Sentinel.* It hadn't mattered too much that the position was with the "Styles" section of the paper; it had been one of the few job offers she'd gotten and the one that paid the best of a rather pathetic lot.

Initially, she'd done a lot of research and fact-checking, with an occasional byline as time went on. She'd written about everything from the latest fashions to museum openings—when she hadn't been acting as a gofer for Leslie, who'd been the *Sentinel*'s resident Ms. Rumor-Has-It.

But then Leslie had run off with her paramour—a fiftyish, thrice-divorced millionaire who'd parted with wife number three to elope with Leslie to Paris—and Kayla had been left holding the bag, albeit a snazzy Versace number in black satin.

Kayla had been summoned to the managing editor's office, which smelled of the Macanudo cigars that Ed O'Neill liked to sneak behind closed doors.

"Jones," Ed had said, "you're up at bat. We need someone fast, and you're perfect—a classy Grace Kelly type with the right prep-school credentials. You'll fit right in covering your old school pals for the gossip pages."

And she had. She'd jumped at the chance to replace Leslie, not the least because Ed had dangled a significant salary raise as inducement. For her that had been enough.

So what if becoming Ms. Rumor-Has-It hadn't been part of her career aspirations? She'd gotten her own column before she'd turned twenty-five *and* she'd stopped worrying about the rent. There'd be time enough, she'd reasoned, for her to segue to the business-news desk.

But that had been three years ago. She'd done her job,

and well. Too well, in some respects. No one was eager to see her move away from the society page.

But, despite the seeming glamour of her job, she'd begun to feel restless. There were only so many canapés that a girl could eat before she felt like regurgitating on Buffy the Man Slayer's Manolo Blahnik heels.

That's why she'd recently started to lobby for an opportunity to cover some real news. Because Ed was right about one thing: she was ambitious and refused to be typecast for the rest of her career as perfect for covering fluff. She was determined to go places.

Unfortunately, today the place that she was heading was Noah Whittaker's front door.

"Well, it's interesting to see how the tide has turned."

Across the boardroom table, Noah gave Allison a disgruntled look. He'd just finished explaining how his recent bad press was baseless. "I know you find this hopelessly amusing, but *try* to contain your glee."

Allison laughed. "Oh, come on, big brother, don't tell me you don't see the hilarity in it all! Women used to chase you the way they'd run to a shoe sale. These days, though, you're more like last year's shoes—still wearable, but you're wondering why you ever bought them."

Quentin and Matt chuckled.

Noah sighed in exasperation.

It wasn't often these days that Noah's whole family was together, but early morning meetings of Whittaker Enterprises' board of directors afforded them the opportunity from time to time, despite their busy lives.

He looked around the room. They were an impressive bunch, and, though he and his siblings could needle each other mercilessly, they had an unshakable bond.

At the head of the table sat his father, James, who, in his retirement, still chaired the board of directors. His mother, Ava—who'd passed along her coloring of dark brown hair and vivid blue eyes to his brother Matt and his sister Allison—was a respected family court judge. Matt, who was older than Noah by two years, was also a vice president at Whittaker, though he'd increasingly been developing his own business interests. Allison had followed their mother's footsteps into the legal profession and become an assistant district attorney in Boston. Quentin, the oldest sibling, was CEO of Whittaker Enterprises.

Missing were Quentin's wife, Liz, who was at home with their baby, Nicholas, and Allison's husband of one month, Connor Rafferty, who ran his own security business.

Noah supposed, given his siblings' penchant for ribbing each other, he shouldn't have been surprised that, once the board meeting had ended, and because they had time to kill before the press conference at eleven, the topic of conversation would turn to the recent headlines about him in the newspapers.

Thanks to Kayla, in the span of two weeks, he'd been branded a philanderer for fooling around with Fluffy, been reported to have had a public scuffle with Huffy during which she'd slapped him and he'd been seen restraining her and, to top it off, been witnessed having an argument with Ms. Rumor-Has-It herself.

He wondered whether Kayla had seen Sybil LaBreck's column that morning and figured she must have. Sybil's headline screamed: Kayla and Noah Kiss and Make Up!

Fortunately, Huffy—er, Eve, he corrected himself, annoyed that now he was unintentionally adopting Kayla's ridiculous names—was in Europe on a modeling shoot and thus probably unaware of the headlines linking her most recent ex to a secret affair with Ms. Rumor-Has-It. Otherwise, he might have had another irate female to contend with.

In any case, he took grim satisfaction in knowing Sybil's column that day had probably riled Kayla. After all, *he* had to suffer through grief from his family.

"Well," Allison continued, "I, for one, would love to congratulate Kayla Jones." She looked at Quentin and Matt for affirmation. "Unlike those vapid, vampish vixens you sometimes date, she's smart enough not to be bowled over by your charm, Noah."

Noah mouthed *vapid, vampish vixens* incredulously while his brothers stifled their mirth. Then he frowned. "Great. I'll let Connor know that, if you ever get tired of the D.A.'s office, you can have a second career as a gossip columnist." He added, "Does family loyalty mean nothing to you?"

"Not since you tried to get me married off to Connor," Allison returned sweetly. "How did you put it to him?" She pretended to try to remember for a second, then snapped her fingers. "Oh, right. I believe your words were 'Why don't you help take her off our hands?'"

Noah grumbled. "Maybe I shouldn't have put it like that, but you and Connor belonged together. *This* situation's different."

Matt's lips twitched. "Ms. Rumor-Has-It does seem to have your number, unlike—uh, how did she put it?—*Huffy, Fluffy and Buffy.* And, on top of it all, your little columnist is undeniably *hot.*"

Noah quelled the sudden, inexplicable urge to slug the amused look off of his brother's face. So, Kayla was hot; she was also a menace, and she was *not* "his" little columnist. "Yeah, and she's also a consummate teller of tall tales in that fiction column of hers."

At the head of the table, his father cleared his throat and gave him a level look. "The bottom line is there's a problem here that you need to fix. Even if there's not a modicum of truth in the recent headlines, they're bad for public relations—both yours and Whittaker Enterprises'."

Quentin nodded. "Dad's right, as much as I'd like to think otherwise. Some people will believe the press, and even those who don't will wonder if you're playing and partying harder than you're working."

Noah watched his mother cast him a sympathetic look that nonetheless managed to carry a hint of reproach. "I know I raised you to be respectful toward women, Noah, so I have no doubt that the recent press about you is just an aberration. Nevertheless, darling, I have to agree with your father and brother. You must fix this. No more headlines, and you should try to do something to repair your public image."

Noah knew his family was right. His philosophy of

working hard and playing harder had long worked for him, but then Ms. Rumor-Has-It had come along.

He had to deal with her and the trouble she'd stirred up in his life.

What was she doing here?

Noah stared in disbelief at the figure slinking into a seat at the back of the roomful of assembled reporters, cameramen and photographers awaiting the beginning of the press conference.

As if she could go unnoticed.

Even if she hadn't been a head-turner with her blond hair falling like a curtain past her shoulders and a figure that was a siren call to every straight guy in the room, she had on a ridiculous outfit consisting of a pale pink sweater made of some clingy material that hugged her breasts, a pencil-thin pinstriped skirt showing off legs that went on and on, and some *come-hither* heels.

Watching as she got a once-over from the guy next to her while, oblivious to any attention, she pulled out a notepad, Noah smiled grimly: *I rest my case.*

Much to his annoyance, the memory of their kiss lingered with him. Her lips had been soft, silky and full beneath his, and their effect had gone through him like a shot of brandy. But so what if the woman had proved she could kiss with real feeling?

He frowned. The last thing he needed to be thinking about right now was their kiss. The press conference would start any minute. He'd resolved this morning to deal with her, but he hadn't expected to be confronted with an opportunity here, now, surrounded by half the press of Greater Boston. Hell.

Anyway, the real question was, what was she doing here? Last time he'd checked, gossip columnists didn't cover breaking business news.

As the clock on the back wall hit eleven, he strode to the podium at the front of the room. He was going to announce the acquisition by Whittaker Enterprises of Avanti Technologies, a small company located along Route 128, Boston's high-tech corridor, and because the acquisition of Avanti impacted Whittaker's computer business—his area of expertise—he'd be doing the initial presentation. Afterward, he and Quentin, as well as the president of Avanti, would field questions.

When Noah got to the microphone, he made a couple of jokes to break the ice, then consulted his notes: "Pleased to announce…welcome the opportunity to work with…corporate synergies involved…"

Throughout his speech, he noticed Kayla kept her gaze fixed somewhere over his left shoulder. *Uncomfortable, eh?* He wondered again what had brought her here and knew that, as soon as the press conference was over, he was going find out.

Focusing again on the assembled reporters, he concluded by saying that additional copies of Whittaker's press release were on a table at the back of the room.

Then, when Quentin and the president of Avanti stepped forward to flank him at the mike, he fielded questions from reporters, eventually calling on a guy in jeans.

The reporter stood up, a smirk hovering at the corners of his lips. "The stock for Whittaker Computing has been down recently. Can you comment on the markets' reaction to the recent bad press about you?"

Noah tensed. Whittaker Computing—one of a handful of companies that made up Whittaker Enterprises—was partly publicly owned. There were any number of reasons why Whittaker Computing's stock had taken a hit recently, as any half-wit could tell you, but the weasel in front of him was obviously trying to bait him.

Noah gave him a semblance of a smile and then, keeping his tone even, said, "The markets have better things to do than follow any spurious rumors written about me."

Noah watched as Kayla slunk farther down in her chair at the back of the room. Feeling a tad self-conscious, was she? *Well, welcome to the club, babe.*

He started to call on another questioner, but the smirking jerk in jeans—probably some overeager new recruit looking to make his mark—persisted. "What about the impression you've given that you can't get along with women? There's been speculation that this could affect Whittaker's ability to recruit female executives."

Noah gripped the sides of the lectern. He'd like to deck the questioning little dweeb. "Maybe it's a question of the ability of a few particular women to get along with me."

This earned him a chuckle or two from the audience.

He held the reporter's gaze until the guy shifted. "Whittaker Enterprises is an equal opportunity employer. We value and welcome female employees. In fact, we're proud we've been rated one of the best places for women to work by a leading Boston magazine. Our on-site day care and flextime schedules are models for the industry. The women at Whittaker who work with me wouldn't tell you differently."

Then, determined this time to cut off the smart-ass, Noah turned to look at another part of the room. "Next question."

Fifteen minutes later, the press conference was over. Immediately, he spotted Kayla scurrying into the hall.

"Excuse me," he said curtly, shoving his way past the milling press and striding out of the room.

He caught up with her halfway down the hall and captured her elbow. "We need to talk."

She started and looked up at him guiltily.

"What?" he asked blandly. "Attempting to make your escape?"

"I'm sure we've said all there is to say to one another," she said, her tone cool enough to freeze penguins in their tracks.

"On the contrary, Barbie," he countered dryly, looking pointedly at her blond hair and pink sweater.

She pulled her elbow away from him. "I'm not going anywhere with you. I may be Barbie, but you're no Ken, Mr. I-Change-Women-with-the-Seasons Whittaker. Barbie and Ken had a committed, monogamous relationship for over forty years."

God, she was maddening. She'd just compared him *unfavorably* to a plastic doll's main squeeze.

He wondered again why he still found her pulse-poundingly attractive. Sick. He was sick.

"As unpleasant as it is for the both of us, we need to talk and I suggest we do it in private—unless you want our public bloodletting to continue?" He took her elbow again.

She looked around. "I'll scream."

Aside from the two of them, no one was in the hallway yet. They were some distance from the room where the press conference had been held, and probably most of the journalists were still gathering their equipment. Still, Noah knew that Kayla could make herself heard.

"I wouldn't advise it," he said dryly. "Not unless you want another newspaper headline about us, and I doubt that."

She opened her mouth.

"Think about it," he said forcefully. "Our names conjoined in ink. Again. *Forever.*"

Three

Upstairs in Noah's office, Kayla still couldn't shake the feeling that this was a bad idea. A very bad idea.

They didn't do well talking to each other. Or even being in the same room together.

Noah gestured her to a seat.

"No thanks," she said.

"Suit yourself," he responded, then sat at the edge of his desk, folding his arms across his chest and crossing one foot over the other at the ankle.

She glanced around his office. It was all chrome and black and glass with two walls displaying great views of nearby hills. Her cubicle at work would have fit into the space behind his desk.

Grudgingly, she admitted that, whatever else Noah was, he did appear to be spectacularly successful.

"What the heck are you doing here?" he asked abruptly, drawing her attention back to him.

"I was filling in for another reporter," she said, self-conscious under his scrutiny. All at once, her skirt felt too short, her top too tight and her heels too high. Damn him.

He raised a brow. "Since when are gossip columnists asked to fill in for business reporters?"

It was on the tip of her tongue to tell him that it was none of his business, when it occurred to her that she'd just been handed a great chance to ask as many questions as she wanted about the acquisition of Avanti—*if*, that was, she acted at least passably civil toward him.

"I've been trying for a lateral move to the business desk at the *Sentinel*," she responded stiffly.

She could see she'd surprised him. "You want to write something other than salacious rumors?"

She checked her temper. "Let's not cross that ground again, shall we? As I think I made clear before, I work hard at my job. It's just that I want to be doing the type of reporting that I got into journalism for."

"And that would be—?"

"Business reporting," she said, her tone clipped. "Are you going to tell me what you wanted to talk to me about, or not?"

He looked at her for several seconds, his green gaze inscrutable. Finally, he said, "I'm calling for a cease-fire."

"What?" It was her turn to be taken by surprise.

"You heard me."

"Oh, right. I suppose now that the empire has struck back, it's okay for *you* to want to call a truce. After all, Sybil LaBreck has just announced *to the whole world* that we're back together!"

"Yeah, well," he said, too placidly to suit her, "you did play straight into my hands on that one."

She stared at him, annoyed. How dare he stand there looking so sexy and so gorgeous—causing an unwanted but very feminine reaction in her—when he was such a calculating sneak. She folded her arms across her chest. "I know I will regret asking, but how did I play into your plans?"

"Yesterday I tipped off that photographer from the *Boston World* so he could snap me leaving the *Sentinel*'s offices looking, uh, contrite after trying to mend fences with you."

"I should have guessed that photographer wasn't just hanging around hoping for a good photo op."

"Little did I know you'd insist on walking out with me—"

"Giving you and him an even better photo opportunity than you were expecting," she finished for him.

The lout.

"So, again, are you willing to declare a truce?"

"What kind of truce?" she asked, suspicious.

He shrugged nonchalantly, rising from his desk.

She forced herself not to take an involuntary step back just to keep some space between them. Over six feet, he had a comfortable height advantage over her—

even when she was wearing heels. But, more than that, he radiated a charisma that was nearly palpable.

"We can help each other."

"Really?" she asked in disbelief, forcing herself to keep up with their war of words because it was easier than thinking about being alone in his office with him. "I can't imagine what help I need from you other than for you to stop sabotaging me."

He arched a brow. "*Sabotage* is a strong word, don't you think?"

"Not if it's accurate." When he was smooth and charming, he was even more dangerous than when he was angry and annoyed. She brushed aside the disgruntling realization.

"You just said you're looking to move to the business desk at the *Sentinel.*"

"Yes…?" She wondered where he was going with this.

"I can give you a news story that will help you get there."

"What news story?"

"An exclusive inside look at Whittaker Enterprises. I'll grant you broad access."

"In return for…?"

He gazed at her speculatively. "In return for your help in rehabilitating my public image."

"Impossible," she responded.

He laughed. "I'm flattered, in a backhanded-compliment sort of way."

"Anyway, you're overestimating my influence on public opinion."

"I don't think so. You damaged my reputation, you can repair it."

"How?"

"By being seen getting along with me."

"I'm not that good of an actress," she retorted.

"Do your best. I'm not looking for an Oscar-winning performance."

His plan was ridiculous, outrageous. So why was she tempted?

Because, she answered herself, he was dangling an irresistible lure, damn him. She'd walk on hot coals to get that business reporter's beat.

"Well?" he prompted.

"Can't. Journalistic ethics. You may have heard of them."

"A little late in the day to be worrying about those, don't you think?" he scoffed.

"Tell that to my boss when he fires me," she snapped.

He shrugged and folded his arms again. "What would it take not to offend your journalistic sensibilities?"

"I won't agree to anything that smacks of you trying to buy me off or of an exchange of favors."

He sighed. "I told you that you'll have broad access to Whittaker Enterprises. You can talk to our employees. Heck, *I'll* talk to you. You can follow me around and see what my routine is. I won't stop you from writing something unflattering. All I'm asking for is that you write a balanced piece."

She continued to eye him, unconvinced.

He sighed again. "Fine, you don't have to pretend to

get along with me anymore than comes naturally, if that's going to trouble your reporter's conscience."

"Thanks."

"And as far as Ms. Rumor-Has-It's column goes, I think you can use the story about Whittaker Enterprises to your advantage. Just tell Ed that you can't write about me in your regular column while you're pursuing an in-depth piece about Whittaker Enterprises because you want to avoid any conflicts. If he's worried, he can assign you an intern. That way, when you do get moved over to the business desk, you'll already have someone in place to take over as Ms. Rumor-Has-It."

He made his plan sound so reasonable—and appealing. Oh-so-appealing. Nevertheless, she had to ask, "What about Sybil?"

He looked untroubled. "What about her? I'll call her up and explain our affair was a hoax. Besides, as long as we spread the word that you're shadowing me in order to write a piece about Whittaker Enterprises, we'll be dispelling the rumor that we're involved."

The thought of Sybil having the rug pulled out from under her *did* make his plan more tempting. Kayla bit her lip, then said, "What's in this for you?"

"For my part, I'm banking your intern won't be as interested in my social life as you are." He gave her a sardonic look. "Besides, since—thanks to you—I'm currently free of models and actresses, there won't be anything exciting to write about."

"Maybe." She refused to concede he likely was right.

"On top of that," he said, warming to his subject,

"once you get your assignment to the business desk at the *Sentinel,* I'm rid of you—at least as a wrecking ball in my social life. And, as an added bonus, I get a balanced news piece about Whittaker Enterprises." He finished triumphantly, "The plan is perfect."

She considered him a moment. "What would be the terms?" she asked, hoping she wouldn't regret this, yet unable to pass up the opportunity he presented.

She saw the flare of gratification in his eyes, but he quickly banked it. "Terms?"

"Yes. I need to know you'll give me access to information soon and won't renege on me." Now that she'd let herself entertain his offer, she wasn't going to be shy about the particulars.

He arched a brow. "Suspicious, aren't you?"

"There has to be a time limit," she said firmly.

"Make your best offer," he countered.

She assessed him, then took a moment to ponder. No doubt he was a shrewd bargainer—after all, he'd just engineered the takeover of one of Boston's leading tech firms by Whittaker Enterprises. "Two weeks."

He shook his head. "Six."

"Three." Nearly a month was fair.

"Five," he said. "These things take time."

"Let's split the difference," she countered. "Four. It shouldn't take long to repair the damage."

"A pleasure doing business with you." He closed the space between them and held out his hand.

Relief, followed by panic, washed through her. *What*

have I just done? She took his hand, felt her own engulfed in his, and experienced a surge of sensation.

Judging by the look in his eye, he felt it, too.

She started to draw away, but he pulled her closer.

He lifted her chin with his free hand and she had just a moment to lower her eyelids before he brushed her lips with his.

The kiss was over in the space of a few heartbeats, but its impression—powerful and disturbing—lingered for her.

He drew back and gazed down at her, his expression inscrutable. "Just checking," he murmured.

"What?" She looked at him, eyes wide, as she strove to clear her brain.

He smiled wryly. "You didn't need to worry about whether your acting abilities were up to the challenge." At her displeased expression, he laughed. "I know, I know. I'm diabolical."

Kayla was grateful he couldn't read her mind—for while *diabolical* should have been the first word that popped into her head, disturbingly, instead, it had been *delicious*.

How does one dress for dinner with a couple of computer geeks from Silicon Valley? Kayla wondered.

The day after the press conference, Noah had phoned her to announce that, if she was going to be shadowing him for purposes of her article, she should attend a business dinner that he had scheduled on Friday night with a couple of young hotshots from the West Coast.

He'd also let her know that, in the meantime, he'd done as promised and called Sybil to say his supposed relationship with Ms. Rumor-Has-It had been a hoax that he'd perpetuated to get even. Ironically, Sybil had been reluctant to believe there *wasn't* a relationship. Perhaps hedging her bets, however, her headline in the next morning's paper had read: Noah Denies Relationship with Ms. Rumor-Has-It.

Kayla figured she'd take what she could get and Sybil's headline was better than nothing. Eventually, the story about her and Noah *would* fade away.

And the good news was she'd been able to convince Ed to do what Noah had suggested. Ed had been pleased Noah had agreed to cooperate on an in-depth profile of Whittaker Enterprises. More importantly, he'd also grudgingly agreed to give her sometime assistant, Jody Donaldson, who was just a year out of college, a greater role in the writing of the Ms. Rumor-Has-It column, including writing anything newsworthy about Noah Whittaker.

So far, Kayla admitted to herself, everything was going according to plan—*if* she could figure out what to wear to this dinner tonight.

She began looking through her closet again from one end to the other. She tossed aside the leather miniskirt that she'd recently worn to the Avalon, one of Boston's well-known nightclubs.

Dress down, Noah had said. Though tonight technically counted as business, Noah had advised her that the term *business* had a whole different meaning among the under-thirty-five, newly rich and geeky set created by the information-technology boom, particularly in Silicon Valley.

She didn't doubt what he had told her. Sure, she herself had been part of the business-casual-attire revolution that had swept corporate offices across the United States in the past ten years. But, as a society columnist, she knew the requirements for her were different from those for some of her contemporaries: she was more high fashion and less grunge fashion. She was expected to blend with the social set she covered and, since she didn't have a trust fund or even a salary that was anything to brag about, she spent a good deal of time haunting outlet stores and consignment shops.

This all, of course, left her lost as far as what tonight required. Exasperated, she kept moving through the hangers in her closet, fretfully passing on her Levi's 501 blue jeans. *I have nothing to wear!* she silently wailed in frustration.

The phone rang and she felt a stab of relief at the unexpected distraction, despite the fact that she had only about an hour left before Noah would pick her up.

"Hello," she said absently, her eyes skimming the disarrayed pile of clothes on her bed.

"You sound as perky as usual," a voice said dryly.

"Samantha?"

Despite being seven years apart, Kayla and her sister shared a close bond, perhaps because they had no other siblings. Technically, they were half siblings, though she never thought of the two of them that way. When Kayla was five, her mother had remarried, and

Greg Jones had adopted Kayla. She had been happy to have a father in her life and even happier when, two years later, a baby sister had arrived. From the beginning, Samantha had followed in Kayla's footsteps, right up to enrolling at Tufts University, Kayla's alma mater.

The pile of clothes forgotten, she asked, "Is something wrong? Did something happen?"

Samantha laughed. "Relax. You sound as bad as Mom. Maybe I just called to say hello."

"Not if you're twenty and a college junior and it's a Friday night," she countered.

"Welcome to my lackluster social life. I'm hoping things will turn around soon," her sister responded. "Why am I not surprised *you're* at home tonight?"

"Actually, I need to leave in an hour."

"Oh?" Her sister's tone brightened. "Hot date?"

"Not really."

"Come on, spill the goods. Who's the guy?"

Kayla hesitated for a second, then resigned herself to the inevitable. "Noah Whittaker."

Silence reigned on the other end of the phone line.

"Samantha?"

"I'm speechless."

"That would be a first."

"Noah Whittaker is hot, hot, hot." Her sister sighed dreamily. "You've come to your senses. Though, if you've finally decided to date guys who are hunk-a-licious, I'm surprised it's Noah. You've been lacerating him in your column."

"Right, and speaking of which…" With one eye on

the clock, she brought her sister up to speed on her agreement with Noah, ending with, "So, what should I wear?"

"What should you wear?" Samantha said laughingly. "Is that all you can say?"

Frowning, she said, "Well, what should I say?"

"How about, this is an opportunity most women would die for! How about, it's not every day a sinfully delicious millionaire asks me to dinner? How about, how can I get Noah Whittaker to carry me off to his lovely penthouse in the sky?"

"How about, get your head out of the clouds?" Kayla countered. "Besides, this is strictly business."

"Oh, Kayla, live a little! Besides, there's no telling where things could go *after* you get your story." Samantha dropped her voice. "Laugh with the sinners for once."

"Coming from my little sister, I find that comment somewhat distressing," Kayla said with mock severity. "But for the record, Noah Whittaker doesn't just prefer to laugh with the sinners. He likes to party with the devil."

"Okay, whatever. Have it your way," Samantha said in exasperation. "Now, let's see.... I know! What about the camisole top that you got at a Filene's sale? Very sexy."

"Too sexy," Kayla said emphatically, thinking of the silky top's spaghetti straps and lace-edged cups. "It's practically lingerie."

"Exactly."

Kayla glanced at the clock again. She was running out of time and getting desperate. If she paired the camisole with some black pants, heels and a wrap, she *would* have an evening look that was dressy but casual, not to mention sexy and cool. She bit her lip.

"Go for it, Kayla," Samantha said, evidently sensing her hesitancy.

She sighed. "You know, you still haven't told me why you called."

Her sister laughed. "I'm not pregnant, homeless or desperate for cash. That's all you need to know. And, really, sometimes I am just calling to talk. I'll call you tomorrow to find out how your date went, and you can hear me gush about my *exciting* evening watching old flicks in the dorm's recreation room. Now, go!"

Half an hour later, Kayla found herself opening her front door dressed in black pants and a silky blue camisole top edged with brown lace, her toes peeking out from high-heeled slingbacks. She'd applied some light makeup and left her straight blond hair loose about her shoulders. Her watch and chandelier earrings were her only adornments.

Noah's eyes widened when he saw her, his gaze raking her from head to toe. He looked ready to devour her on the spot.

A shiver ran through her that had nothing to do with being cold. He looked devastatingly attractive in a blazer and a dark gray T-shirt paired with hip-hugging jeans, a five-o'clock shadow darkening his jaw.

"You look great."

She glanced down at her clothes, pleased he approved. "I wasn't sure what you meant when you said tonight was casual."

He tapped a finger on his chest. "*This* is what I meant."

As his blazer gaped open, she noticed the writing printed in black across the top of his T-shirt: Plays Well with Others.

"Geekdom values nonconformity over social acceptance. It's the pursuit of neophilia in its purest form."

At her confused look, he explained, "Neophilia means being excited by novelty. Geeks are big on novelty."

"Oh." Her brow furrowed. "In that case, I'm *not* dressed right."

A smile hovered at the corners of his lips. "No, you're dressed just right. At the risk of sounding sexist, the dress code doesn't apply to women because even computer geeks want to be seen with a babe on their arm. It all goes back to the high-school fantasy of dating the most popular girl in the class."

"That *is* sexist." But he thought she was a babe? She quelled the flutter that gave her.

He nodded, still standing in the doorway.

Inviting him in was too dangerous, and they were running just on time as it was. She held up her hands, one of which clutched a small handbag and a light shawl. "I'm ready when you are."

As she brushed past him, she ignored the grin that spread across his face, one that was all blatant male appreciation and said *ready for what?* Fortunately, he resisted the urge to give voice to what she could read on his face.

When they got downstairs, her attention was drawn to the sleek black Jaguar parked at the curb.

"Welcome to the Batmobile," Noah said with a grin, opening the passenger door for her.

When he'd gone around the car and gotten behind the wheel, she glanced around the luxurious interior and asked, "Why do I suspect that the doors lock, the windows fog up and the passenger-side seat drops back at the driver's command?"

As he turned the ignition, he tossed her a wicked grin. "I refuse to incriminate myself."

Four

When they arrived at Ginza, a trendy Japanese restaurant, Noah introduced her to the two "executives" from Silicon Valley as a news reporter who was shadowing him for a profile on Whittaker Enterprises.

Tim and Ben, who looked no older than twenty-five, had attended the prestigious California Institute of Technology together. Neither was geeky in the obvious glasses-and-pocket-protector way, but Tim was wearing an orange T-shirt paired with a dark-red blazer, and Ben had used a safety pin to replace a missing button on his shirt.

Kayla discovered they had spent three years toiling away in the bowels of established high-tech companies, working eighty-hour weeks, before they'd decided to strike out on their own—so they could still work eighty-hour weeks but be their own bosses.

Over dinner, the conversation moved across a variety of topics, from which tech company had recently lured a top employee from a rival to which new computer software products would soon be launched onto the market. To her disappointment, however, there were no hints as to what sort of business relationship, if any, Noah was contemplating with Tim and Ben's company.

However, if tonight was any indication, it didn't seem as if Noah would have any reason to be interested in nefarious offshore investments in the Cayman Islands or elsewhere. He had enough people with legitimate businesses knocking on his door.

Soon, the conversation at dinner veered to her job at the *Sentinel.* Both Ben and Tim were fascinated by her position as Ms. Rumor-Has-It, which they viewed as glamorous.

It made her want to laugh. She earned a fraction of what they made—and what they could make in the future. She wondered how glamorous they'd think her life was if they saw the small apartment she lived in and the car she'd been driving since her high-school days.

Noah, she noticed, didn't say anything. Not even a peep about being a favorite target for her column. That was, until Tim asked how she chose her stories. "Yes, Kayla," Noah interjected in a bland voice, "how *do* you choose your stories?"

She ignored him, keeping her attention instead on

Tim and Ben, who seemed unaware that Noah was one of her favorite targets. "I try to write stories that people want to read." She shrugged. "But I suppose personal taste comes into play in deciding whether the focus is going to be on politicians, celebrities or other figures."

"So what do you focus on?" Ben asked.

"I look for stories that are humorous—it's always amusing to poke fun at egos and pretensions."

Next to her, Noah guffawed and shifted in his chair, his leg brushing hers.

She tensed but forced herself to keep looking at Tim and Ben. "Of course, sometimes I don't have to look. The stories come to me."

"People want to appear in your column?" Tim asked curiously.

"You'd be surprised. There's a love-hate relationship between journalists and celebrities' publicists or press agents. Sometimes handlers want publicity in order to keep their celebrity in the public eye. But if a celebrity gets caught in a scandal-worthy situation, his publicist will be on the phone faster than you can say 'libel suit' to try to get you not to print the story. That is, if they don't have a hope of convincingly denying the truth of the story outright."

Tim laughed, and Ben said, "Marvelous!"

"How do you get the dirt on your victims to begin with?" Noah asked.

She turned to look at him fully. Mild annoyance was stamped on his face. "Now that would be telling, wouldn't it?"

"I thought *telling* was what you did for a living," he retorted.

She could come up with an appropriate rejoinder to that, but, she reminded herself, she had to do a passable job of getting along with Noah. At least until she got this story. Then all bets were off.

She smiled brightly at the younger guys facing her. "Just about anyone can be a source. Doormen, bouncers, waiters. Sometimes rivals or so-called friends call in tips, and then, of course, there are the anonymous tipsters."

"Have you gotten any good tips from anonymous sources?" Ben asked.

"Yup." She took a sip from her glass of sake. "I've broken a few stories because of them, too."

Ben raised his eyebrows, and Tim said, "Wow."

"The last story I broke was about the CEO of a troubled department-store chain—"

"I remember when he hit the papers," Noah interjected.

She nodded. "It turned out he was buying five-thousand-dollar shower mats for his penthouse while his shareholders were bleeding money."

"Ouch," Tim said.

"What happened?" Ben asked.

"He's no longer CEO," Noah said, answering for her. "Just like, if Kayla has her way, I'll no longer be the playboy of the northern hemisphere."

Tim stifled a smile, while Ben looked from her to Noah and back.

Kayla groaned inwardly. Great. Tim and Ben obviously thought something was going on between her and Noah.

After dinner, they headed to a karaoke bar. Though going to a bar where the patrons were encouraged to stand up and sing popular tunes wasn't her thing, she was soon laughing and clapping along with everyone else as one guest after another tried to carry a tune, assisted by a microphone, a DJ who loaded the right soundtrack and a TV monitor that displayed the song's lyrics.

The dim lighting in the bar, as well as the intimacy of their seating arrangement at a small table, kept Kayla acutely aware of Noah, who was seated next to her.

So intent was she on the accidental brush of his leg against hers that she was startled when Noah spoke. "So what's it going to be?"

"What?" she asked uncomprehendingly.

He indicated the small stage with a quirk of an eyebrow. "What are you going to sing?"

"No," she said, shaking her head.

"Chicken," he teased.

She straightened her spine. "I haven't sung since I was in the junior-high-school chorus."

"Not even in the shower?"

"That's not in public."

"So you do sing in the shower?" he asked. "Funny, I didn't think you were the singing-in-the-shower type."

"And you are?" she parried.

"I've done many things in the shower," he said, his look wicked. "Singing is just one of them."

"The question is, are you good at any of them?"

Noah threw back his head and laughed, drawing the momentary attention of Ben and Tim, who were seated in front of them, closer to the stage, watching someone do a torturous rendition of "Midnight Train to Georgia."

Kayla felt Noah's laugh to the tips of her toes. It was low, rich and seductive.

"Come on," he said. "I'll get up there if you will. It's practically required. Even Ben and Tim are taking a turn."

As it turned out, Ben and Tim did a passable rap duet.

She was sort of stunned actually, but all Noah said was "Like I said, the name of the game is novelty."

"Where do they find the time with their work schedules?"

Noah shrugged. "Rapping helps them attract women."

Her turn came a few minutes later. She walked to the stage and, in a snap decision, told the DJ to change her song selection.

If the name of the game was doing something out of character, she knew how to oblige.

As the first notes of the song vibrated through the room, she closed her eyes for a few seconds and let herself get caught up in the mood.

Finally, she opened her eyes and began singing "Come Away with Me." Norah Jones's hit song was slow, romantic and suited to her own husky singing voice.

For the first minute or so, she avoided looking at Noah. When she did chance a glance at him, her eyes locked with his and she almost stumbled over a note.

At that moment, the strangest set of feelings passed over her. She felt the exhilaration of racing with the wind in her hair alternating with the languor of lying in a hammock on a hot, sunny afternoon. The sensations thrilled and warmed her at the same time.

She sang on about walking together on a cloudy day and a love that would never stop.

Noah's gaze flickered, though the rest of his face appeared etched in cement, and sexual awareness wrapped itself around her like a blanket.

When she was done, her eyes lingered on his. He gazed at her intensely, as if he was stopping himself from bounding onto the stage, sweeping her up and making a beeline for the door.

The thought gave her goose bumps and she told herself to stop being ridiculous. She replaced the microphone on its holder and headed back to their table.

Noah met her in the middle of the room as he made his way to the stage. "Impressive," he murmured. "You should do more than sing in the shower."

"Th-thanks."

When she'd taken her seat again, the DJ began Noah's selection. She recognized the song within a few notes and tensed.

He wouldn't.

But he did.

She felt hot all over as Noah began singing Billy Paul's "Me and Mrs. Jones." Tim and Ben turned around to toss her amused looks, but her gaze was caught and held by Noah's.

As Noah sang about how he and Ms. Jones had a thing going on even though they knew it was wrong, she resisted the urge to fan herself. He had changed the lyrics to "Ms." instead of "Mrs." and she was in danger of dissolving into a puddle under the table.

She lowered her lashes and tried to look around the room. She hoped no one here knew either of them, because he was practically inviting headlines in tomorrow's paper!

Her gaze moved back to his. The look on his face matched his voice: smoky and full of sensual promise.

Oh, God.

Kayla wasn't sure how she lasted through Noah's song, but, helped by a few fortifying sips of a martini, she did.

When the song ended, Noah grinned, breaking the spell, and then thanked the DJ. As he made his way back to their table, several of the women in the room cast him inviting looks.

Well, she concluded glumly, Noah had proven he *was* good at one thing in the shower. She couldn't prevent herself from thinking about what else he was good at.

Bed. That was Noah's first thought. The second was: he had to ditch his Silicon Valley sidekicks.

As he approached their table, he noticed Kayla appeared flushed and flustered. She seemed to look everywhere but at him.

The air was so sexually charged between them that he was almost afraid to touch her. As it was, he gave them two-to-one odds of winding up in an empty cloakroom, tearing each other's clothes off.

He'd chosen "Me and Mrs. Jones" on a whim, thinking he'd have some fun with her. But along the way, while he'd been singing about hopes being built up too high, the mood had turned from playful to hot and intense.

He couldn't remember the last time he'd had a connection that strong and fast with a woman. The realization left him bemused.

As he neared, Ben turned to Tim and cracked, "And he can sing, too."

Tim looked up and shrugged, a wry look on his face. "Okay, dude, the T-shirt, the Billy Paul imitation…I guess I've gotta concede."

Noah noticed Kayla continued to remain silent, sipping her drink. To Tim and Ben, he said easily, "If I couldn't top you guys on my home turf, I'd have to toss in the towel." He withdrew some bills from his wallet and threw them down on the table. "Since we've got a victor, let's call it a night."

While Ben and Tim thanked him for picking up the tab, Noah cast a covert look at Kayla. She seemed to be getting her bearings.

"You okay?" he asked.

For the first time, she looked directly at him. A range of emotions flickered across her face before she seemed to school it into a polite smile. "Yes, of course."

He moved back so she could precede him to the door. A part of him couldn't wait to get rid of Ben and Tim. The other part warned him that being alone with Kayla right now was not a good idea. He was supposed to be giving her a story. Instead, he was thinking about the shortest route to the bedroom.

He didn't have time to dwell on his thoughts, however, because when they got to the front of the bar, Tim suddenly turned and motioned Noah over. "Bad news," Tim said. "The valet mentioned that a paparazzo with a camera has been spotted outside. The staff here have been telling everyone who's leaving in case they're the reason the guy is here."

Noah muttered a curse under his breath.

Next to him, Kayla tensed.

"Friend of yours?" he asked.

"Don't be ridiculous," she retorted. "Besides, if there's anyone who has a history of siccing journalists on the two of us, it's you."

"Just checking."

"Anyway," she added, "we don't know it's us that he's waiting for. This street has lots of trendy places. He could just be on a fishing expedition, hoping he'll get lucky and snap someone good."

Noah pulled his car keys from his pocket. "Maybe," he said, because he thought she was engaging in wishful thinking, "but the fact is he's out there now, and he may spot us when we walk out of here." Catching the panicked look on her face, he asked, "What's the matter?"

"We can't be photographed together! At least not yet, and definitely not leaving a bar and driving off alone together! Not so soon after Sybil published your denial of a relationship between us. It will undermine everything."

"Ah," he said, because he understood her predicament, having been there one too many times himself. "Welcome to my world, baby doll."

"We can't go out there!" she reiterated.

"Throwing yourself on my mercy, are you?" he said, then added, relenting, "Fine. We'll make the most of the fact that he may not know we're in here." He looked toward the rear of the bar. "There should be a fire exit at the back."

"What—?" As comprehension dawned, she shook her head. "Oh, no."

"Don't worry," he said, then pretended to grin lecherously. "If there are any walls to scale, I'll give you a boost—unless you have a better idea?"

She sighed.

"Great." He shook hands with Tim and Ben. "Gentlemen, I believe this is where we part company. Kayla and I are going to use the back exit to make our getaway. I doubt our cameraman is after either of you, but your leaving will provide a distraction in case Kayla and I need one."

Tim and Ben nodded, and Tim joked to Ben, "Have you noticed he always gets the girl at the end, too?"

Noah chuckled and said, "Not always."

Kayla rolled her eyes. "Infamous on the West Coast as well, hmm?"

He winked at her because he knew it would irritate her, and he wasn't disappointed.

They left Tim and Ben then and, with the help of the bar manager, made their way to the back of the bar and out the fire exit.

As it turned out, they didn't have to worry about scaling walls. There was an alley that ended at a side street. From there, they walked to where Noah's car was parked.

Once they'd hit the road, Noah said wryly, "Tonight was the sort of thing that passes as business entertainment among the wonder boys of high-tech. Just be glad there wasn't a *Star Trek* convention in town."

"Tim and Ben are nice guys."

Her comment amused him. "And I'm not?"

"You're grist for the rumor mill."

He laughed, then sobered. "When your life is fodder for the tabloids, you become familiar with back exits."

When she made no response, he changed the subject. "Seems like you have an interesting job. Makes me wonder why you want to trade it for a hard news beat."

The look she gave him said she hadn't expected him to admit her job had any redeeming qualities. "My job has its moments, but my column is mostly news about local figures because the *Sentinel* doesn't have a hope of competing with national tabloids and magazines."

He flashed her a look. "I figured ambition had to have a place here somewhere. So why don't you apply for a job at one of the national tabloids?"

She didn't answer for a minute, as if weighing what she wanted to reveal. "I'm ready for something besides gossip," she said finally. "Believe it or not, it's tiring to report on Buffy the Man Slayer's latest conquest. And, reporting on celebrities' bad behavior also requires a thick skin."

"How so?"

She slanted him a sideways look. "When you print things that upset people, there's sometimes fallout. And, besides, I don't take pleasure in printing stuff that winds up hurting someone."

Her admission surprised him. In fact, the entire discussion this evening about her job had surprised him. While he was still angry about his own appearances in her column, he was willing to concede he might have been too judgmental in characterizing what she did for a living as telling lies.

While he still wasn't sure whether her column could be thought of as social satire, he could concede there were some areas of his social life—and, God knew, of those of the women he dated—that could easily be mocked.

Yet, he was glad she'd gotten an unexpected taste tonight of dodging paparazzi. He'd seen the worry in her eyes and had felt a modicum of satisfaction in knowing she was stressed over the possibility of being caught with him and of having to stomp out the inevitable flames in the media.

When they got to her apartment complex, he parked and helped her out, then walked with her to the front door of her building, which had a security camera but no doorman.

She took out her keys, then looked up at him. "I'm not sure what to say under the circumstances, but thanks, I had a good time. It was a good intro to how the computer industry works."

"You're welcome."

Her air of vulnerability both attracted and amused him. He wondered whether her regular dates ended with awkward moments like this.

Abruptly, he pulled his mind back from the irritating thought of her out with other men. To hell with other guys and what they'd done or hadn't. *He* wanted to kiss her.

He leaned in, but she dodged with a nervous laugh. He looked at her quizzically.

"You haven't been keeping to your part of the bargain," she said.

"Huh?" He blinked.

"Even though I learned a lot tonight about the computer-software industry in general, I didn't get a smidgen of information about Whittaker Enterprises in particular." Her chin came up. "What's your interest in Tim and Ben's company?"

And what an attractive chin it was, he thought. Attached to a long and graceful neck that led down to breasts straight out of an erotic fantasy. *His* erotic fantasy.

"Are you paying attention?"

"Mmm-hmm. Yeah." He focused his gaze on her face again. "I agreed to give you broad access, but *not* to give away confidential information about Whittaker's possible future plans. For one thing, you're the press. For another, that information could be very valuable on the stock market."

"Are you suggesting I'd do something illegal like purchasing company stock on an inside tip?" she asked crossly.

He tapped her nose. "Not you personally, no, but the policy still stands. The last thing I need is for inside information to inadvertently leak, so the fewer people who know anything, the better." She was too cute standing there, looking all mad at him. "But here's a hint I'm willing to give—nanotechnology."

"That's it?" she said disbelievingly. "One word?"

He couldn't help smiling as he leaned down again. "Yeah," he murmured. "But don't worry. There's more where that came from."

The kiss he gave her was brief, yet still powerful and disturbing, and he wondered again what he was doing getting mixed up with a journalist who just saw him as a convenient ticket to a promotion.

"I can't believe it!" her sister said. "Two guys who have great odds of seeing their bank accounts shoot into the multimillions and you didn't even mention you had a single and unattached younger sister? Did it even cross your mind that I have student loans to pay off? No, of course not," Samantha answered herself, before slumping into a chair. "You were too focused on Mr. Naughty-and-Nice."

"I was not focused on Noah," Kayla said absently.

Samantha snorted. "Yeah, right. I suppose that's why you've mentioned him about fifty times in the past hour?"

Kayla closed out of the website that she was viewing and looked away from the screen. It was a sunny Sunday afternoon and, as happened from time to time, Samantha had crashed at her place the night before, not wanting to take a late train back to school after an evening out on the town. "You're a real smarty-pants, you know?"

"Smart and *poor,*" Samantha replied, then nodded at the computer. "What have you been doing?"

"Looking up everything I can find on the Internet about nanotechnology. As I said, it's the only hint he gave me."

If Noah had held better to his part of the bargain on Friday night, she wouldn't have to be looking up stuff. She couldn't believe he'd left her with a one-word hint!

They had just over three more weeks ahead of them, and he'd pony up or there'd be consequences. And, there wouldn't be any more kissing. If he hadn't caught her off guard, the kiss on Friday night would never have happened. She was a reporter doing a story, and he was her subject, for Pete's sake.

Still, truth be told, wasn't she partly to blame? She'd let herself get swept up in the mood of the evening.

She'd become attuned to every brush of his leg against hers, every smile that lit up his face, every nuance of conversation. So much so that she'd lost track of her mission, which was to get information on Whittaker Enterprises.

Of course, then there'd been that near brush with a photographer to distract her. She'd been hoping she could shadow him for a story without attracting the attention of the press. She definitely hadn't anticipated drawing media attention on their first outing together.

And then, to top it off, he'd kissed her—and she'd enjoyed it. *She'd wanted more.*

Good grief. She had to get a grip. She reminded herself that Noah Whittaker was a smooth-talking and accomplished seducer.

"So what's wrong with Noah?" Samantha asked.

"Nothing!" Then, because she realized she'd practically shouted, she took a deep breath. "Nothing."

"He's only wealthy, good-looking, smart—"

"Stop! He's also irritating, smug, arrogant, born with a silver spoon in his mouth and way too used to having women fall at his feet. I'm only trying to get a story here, okay? I am *not* interested in Noah."

"If you say so. You know, denial of physical chemistry is often the first step in a romantic relationship."

"Argh!" Kayla exclaimed in exasperation. Ever since Samantha had started majoring in psychology—supplemented by a steady diet of popular self-help books with titles such as *From Toxic Dates to Toxic Hate*—it had been "get in touch with your emotions" *this* and "express your feelings" *that*.

Her sister regarded her thoughtfully from her position in an overstuffed armchair. "You know, not every rich guy is a cad. Just because Mom made a mistake—"

"It wasn't a simple mistake. It was a catastrophe that sent her life reeling off course."

"Yes, but she got you in the process, and I don't think she's ever regretted that."

Kayla tamped down the wellspring of feeling that her sister's comment aroused. True, she'd always had a great relationship with her mother, but she couldn't forget the hard years they'd endured, years during which her mother had completed her college degree at night *and* raised a child as a single parent. Even with the help of her family, it had been hard.

"Have you heard anything about him recently?" Samantha asked.

"Who?" she responded, though she knew perfectly well what her sister meant. "Bentley Mathison IV?" She hadn't thought about her biological father in a while.

Her sister nodded.

"No." She busied herself straightening the papers on her computer desk. "He and his wife retreated to a luxury cottage on Martha's Vineyard after he was released from prison. He's been keeping a low profile ever since."

Which was fortunate for her. The chances she'd run into him at some gala or other that she had to cover for the *Sentinel* were slim—though, of course, he wouldn't recognize her since he'd never been involved in her life and she now used the common surname Jones.

When the apartment's buzzer sounded, Samantha said, "I'll get it," and popped out of her chair.

"Who is it?" she said into the intercom mounted on the entryway wall.

"Noah Whittaker," came the reply, unmistakable even though garbled by static.

Samantha turned, eyes wide with excitement. "It's—"

"I heard," Kayla said dryly. Her stomach did a somersault. Why was he here?

Samantha spoke into the intercom again. "Come on up." She pressed a button to let Noah in.

Kayla looked down at her sweatshirt and tights. She

was a mess and Mr. Lady-killer was coming up in the elevator.

"Quick!" Samantha said, jumping into action and pulling Kayla out of her chair. "Into the bedroom," she said, shoving her along. "Jeans tight, blouse low-cut, and put on some lipstick! Think *Cosmo* ad—casual but ready to frolic."

Thrust into her bedroom, Kayla turned around and started to protest.

"I'll stall him as long as I can," Samantha said and shut the door in her face.

Five

Noah knocked and, a full minute later, the door to the apartment opened and a knockoff of Kayla stood in front of him. She was wearing a T-shirt that had Tufts Field Hockey in big letters on the front, and her hair was caught up in a ponytail.

"Wow, look who has a license to thrill," she said, leaning against the door jamb. She stuck out her hand. "Hi, I'm Samantha, Kayla's sister."

Noah broke into a grin as he grasped the proffered hand. "I'm—"

"Mr. Naughty-and-Nice," she finished for him. "I know."

"What?" he spluttered on a laugh.

"Never mind," she said, pulling him in. "Can I get you something to drink? Beer? Wine? Sangria?"

"A beer is fine. Thanks."

"Kayla's in the bedroom changing into something comfortable," Samantha said as she walked into the small kitchen next to the entry. "She's been working all morning."

Noah noticed she didn't say Kayla had been *at* work all morning, but he limited himself to saying, "She's too intense."

"Well, she's going through her blond-ambition stage," Samantha said, opening the fridge.

Noah leaned a shoulder against the archway to the kitchen. "Don't you mean blind ambition?"

"That too." Samantha took a beer out of the fridge. "She's a real blonde by the way, in case anyone's interested." She opened a drawer and pulled out a bottle opener. "Ask me anything. I'll tell you everything you want to know. Well, almost everything."

"Samantha!" Kayla exclaimed aghast.

Noah glanced through the pass-through between the kitchen and the dining/living room. Kayla had emerged dressed in blue jeans and a short-sleeved, deep-red top. The scoop neck, he noticed, did amazing things for her cleavage.

"What?" Samantha asked, directing her question at her sister.

Noah felt his lips curve at Kayla's answering frown. "I like your sister," he said. "She's a firecracker."

"Really?" Samantha said.

At the same time, Kayla muttered, "That's not all she is."

Samantha leaned against the kitchen counter. "I hear you know a lot of up-and-coming types in the computer industry." Without missing a beat, she added, "I'm five-seven and a college junior, and I *love* meeting new people."

The hint was as subtle as a sledgehammer. "Yeah, I meet with some Silicon Valley types," he responded, enjoying himself, not the least because Kayla continued to look discomfited, "but most of them are, uh, wardrobe challenged." And that was the tip of the iceberg.

"I'm great with clothes," Samantha countered. "In fact, I sometimes advise Kayla."

"Do I have you to thank for the baby-doll top?"

"That's right. You owe me one." She handed him an open beer.

"All right, that's enough," Kayla said.

"Is she always like this?" Noah asked Samantha.

"Not always, no."

"She's too serious," Noah said, and they both looked at Kayla.

"And you're never serious," Kayla retorted.

"I'm studiedly unserious. It takes a lot of work," he replied lazily, pushing away from his spot in the entryway to the kitchen and moving into the living room.

"Right. Well, I prefer the terms *sensible* and *level-headed.*" With a pointed look at him and her sister, she added, "Some of us need to be."

The first thing that caught his eye in her living room was the bouquet of roses on an end table. *His* roses.

She followed his gaze and stiffened. "They were too beautiful to throw out, but I didn't want them sitting around the office drawing attention." She shrugged. "Why look a gift horse in the mouth?"

He pulled his gaze away from the flowers. For some reason, he felt ridiculously pleased she hadn't chucked them in the trash bin. And the fact that he felt that way was, well, ridiculous.

"Here," he said, holding out a shawl. "You left this on the back seat of my car on Friday night."

"Thanks." She took the flimsy, sparkly material from him.

He shrugged. "I was driving through your neighborhood and figured I'd drop it off." He also hadn't been able to stop thinking about her. "I'd have called first, but I couldn't locate a number for you other than work."

From the corner of his eye, he noticed Samantha was following the conversation while pouring herself a glass of orange juice.

"Also, it gives me an opportunity to mention an event I have coming up."

"Oh?"

"Juice, Kayla?"

"Thanks, just water." To him, she said, "Have a seat."

He took the couch while she sat in an armchair.

He glanced around the apartment. It was small but thoughtfully furnished. On the walls hung framed black-and-white photo reprints of cityscapes: New York, Paris,

Boston, Miami, Sydney. Near the pass-through to the kitchen sat a black lacquer-and-glass table. The rest of the room consisted of an armchair, a cream-colored couch, a small television and a computer desk. The computer was a late-model Apple with a flat screen, salsa music emanating at a low volume from its two small speakers.

He nodded at the computer. "You've got some eclectic musical tastes. From Norah Jones to salsa?"

"We were raised on salsa," Samantha piped up as she walked over to Kayla with a glass of water. "Our grandmother is a big fan." Samantha looked at him. "She was born in Cuba."

"Was she?" Noah took a sip of his beer, amused that the expression on Kayla's face said she wondered whether her sister was planning to give him details about their *entire* family.

"Yup," Samantha said, ignoring her sister's pointed look and sitting down on the couch next to her. "Bolero, salsa, merengue—*Abuela* likes it all. Kayla and I could barely get anything else played around the house since our grandmother was often there. Fortunately, Ricky Martin hit it big, and we finally found a middle ground."

"Interesting," he murmured, looking at Kayla.

"*Abuela* sang around the house, too," Samantha continued, then laughed before turning to her sister, "but Kayla only sings in the shower."

"Yeah, I know."

"So, you mentioned an event a minute ago," Kayla said, clearly looking to change the subject. "What event?"

"There's a black-tie benefit for the Boston Esplanade being thrown on the banks of the Charles River next Saturday night by the Charlesbank Association. I'd like you to come with me. You'll get to listen in on some interesting conversations."

"Unless it's a costume ball with Venetian masks, the answer is no. We had one near brush with paparazzi on Friday night. I'll follow you around but in a more low-key way from now on."

He sat back and tilted his head. "Somehow I thought that would be your initial reaction."

"Good, then you weren't disappointed," she countered.

Samantha was looking like she longed for a big tub of popcorn so she could watch the gathering storm with the same intensity she'd view an absorbing TV drama.

"Instead of inviting me to charity benefits," Kayla continued, "if you really wanted to help me, you'd be inviting me to tour Whittaker Enterprises' offices and giving me a list of employees to speak with."

"Fine. I've been too busy this week to get to that," he responded. "Call my office on Monday. We'll set up a time for you to come by and I'll have some names for you. But I still want you to go to the Charlesbank Association event with me."

"Going to a charity benefit with you would be like waving a red flag in front of the gossip columnists in this town—they're sure to charge, and odds are we'd be gored."

"I'll introduce you as the reporter who's researching an in-depth piece on Whittaker Enterprises," he said with patience. "Everyone will buy it because the alternative—that we're flaunting a relationship that I just publicly denied existed—will seem too outrageous."

Kayla rolled her eyes. "Wow, you sure know nothing about gossip columnists. Stories about three-headed aliens landing on top of city hall aren't too outrageous." She leaned forward. "And if the mayor refutes it, of course, the headline is Mayor Denies Aliens Landed on his Roof."

Samantha laughed.

Noah stared at Kayla, and she stared right back.

Sighing, he turned to Samantha. "Feel free to chime in any time, kid. I could use all the help I can get."

"No way." Samantha shook her head. "Kayla's wearing her 'look.' She can be very stubborn when she wants to be."

"You don't say?" he said, not taking his eyes off Kayla.

"Yup. She's been known to camp out overnight for concert tickets."

"Everyone has his price," he said.

"You couldn't afford me," Kayla retorted.

"How do you know what I can afford?" he responded coolly. "Done a lot of research on me?"

She looked away.

He wasn't sure why he was pressing her to accept his invitation, except somewhere along the way getting close to Kayla had taken on an importance equal to rehabilitating his image. "You need to be there. It'll be full of glitterati and beautiful people."

"I can get a press pass."

"I'll introduce you to people who are worth knowing. I'll even put in a good word. Some of them have a natural aversion to goss—uh, journalists."

"Who?" she asked doubtfully.

Ah, finally, Noah thought, a chink in the armor: getting the upper hand in her ongoing rivalry with Sybil LaBreck was enticing. "Susan Bennington-Walsh," he said, naming one of Boston's leading hostesses.

She shook her head. "Already know her."

"You don't say." Surprising. "Susan disdains the press, and gossip columnists in particular."

"That's what they all say, at least publicly," she replied dryly.

"Are you saying she secretly feeds information to you?"

"No comment."

Well, well. He filed away that bit of information and reminded himself not to say anything too revealing at one of Susan's future parties. "The mayor then," he offered, switching tactics.

"You know the mayor?" Samantha said, looking impressed.

"Of course he knows the mayor," Kayla responded.

"I contributed to his last election campaign."

"Handsomely, I'm sure," Kayla jibed.

"Naturally." He could tell Kayla was mulling over how a personal introduction to the mayor would benefit a would-be business reporter.

Finally, she said doubtfully, "Black tie or business attire?"

He masked a grin. "Black tie."

"Great!" Samantha clapped her hands together, not giving her sister a chance to shy away again. "Now that that's settled, tell me about your racing career, Noah. I'd love to know what it's like to race at two-hundred miles an hour."

Noah gave her a quick grin. No doubt about it, he thought, the kid had charm in spades. Too bad he had a major case of the hots for her sister, who seemed determined to keep him at arm's length.

"I'm sure Noah has better things to do," Kayla interjected.

"Trying to get rid of me?" he asked.

Their eyes met and clashed.

"Don't be silly," she retorted. "I'm only thinking of you and your busy schedule."

"Come on, Noah," Samantha pleaded, ignoring her sister. "It all sounds so thrilling."

"Thrilling and dangerous," he corrected. Certainly no one knew that better than he did. Danger—of the fatal variety—was what had convinced him that it was time to put away his racing suit.

Samantha curled up on the couch. "How did you get started?"

He shrugged, having fielded similar questions countless times before from fans, acquaintances and the merely curious. "At a racing school, like a lot of other professional drivers. I got the appropriate racing licenses and started driving in some of the lower-level series and then worked my way up to an Indy car."

"Did you race in the Indianapolis 500?"

"Yeah, I had a couple of starts there." More than that, he'd had a top-five finish in his rookie season. He'd been red hot until the crash that had changed his life and put an end to his professional racing career at the relatively young age of twenty-six.

Samantha continued to look impressed. "How do you get into the big leagues?"

"It's tough," he admitted. "You need high speeds even to qualify for the big events. Then you throw in finding a racing team that will give you a car, lining up sponsors, putting together a pit crew, and everything else."

"So why bother?" Kayla asked.

He glanced over at her. "The thrill."

There wasn't anything like taking a turn at two-hundred miles an hour, fighting to stay in control of the car, and making split-second decisions that meant the difference between winning and losing.

He didn't expect her to understand. His family hadn't, though they'd come to accept his dream of racing cars.

The love of speed, he'd found, was something you were either born with or weren't. In his case, there must have been a genetic mutation because no one else in his upper-crust Boston Brahmin family thought that hurtling yourself through space at two-hundred-plus miles an hour was a pleasant way to spend a sunny afternoon.

He caught Kayla observing him with a thoughtful expression on her face.

"For me, a thrill means finding a Stella McCartney designer top in my size at a thrift shop," Samantha said.

Noah laughed. "Can't say I can relate, but I'm often appreciative of the results."

Samantha grinned back; Kayla scowled.

Holding Samantha's gaze, he nodded his head at Kayla. "She doesn't like my playboy ways."

"Maybe I just don't like you," Kayla retorted.

"Ouch." He pretended to wince.

Samantha leaned forward confidingly. "It's not personal. She just doesn't like any rich—"

"Okay!" Kayla said, then stood up and shot her sister a dire look.

Samantha clamped her mouth shut.

Baffled, he looked from Kayla to Samantha. "She just doesn't like any—?"

"Rich men who ask probing questions," Kayla finished flatly.

He looked up at Kayla and knew, just knew, he needed to know more. He needed to know everything about her, to know her intimately. And he wasn't giving up.

On the following Wednesday morning, Kayla showed up early at Whittaker Enterprises' headquarters. She'd arranged with Noah to tour the company's offices, talk to people, follow him around and, basically, see how things operated.

She'd taken extra-special care with her clothes and makeup. She'd already discovered the hard way that, for a good chunk of the world, *young single female* meant *not to be taken seriously*.

So, today she'd paired navy flare-leg trousers with a striped blue-and-yellow open-collar shirt. Her jewelry was discreet and understated, just a watch and some small cubic-zirconia stud earrings.

The look was classy but professional, or at least she hoped so. As Ms. Rumor-Has-It, she had to dress the part, but this was something different altogether.

On the drive over to Noah's office, she'd reflected again on the research she'd done and the articles she'd read on Whittaker Enterprises—and on Noah himself—in preparation for today's visit.

Whittaker Enterprises had been started by Noah's father back in the 1960s and had since metamorphosed into a conglomerate with interests primarily in real estate and high technology. Noah's oldest brother, Quentin, had taken over the reins of the family company a few years back, when his father had moved into semi-retirement. At the same time, Noah had become the point person for Whittaker Enterprises' computer business. That was, as soon as he'd quelled his maverick tendencies. After graduating from M.I.T. with a bachelor's degree in computer science, instead of joining the family business, he'd headed off to pursue a race-car driving career.

She'd found news articles from the time that detailed the surprise with which Noah's move had been greeted in Boston social circles. It was as if he'd announced he'd rather be the jockey than the horse owner. *It just wasn't done.* Not in the rarified circles of Boston old-line families.

Still, he'd entered the Indy car-racing circuit. After three years of heady success had come the accident that had marked the end of his career. Precisely, it had happened on turn three at the Michigan Indy 400. Noah had been fighting for the lead with Jack Gillens, one of his racing buddies. Just as Noah was going by him, Jack had lost control of his car and hit the barrier wall on the racing oval head-on; car debris had gone flying everywhere.

Attempts at resuscitating Jack had proved futile. Minutes after the crash, the race had finished under a yellow flag. Noah had won, only to learn Jack had been taken to the hospital but had been declared dead upon arrival. A later investigation had concluded Noah wasn't to blame for the crash.

Until the accident seven years ago, Noah had been in the news a lot. He had sex appeal in spades, and that, combined with his high-testosterone racing career, had been enough to net him a dozen magazine covers and have him named one of *People*'s Sexiest Men Alive.

But after the accident, he'd holed up. Then, after a few months, he'd made a public announcement that he was retiring from racing. He'd gone back to M.I.T., gotten his doctorate in computer science and then joined the family firm.

He dropped out of the public eye for a short time after the accident, but he came back with a vengeance. In his new incarnation as a playboy, he was seen squiring around models, actresses and, yes, even a reality-show contestant. He was back making regular appearances in *People* magazine, in *Us Weekly* and in the local gossip columns.

Kayla had known about the accident, of course. People talked, still.

But she hadn't known the details of the fatal crash or of Noah's life at the time. She'd still been in college at that point. However, having read the news articles, the past—Noah's past—was all very fresh for her.

She remembered his reaction back at the book-launch party when she'd brought up the racing accident—he'd shut down immediately—and she cringed inwardly again.

And, as she walked around Whittaker Enterprises with Noah, everything she'd read was at the back of her mind.

"I've been doing some research on nanotechnology," she said conversationally.

"Really?" he said. "What have you discovered?"

"Probably lots of things I should have been hearing from you instead."

He laughed.

"So," she said, "instead of my telling you what *I've discovered,* why don't you tell me what *you know*?"

"All right. Have you heard of Moore's Law?"

"No."

"Okay, well, Moore's Law basically says data density in computers will double about every eighteen months or so."

She nodded. "How does Moore's Law relate to nanotechnology?"

"I'm getting there," he said, giving her an amused look. "If you've done your homework, you know nanotechnology concerns the manipulation of atoms. It gets its name from the fact that the structures it studies—atoms and the like—are measured in nanometers. A nanometer is one-billionth of a meter."

"Right." So far everything he'd said was in line with her research.

"The potential applications for nanotechnology are practically limitless, from handheld supercomputers to faster diagnoses for cancer."

"Wow."

"Exactly. People in the computing field are racing each other to harness and use nanotechnology, even though it's still a young field. It wasn't until the mid-1980s that a scanning tunneling microscope was developed that could study atoms. But now nanotechnology is the biggest thing since computers."

"Are you saying that Whittaker Enterprises has developed a product that uses nanotechnology?"

He smiled. "I haven't gotten to that part of the story yet. You'll have to stay tuned."

"But—"

"Come on," he said, interrupting her, "let me introduce you to people and then get out of your way. You'll start to get a picture of what we're all about."

She sighed. At least she'd made some progress. "Okay, great."

Noah, she soon learned, had organized the computer side of the business into project teams, each headed by a team leader. The teams were small groups flexible enough to make things happen.

She jotted notes as she talked to people. One group

had developed a new, ultra-slim handheld PDA that was about to launch on the market. Another was testing a super-light portable DVD player. *Small* seemed to be the name of the game. However, no one brought up nanotechnology in any detail. She got the sense *that* information was rather sensitive.

Everyone, however, sang Noah's praises. He was smart, easy to work with, unflappable and had enough stamina to work around the clock if necessary—all of which, of course, she felt compelled to bring up later when she caught up with Noah outside his office.

"So, apparently your reputation is that you work hard and party harder."

He smiled. "You sound annoyed."

"It's the kiss of death for reporters. No dish, no dirt, no anything."

He held up his hands. "Hey, I didn't tell them to hold back, just to keep their mouths shut about confidential business information."

"Everyone's afraid of antagonizing the boss, I bet."

He shook his head. "Our attrition rates are very low for the industry, and we pay top dollar. People are here because they want to be here." When she had no ready reply he said, "Come on, I'll take you to lunch."

She reluctantly accepted. Lunch, as it turned out, was not in the building's well-stocked cafeteria, which she'd passed earlier in the day, but in Carlyle, at a charming little bistro.

She ordered the French onion soup, a half sandwich and a healthy serving of information from Noah.

He just laughed and ordered the crab cakes.

"So," she said after their food had arrived and they'd dug in, "I've been reading a lot about you."

He raised his eyebrows. "You're not writing about me anymore in your column, so what's there to read these days?"

"I meant about your past. I've been coming across articles while researching Whittaker Enterprises."

His eyes flickered. "The past can't be changed, so I don't spend too much time examining it myself."

"You had a great racing career going," she said. "I didn't realize how successful you were until I went back through the news reports."

He wiped his mouth with his napkin and took his time answering. "What? Would it have changed how you wrote about me in your column?"

"I don't know," she admitted. She hadn't realized Noah had been such close buddies with the driver who'd been killed. It made sense though: they'd belonged to the same racing team. "It would have given me a different perspective though."

He seemed to wait for her to go on.

"Auto racing seemed like an odd choice for you."

He shrugged. "You're not the first person to make that observation. The truth is, though, there are a lot of similarities between auto racing and what I do now. Professional auto racing is all about the technology."

"How did you even get interested in it?"

"In a word?"

"Yes."

"Go-carts."

She raised her eyebrows. For once, he was looking earnest, instead of using his customary half-amused expression.

"It was a friend's birthday party," he explained. "It took place at a racetrack, and we got to race around in these little carts. I was hooked."

"And you were how old?"

"Ten. I moved up to real cars in my teens. Took a hiatus from competitive racing for a while in college, and then I was back at it."

"Until the accident," she corrected.

He sat back, took a breath and then expelled it slowly. "Yeah?"

He said it like a challenge.

"Why did you choose to quit? From the articles I read, you were a hot commodity, poised for a great career if not the record books."

"Maybe it wasn't a choice. Some things aren't. If the highest card you're dealt is a ten, you can't put a king in play."

She looked at him. Was he kidding her? He was gorgeous, wealthy and talented. "Most people would look at you and say you definitely got dealt a king in the card game of life."

"Most people don't know me," he said, then added pointedly, "even if they think they do based on what they read or write about me."

She took the jab and kept going. "They don't need to know you to understand you grew up privileged—"

"Yeah, but sometimes it doesn't matter how wealthy you are, you still have to deal with the irrevocable moments of life."

"Is that what the accident was? Something you wish you could take back if you could? Is that why you threw away the racing career?"

He motioned the waiter for their check, then looked back and studied her for a second. "Maybe it was the other way around. Maybe the racing career threw me away. Or, maybe, *Kayla—*" he said, drawing out her name "—I just decided I didn't want to race for the next ten or twenty years and that developing cutting-edge technology was more appealing."

He was the closest to really ticked off that she'd ever seen him, and that included the time of their confrontation at the book-launch party. She shifted in her seat.

He narrowed his eyes. "I hope there isn't some sort of strange reporter's instinct at play here. You know, digging for some weird psychological profile for your article."

She hadn't been thinking about that—had only wanted to have her curiosity slaked—but now that he mentioned it…. "And what if there is? Is the accident the reason you became the hard-partying Noah of the past few years?"

After signing the check, he looked up. "You're barking up the wrong tree. If you really want to understand what makes the techie guy in me tick, then look at my experiences at M.I.T. and at the office, not on the racetrack."

She wasn't so sure about that. Not so sure at all.

Six

There was no place to hide.

She'd looked.

A party hosted under a white tent afforded no inviting nooks and crannies into which a single woman seeking to avoid a fate worse than death could cram herself. Particularly a woman dressed in a sequined halter top and black sheath skirt and two-and-a-half-inch heels. For the sake of future events, she'd have to make a polite suggestion to the Charlesbank Association.

The evening had started off innocuously enough. Noah had picked her up, appearing more sinfully good-looking in a tux than any man had a right to look. Her pulse had kicked up a notch, a response that she was growing used to. She'd come to admit to herself that, yes, okay, she did find him very attractive—who wouldn't? But she knew better than to think that acting on any attraction between them was a good idea, recent kisses aside.

Once they'd arrived at the charity benefit, Noah, as promised, had introduced her to the mayor as a journalist who worked for the *Boston Sentinel* and who was gathering material for an in-depth profile on Whittaker Enterprises. Fortunately, the mayor had not seemed to connect her face to the Ms. Rumor-Has-It column. And Noah had been right: with his introduction and implicit endorsement, the mayor had been friendly and approachable.

Unfortunately, though, after that brief interlude, the evening had turned from one where she was playing with nice, friendly dolphins to one where she was swimming with the sharks.

First, she'd run into Fluffy, who'd been eager to make sure Kayla would mention her in Monday's column.

Then Buffy the Man Slayer had homed in on Noah. Evidently, she'd taken to heart the hint in Kayla's column and decided Noah would make a lovely addition to her all-male menagerie.

Kayla was thankful Huffy, at least, wasn't around to add to the drama. According to word of mouth, she was still in Europe, presently flirting with a German count who was dancing attendance on her. Kayla had no doubt the two of them would soon hit the European gossip magazines.

Kayla wondered whether Noah would be crushed by

the news. She glanced over at him now and caught his look of mild irritation from across the room, where Sybil LaBreck had run him to ground.

Under other circumstances, Kayla might have felt some pity. Under present ones, however, she was too busy dealing with her own problems.

Because, just as she'd been breathing a sigh of relief, she'd turned around and spotted Bentley Mathison IV.

For an instant, she'd frozen. Then she'd embarked on her present and so-far-fruitless search for a hiding spot.

Bentley Mathison and his wife wouldn't recognize her, but she still had no interest in encountering them. Particularly here. Particularly now.

Giving up on the tent, she headed toward an exit. She could take a moment outside to collect herself.

As she made her way toward a gap in the tent, she recognized Noah's siblings as they entered along with their spouses, and groaned at the timing.

Trapped, she made a complete 360-degree turn, looking for at least a potted plant that might afford some camouflage.

Noah, she noticed, had disentangled himself from Sybil's clutches and was heading her way. His family, with Allison Whittaker in the lead, was bearing down on her from the opposite direction. And, she noticed, Bentley Mathison and his wife were making their way toward all of them, too.

She dredged up a smile. It was the least she could do when her life was bearing down on her with all the horror of an impending train wreck.

"Noah!"

"Allison!"

"Kayla!"

Help! Kayla thought.

"Well, isn't this a pleasant surprise," Allison said. "We didn't know you'd be here, Noah." Allison looked for affirmation at the dangerously good-looking man next to her.

Kayla knew Connor Rafferty by sight. Rumor had it that he'd carried a torch for Allison for years before they'd recently begun seeing each other and gotten married.

Bringing up the rear, behind Connor, was a tall, dark-haired man who looked as if he'd stepped off the pages of *GQ* magazine and whom Kayla knew by sight to be Noah's older brother Matt.

Behind Matt, Kayla noticed that Noah's other brother, Quentin, and his wife, Liz—whom she knew from various social functions that she'd covered in the past for the *Sentinel*—had already been waylaid by a couple of other guests nearer the tent's entrance.

Noah shrugged. "Until recently, I wasn't sure I'd be showing up either."

Allison looked from Noah to Kayla, zeroing in on the arm that Noah had just slipped around her waist and was using to guide her forward.

She couldn't blame Allison for looking confused. After all, mere days ago, Kayla had been the bane of Noah's existence.

"Allison, Connor, Matt, this is Kayla."

Allison reacted first. "Kayla and I have been introduced to each other before." She looked at her brother, her lips twitching upward. "I'm just surprised Kayla's here with you."

Kayla felt herself grow warm, but Noah said, "I guess you haven't heard that Kayla is shadowing me because she's doing a profile on Whittaker Enterprises for the *Boston Sentinel*."

Allison raised her eyebrows, and Connor and Matt, though they refrained from making any comment, wore looks that said they found it all highly entertaining.

Allison opened her mouth to speak, but, before she could say anything, a voice caused all of them to turn.

Bentley Mathison, who until now had remained quiet, spoke up. "Noah and Matthew Whittaker." He stepped forward, hand outstretched and chuckling too heartily to sound sincere. "How long has it been?"

Kayla winced. Bentley Mathison's audacity was stupendous, especially in light of the fact that, if it had been a long time, it was entirely due to his thirty-six months spent behind bars for tax evasion and misappropriation of funds.

"Bentley," Noah said, nodding in acknowledgment and, reluctantly, it seemed to Kayla, accepting the proffered hand. "Yes, it's been a while."

"Too long," Bentley said jovially. He then turned to greet the other Whittaker siblings and introduce them to his wife, Margaux.

Allison, Kayla noticed, appeared cool during the introductions. And, no wonder, Kayla thought. As an assistant district attorney who'd recently been harassed by a defendant in one of her cases—before Connor had reportedly led the police to the culprit—she doubtlessly did not suffer criminals, past or present, gladly.

When Noah turned and introduced Kayla to the Mathisons, she tried to appear unaffected. Nevertheless, her hand was clammy and cold as it was grasped by Bentley Mathison's.

Her biological father.

She looked into his pale blue eyes—as clear and cold as a winter sky—and could not believe this was the man who'd set her life on its trajectory, and, in fact, the man responsible for her very existence.

Unbidden and uninvited, her mind busied itself looking for resemblances. She dreaded finding any.

She caught Noah looking at her oddly.

It was then she realized she'd been holding on to Bentley Mathison's hand.

Embarrassed, she murmured, "Nice to meet you," and then withdrew her hand.

She was vaguely aware of conversation continuing to flow around her, but she was in a weird state where she heard everything but took in nothing. Mostly she faintly discerned that Bentley was attempting to ingratiate himself with the Whittakers—probably in the hopes of resuscitating business contacts—and that the Whittakers were responding with varying degrees of polite detachment.

No one apparently noticed how uncomfortable she'd become. No one except Noah, apparently, since she caught him tossing her a quizzical look or two.

At some point, she heard Noah say, "Excuse us." Then, without waiting for a response, he tugged her toward the dance floor. He guided her into his arms and they started swaying to a slow tune.

"What was that all about?" he asked finally against her hair.

"What?" She tilted her head back to look up at him.

"Your Medusa impersonation when you were introduced to Bentley Mathison. I thought you were going to turn him to stone."

"Don't be ridiculous. If I did have a reaction, it's only because the man is a shameless unreformed criminal."

He raised his eyebrows. "Strong words."

"Your sister seemed to have a similar reaction."

"Yeah, but she's in the business of being the scourge of society's criminal element. You, on the other hand, are in the business of getting information however you can get it."

"Not from Bentley Mathison," she said sharply. Then added less stridently, "And since when are you befriending former criminals?"

"Hey, hey," he said soothingly. "I didn't say I like the guy. I just wasn't going to create a scene when he approached me in the middle of a charity gala. Besides, he paid his debt to society by serving his prison sentence."

She looked away. "Maybe there are other debts that are still outstanding."

"What?" Noah asked.

Realizing she'd muttered aloud, she said, "Never

mind. I don't want to talk about it." The last thing she wanted to do was give Noah Whittaker more personal information about herself.

He looked like he wanted to argue with her, but then he simply nodded.

They danced in silence. And, despite being distracted by the presence of Bentley Mathison, she felt an electric awareness course through her at Noah's nearness. Being pressed against his muscular frame, she experienced a strange fluttery sensation in her midsection.

When the song ended, he guided her off the dance floor. "Now, let's get back to you and Bentley Mathison."

It took her a second to digest what he'd said, caught up as she still was in the sensation of having been held against him. She gave him a sidelong look. "There's nothing to tell. It's just too bad even a prison sentence doesn't mean social disgrace anymore."

He shrugged. "Maybe disgrace is in the eye of the beholder."

"Too true," she said, half to herself.

Just then she noticed Bentley Mathison was standing in their path along with his wife and another couple. If they continued walking on as they were, they'd be forced back into conversation with him, and from the looks of it, that's what Mathison was hoping for.

She stopped and clutched Noah's arm.

He looked down at her, a question in his eyes. "What?" He cut himself off as he looked up again and caught sight of Bentley Mathison.

Glancing back at her, he muttered, "All right, you want to come clean about this?"

She gave a small defeated nod. "But first get me out of here." Her voice sounded strained to her own ears.

In a deft maneuver, he turned, pretended to recognize someone across the room, and half pulled, half dragged her along with him as he strode past several tables.

They were outside the tent within minutes, and she took a deep breath.

"You okay?" Noah asked, and she was surprised to see genuine concern etched on his face. "You look pale."

"Fine…I'm fine." She took another breath, then said in a rush, "Bentley Mathison is my biological father but he doesn't know it."

Noah raised his eyebrows, then stuffed his hands in his pockets. "Your secrets pack a punch, I'll say that."

"Sometimes I wish I didn't have any."

"Then why keep any?" he said.

She looked at him askance. "It's not easy telling someone that my ancestry is one-quarter Cuban, one-quarter English, and one-half jerk."

"You're not the jerk. He is," he said with conviction.

She was close to tears and wondering now what had possessed her to blurt out one of her most closely-held secrets. And to Noah, of all people! Why, all he had to do was relay that juicy tidbit to Sybil LaBreck and Kayla would be cooked, roasted over the open fire of the public's flaming need for scandal.

As if reading her mind, Noah said, "Don't worry, I

won't tell anyone, and especially not Sybil LaBreck." He looked around. "Let's get out of here. I'll take you home."

"But we arrived only a short time ago."

He took her arm. "You're in no shape to go back in there and face Bentley and company, not to mention Buffy the Man Slayer. And, for the record, neither am I. Let's go."

"Thanks." She was relieved he was taking charge, and surprised at his understanding.

She stole a glance at him. He was frowning and looking formidable. Yet, strangely, right this second, she found she liked him better than she ever had.

Noah flipped the light switch as they entered her apartment.

What a night. First, he'd been cornered by Buffy, then Sybil LaBreck had stopped him to ask irritating and probing questions about the true nature of his relationship with Kayla. She suspected all was not as it appeared, or at least as he'd been insisting publicly. He'd finally gotten rid of her with a dismissive comment.

And, to top off the evening, of course, he'd never have guessed Kayla was Bentley Mathison's biological daughter.

No wonder she seemed to have issues with men. Particularly rich, to-the-mansion-born types, a class into which he fell.

What was it that her sister had started to say before being cut off? Something about Kayla's dislike for him not being personal. After tonight, he understood why:

Kayla's issue was with all guys who bore a superficial similarity to Bentley Mathison.

Yet, the joke was on him. Because he'd been checking his symptoms and there was no doubt about it: he had a major case of lust for Kayla.

He watched as Kayla set her sequined purse on the table. With her back still to him, she lifted the hair from her neck and shook her head. He lapped up the view of her smooth, bare back before the curtain of sleek hair fell back into place.

He cleared his throat and she glanced back at him over her shoulder.

She looked doe-eyed and lost for a second. Her shoulders lowered. "Sorry, I'm being rude," she murmured.

"I was just going to ask if you needed anything. A glass of wine, coffee." Me.

He tamped down the well of lust that came unbidden with that last thought.

She forced a little laugh as she turned fully toward him. "Quite a role reversal. Those are things I should be asking you."

He just looked at her. She was good to look at, her shoulders toned in the top that she wore, her breasts round and full and her calves shapely beneath her longish skirt.

She broke the awkward silence by starting toward him. "I'll just get us both a drink. How's that?"

"Yeah, sure."

He should have moved back. Instead, he let her brush by him on the way to the kitchen.

The effect was electric. On him, anyway. Had he imagined the quiver that had gone through her?

He shoved his hands in his pockets to keep from grabbing and kissing her. Instead, he watched as she poured him a scotch on the rocks.

She set it on the kitchen counter near him. "There you go," she said without glancing at him.

Had she been afraid to touch him? He couldn't tell because she refused to look up.

He took the drink, then walked into the living room as he heard her open and close the refrigerator. He took a sip, felt the burn, then loosened his tie with one hand before raking his hair.

He felt more than heard her enter and turned to look at her. She came toward him, all cool Grace Kelly allure dressed up as 1950s bombshell, her stiletto heels clicking on the wood floor before hitting the area rug in front of the couch.

She held up her glass. "Cranberry juice with a splash of vodka." She clinked her glass to his. "Cheers."

A smile pulled at his lips. "Feeling reckless, are we?"

"Hmm." She shrugged. "Aren't you the expert on living dangerously?"

He took another sip, regarding her through narrowed eyes. "If I lived dangerously, I wouldn't be standing over here and you wouldn't be standing over there."

She smiled, a gleam in her eyes. "But I'm only inches away."

"Exactly." Tonight, it seemed, was the night for her to confront all the disreputable males in her life: her biological father, *him*. "Let's get to the bottom of what this is about, okay? Running into Bentley Mathison threw you for a loop."

"Mmm." She licked her lips.

He forced his mind to stay on topic.

She walked away. "So boring. Can we talk about something else?" She sat on the couch, crossed her legs and patted the seat next to her. "I don't understand how you got your reputation as a great seducer when you use lovely conversation starters like deadbeat, jailbird fathers."

He was tempted to show her just how he'd gotten his reputation, but her current performance could have rivaled Buffy the Man Slayer's. And, that's exactly what it was: a performance. She was playing the seductress—did she realize how naturally the role came to her?—intent on conquering him, the great seducer.

He swirled his drink. "Tell me how your mother fell under the spell of the great Bentley Mathison."

Kayla wrinkled her nose, then took a sip from her glass. The reckless gleam hadn't disappeared from her eyes. "It's a tragedy in three parts. I like comedies better, don't you?"

"How does act one begin?"

She heaved a sigh. "Act one begins with a young woman from a close-knit family going off to college on a scholarship."

"Your mother?"

"Mmm-hmm. She gets a summer job at a financial

services firm. Happily, it pays well and will help with the rest of her college bills. One of the partners takes a liking to her."

"Bentley."

"Yes, and reportedly quite the smooth operator even when he was younger."

"So," he guessed, "the summer intern proceeds to get pregnant by said partner, basking in the thrill of his attention."

"Yes, that would be act two." She swirled her drink. "You're too smart not to know act three."

"He refuses to have anything to do with her," he said flatly.

"Right," she confirmed, her tone harsh. "You see, Bentley was about to become engaged to the daughter of a well-connected financier. Of course, a connection like that was going to make his career."

"What happened to your mother?"

"Well, she was too afraid to tell anyone about the affair at first. Who would have believed her? Bentley had encouraged her to keep their relationship under wraps in order not to raise eyebrows at the office."

She shook her head, then went on. "But eventually she told her family. They took her in. She dropped out of school for a time to have the baby. With her family's help, though, she finally finished her degree."

"And your sister?"

"Well, there's the happy postscript." She put down her drink on the end table. "Several years on, the woman meets a man who's her soul mate. They fall in love and marry. He adopts her child and, later, they have a daughter together."

"Understood," he said, "except for one small detail."

"What's that?"

"I'm not Bentley," he said deliberately.

"I never said you were."

"No, but you act like it."

She uncrossed her legs and stood up, armor in place. "I get enough pop psychology from Samantha."

He wasn't letting her off the hook. "I got it wrong, didn't I?"

"Got what wrong?"

He shook his head and set his glass down, then let his gaze rake over her. "I'm not the favorite whipping boy of your column because you're secretly attracted to playboys. Just the opposite, in fact. Players remind you of your biological father, so you're determined to rake them over the coals."

She tossed her hair over her shoulder. "Believe what you want. You don't know me."

He sauntered closer. "Of course, that's too bad for me," he mused. "I prefer the story about your secret attraction to playboys."

She threw up her hands in exasperation and he caught her chin in his hand.

The air went out of her and her eyes widened. "What are you doing?" she said, stumbling over the words.

"Putting you to the test," he muttered, his gaze focused on her mouth.

"W-what test?"

"You know, the one where you prove that, unlike your mother, you can't be taken in and seduced by the cads of the world."

He raised his eyes to look into her stormy brown ones, and then he kissed her.

Seven

The second Noah's lips touched Kayla's, she felt herself yield. His kiss this time was not a fleeting brush, but a command. It took her breath away and her mouth opened under the pressure of his soft, coaxing lips.

He took the kiss deeper, his hands stroking up and down her arms, forcing her to deal with the emotions roiling inside her, forcing her to deal with *him*.

He was *so* wrong about her. She didn't write about him in her column because she had an ax to grind with player types who reminded her of Bentley Mathison.

If she wrote about Noah in her column, it was only because he led the type of glitzy private life that people liked to read about. Nothing more, except perhaps her own prejudice against someone whose glamorous and charmed life seemed so far from the everyday concerns of an average person like her.

She supposed he expected her to push him away now and break their kiss. Instead, she slid her arms around his neck.

She met him kiss for kiss.

She wasn't going to run away from his challenge. She'd seen the way he'd looked at her tonight. He'd eaten her up with his eyes. No, Noah was far from immune to her, and she knew she had good odds of being the seducer rather than the seduced.

His arm snaked around her and pulled her flush up against him. He was all hard planes and muscles, big and male. And aroused, she thought, as a shiver went through her.

He lifted his head and sucked in a breath. His gaze was hot and intent. "You're weakening," he said, his voice raspy and hoarse with sexual excitement.

"So are you." She sounded breathless.

"Just the invitation I needed," he murmured.

"It wasn't an invitation. It was a warning."

He laughed softly and nuzzled her temple, then trailed whisper-light kisses along the side of her face. "I'm a risk taker, remember?"

He blew lightly into her ear and she shuddered. She felt sensitized to his every move.

He kissed and then sucked on her earlobe before nibbling along her neck. One hand was splayed on her bare upper back; the other had gone to cup her backside, nestling her closer to his arousal.

Her head fell back to afford him better access and she closed her eyes. It was becoming harder to tell who was the seducer and who the seduced as they both became caught up in the moment.

Only when light fingers of cool air caressed her did she realize he'd lowered the zipper on her halter top, which now gaped around her to reveal her strapless black bra.

She sought his gaze.

His face was flushed, his gaze taking her in. "You're beautiful." He trailed his fingers along the satiny fabric of the bra. "Sexy. Like a Christmas package just waiting to be unwrapped."

Her breasts felt hot, heavy and tight under his hungry gaze, and a quivery warmth settled in her middle.

Then he was kissing her again, and she soon discovered that, not only was it unclear who was seducing whom, but it no longer seemed to matter.

All that did matter was that he continue to do wickedly pleasurable things to her. Because she wanted him with an intensity that surprised her.

When he'd finished unhooking her bra, he broke their kiss and sat on the edge of the couch behind him to kiss and nuzzle her breasts.

She ran her fingers through his hair, which felt soft, thick and inviting, and caressed his thigh, which felt hard and sinewy, the muscles bunched.

She moaned as he laved one nipple and then blew softly on it, sending all her nerve endings into overdrive in the process.

"Noah…"

"Shh," he said. "Don't think. Just feel."

He moved to her other breast, repeating his attention, as she shuddered against him.

It was too much and not enough.

Finally, he lifted his head. "You've got the most beautiful breasts I've ever seen," he said thickly. He traced the edge of onc nipple, then the curve of her breast until she wanted to moan in response. "They're full but firm and uptilted. The nipples are tight and hot. Gorgeous."

His words sent heat coursing through her veins, arousing her even more. She tugged at his tuxedo tie until it hung loose and undone. "Let me see you."

Her hands went to the buttons of his shirt, while he shrugged out of his tux jacket. Once he'd gotten rid of his jacket and shirt, he pulled his white undershirt over his head and she was greeted by the sight of his smooth chest with its flat abs and defined muscles.

"Tit for tat. We're even," he said, his voice husky.

She ran her hands over his biceps, then trailed them over his chest. "You're in fantastic shape."

"I try even with my work schedule," he murmured back, cupping her face and drawing her down to him.

He kissed her deeply, giving her his tongue again and again, his hands on her breasts, then caressing her back, and then hiking her skirt so she could straddle his bent leg.

She moaned, her fingers tangling in his hair.

On and on, it went. Their movements more feverish, the slide of his leg against the juncture of her thighs sending her higher and higher while the brush of her leg against his arousal brought him more fully erect.

Finally, when she thought she could stand no more, he lifted his head and gazed at her. “I want you. Badly.”

She shook her head, sanity returning with a *thunk*. “We can’t.” She started to pull away but he held firm. “We shouldn’t even have kissed! I’m writing an article about your company. I need to remain impartial.” Not to mention the fact that she had an absolute rule against casual flings; they just didn’t agree with the women in her family.

He grimaced. “Believe me, I don’t think you’ve shown any problem remaining *impartial* where I was concerned in the past.”

“I don’t know what’s wrong with me tonight.”

He looked into her eyes. “I’ll tell you. Bentley Mathison. You were thrown for a loop.”

He saw too much, and she still didn’t want to talk about it. She gave him a shove, intending to get him to loosen his grip, but instead, she threw off his center of gravity, and he fell backward onto the couch, taking her with him.

They landed in a heap. Her breasts pressed against his chest, his erection nestled against her and their legs tangled together.

She froze. She felt him everywhere, and he felt *so* good. It had been months since she’d had sex, and before that she’d hardly been a swinger. Despite her seemingly glamorous life, a lot of her socializing was work-related.

And now here was Noah Whittaker: Heartthrob. Former racing stud. Playboy millionaire. Scion of one of Boston's leading families. Underneath her. On her couch.

Oh boy. She lifted her head and her eyes connected with his green ones.

The sides of his mouth had teased upward. "If you wanted to be on top, all you had to do was say so." Then he kissed her.

It was easy to kiss him back. After all, gravity was in Noah's favor. All she needed to do was relax—relax into him. It was all too easy.

He didn't grope. He didn't come on too strong or too fast. It was all seamless and smooth. She realized it took a lot of skill to make things seem so natural.

She was barely aware of his fingers slipping up her stockinged thigh, raising her skirt in the process, until his hand slid between her legs and made contact with the spot that was already hot and wet and wanting him.

She felt his touch—light, feathery and quick—and tensed against it. They really shouldn't be doing this.

Still, he was evoking a response from her. She moaned, pressing into his hand. Being with Noah felt delicious, wicked and, yes, forbidden.

"Let go, Kayla," he breathed into her ear. "Let go."

Yes. The whisper of his breath in her ear was the last push that led to her unraveling. She came then, responding to the sure touch of his fingers at her center, the tension of the evening rolling away from her, leaving her sapped and languid.

Slumped against him, she let out a shaky breath, surprised to find tears pricking her eyes, her head relaxing on the curve of his shoulder.

He stroked her back, not saying anything. At some point he caressed her hair, moving the sheet of it back to uncover her face.

She found it all very soothing—tender, really, which was the last emotion that she would have expected to experience with Noah.

"All right, now?" he said, his voice deep, and she felt his question as it rumbled up from his chest.

"Yes," she said quietly. And yet, she'd never been less all right in her life. A lot of things that she'd accepted as fixtures in her life had come unstuck tonight, and there was no putting them back into place.

Over the next few days, Kayla had a lot of time to ponder what had *almost* happened in her apartment on Saturday night and what, in fact, *had.*

Noah had taken down her defenses and had had a glimpse of what lay behind them, and there was no undoing that. He'd just been so *persistent,* but she couldn't seem to find it in her to get mad about it.

She'd also seen a side of him that, she was sure, was rarely on public display. He'd been amazingly kind and concerned when he'd seen her reaction to Bentley Mathison.

The only problem was that along with the newly found peace that had descended on her relationship with Noah came the realization she'd gotten intimately involved with the subject for her news story. A definite no-no in journalism.

And, she couldn't let herself forget, Noah was well skilled at seduction, just like Bentley Mathison had been twenty-eight years ago.

Therefore, there was no doubt in her mind, as she followed Noah around Whittaker Enterprises later that week, that she had to lay down the law: no kissing, no sexual touching and, above all, *no orgasms.* Just thinking about how she'd responded to him on Saturday night caused her to heat.

She jotted notes as Noah kept up a running monologue about nanotechnology, among other things, as they strolled the halls, occasionally stopping to talk to a team leader or other tech employee. The conversations were sprinkled with references to proton-powered molecular biomotors, zero-dimensional objects, quantum computing and entangled particles.

Finally Noah stopped and slanted her a look. "Are you getting all this?"

She looked up from her scribbling. "Yes."

"Great." He looked at his watch. "It's already after six. Want to catch some dinner?"

She took a deep breath. *She had to do this.* "Sorry. I can't."

"How about tomorrow night then?"

She shook her head.

Following him around today had been doing fluttery things to her pulse, not to mention making her all nervous and quivery. Being so close to him now, looking into his deep green eyes, she felt the full force of his compelling charisma, the type of charisma shared by the best sports stars and that sent their fans into paroxysms of screaming worshipfulness.

Plus, now that she'd experienced his warm and caring side the other night, she'd just lost her best defense against him. But resist him, she had to.

"Okay," he said easily, "what about the night after next?"

She took another fortifying breath. "Noah, we—I can't. It would be wrong. I'm here to do a story about Whittaker Enterprises. I can't compromise that. Thank you for being so supportive when I needed a shoulder to lean on after the charity benefit on Saturday night, but what happened afterward..."

"Shouldn't have?"

"Right." This was so hard, especially since she wanted him like crazy, and even though she was *crazy* for wanting him.

He took his time answering, shoving his hands into his pockets. "You should know I don't give up easily. Saturday night something started between us. I don't know about you but I vote for doing some more exploring."

She experienced a little thrill at his words despite herself. *Stop it,* she warned herself. Aloud, she said, "You promised you'd cooperate for this story."

He smiled wolfishly and leaned down toward her. "Yeah, but I didn't promise not to pursue you."

Suddenly she felt as if she'd been caught in a Venus

flytrap. From what she'd already seen, Noah's seduction skills were well honed. And she was weak. *Weak.*

He searched her face, then sighed and straightened. "How much more time did I promise you for this story?"

"Two weeks."

"Okay, you've got them, but after that, sweetheart—" he gave her an intense look "—the gloves come off. You've got two more weeks to finish this story. After that, I'm coming after you."

She should have responded that he could pursue all he wanted—she had no intention of giving in—but the words wouldn't come. Weak. *Weak.* All she managed to say was a lame "But people will think we were involved while I was writing this story, despite all our denials up until now. It'll undermine everything."

He took a step forward and rested his hands on the cubicle wall behind her so that she was trapped between his outstretched arms. Fortunately, it was after regular business hours and most of the staff had already departed.

"Let people think what they want," he said, gazing into her eyes. "I got used to ignoring most of what people say a long time ago."

"But—"

He ducked in for a quick kiss. "But nothing. Are you going to deny you're attracted to me?"

Unfortunately, she couldn't. And, if it was up to her to hold out against jumping into bed together, they were in big trouble.

* * *

Noah made his pursuit of Kayla more dogged as the days passed. He lured her to dinner one night. Two days later, when she was at Whittaker Enterprises again, he coaxed her into having a drink with him after work.

He was fiendishly persistent. But, because he'd promised not to, he didn't put any heavy moves on her—as much as it killed him not to. Now that he'd had a taste of her, he found himself wanting more.

Yeah, she was still a gossip columnist, and he was often gossip fodder. But she was also a leggy blond with a great shape, and he was weak. *Weak.*

Not only that, he liked the way she challenged him, refusing to be cowed. Sometimes, he admitted to himself, he worried about losing brain cells when talking with Huffy, Fluffy, Buffy or any of the rest of them. He remembered Kayla's jibe at the book-launch party about his taste in women, and now he let himself admit that what she'd said may have contained an iota of truth.

Still, he was patient with her. He bided his time. After the night at the Charlesbank Association event, he knew that building trust with Kayla was key. Now that he understood the nature of her relationship to Bentley Mathison, he figured being left by her biological father—even if she was too young to remember when it had happened—had done a lot to influence her relationship with men. Particularly men like him.

So, he pursued her unfalteringly but quietly. On Saturday afternoon, he got her to go out with him to a racetrack near the New Hampshire border where he still occasionally raced cars for fun. She'd tried to demur, but he'd argued it would give her a fuller picture of Noah Whittaker, computer guru.

So, she'd agreed to come along, ostensibly for research purposes, and he'd tamped down the well of satisfaction at having her along. If nothing else, it meant he could keep an eye on her. Because he'd be damned if he held back only to see some other guy take advantage of her availability.

When they arrived at the racetrack, he watched as she looked around. "Do you come here to keep your driving skills honed?" she asked.

"That, and doing a few laps around the track is a good way to blow off steam. It gets my mind focused on something different." He didn't expect her to understand about his love affair with fast cars. Nevertheless, he cocked his head and said, "Want to tag along and find out what it's like?"

"How?" she said. "Don't Indy cars have room only for the driver?"

"There are two-seater stock cars here at the track that they keep for instructors and students." Unlike low-to-the-ground, bullet-shaped Indy cars, stock cars superficially resembled regular cars on the road; they could be modified to include a front passenger seat.

"Didn't you race Indy cars professionally?" she asked quizzically.

He shrugged and gave her a wry smile. "Sometimes I race stock cars down here. I like the variety. Besides, stock-car racing's taken off in the past few years." He slipped his hands into the front pockets of his jeans. "So, are you game?"

She looked at him, then shrugged. "Sure, why not?"

"Yes?" He couldn't keep the surprise out of his voice.

"Mmm-hmm."

"Why?"

"Because you expected me to say no," she said wryly, her lips quirking.

Well, well, he mused. Apparently, his Ms. Rumor-Has-It—he didn't stop to analyze when she'd become *his* Ms. Rumor-Has-It—didn't shy away from a challenge. He found he liked that about her, and he filed the information away for future reference as they went to get the correct protective equipment and wait for their race car to be pulled out.

At the administrative office, they signed the required forms, and then he grinned as she tried on a helmet.

"How's this for a fashion statement?" she asked, amused.

"Would you believe *sexy?*" he replied.

The moment stretched out between them—fraught with need and suppressed desire—until she cleared her throat and said, "We should be getting back outside. The car's ready."

He had it bad. Since when did a woman in a helmet send his temperature shooting up?

When they'd walked back outside and were strapped into the race car, he said, "Last chance to bail. You know, no one will fault you for reporting from the sidelines on this one."

"Forget it."

"If you beg for mercy, I'll stop," he teased.

"Fat chance," she retorted.

He grinned. "Anyway, I plan to go easy for the, uh, virgin riders in the car."

She lowered her visor with a click and, chuckling, he angled the car onto the track.

The ride was like it usually was for him: the next best thing to sex. He accelerated to a cool one-hundred-fifty miles an hour, and they were jostled and bumped as the well-tuned machine roared beneath them and raced over the asphalt. His attention was focused on the racetrack ahead and on every pull and jerk of the car beneath him. Everything else faded into a peripheral blur as he took oncoming turns with smooth calibration, correcting for the car's tendency to head in a straight line.

It was fifteen minutes later when he finally pulled into the pit and stopped. When they got out of the car, he looked over at Kayla. Whatever he'd been expecting to see, it wasn't the grin that greeted him. She looked exhilarated.

"That was great!" she said, still holding her helmet.

His lips quirked up. Not a single one of the women he'd dated had shown any interest in racing, let alone riding in a car with him. The helmet alone would have ruined their hair—but Kayla was apparently a different breed.

"Are you sure you're not a speed addict?" he teased.

She arched a brow. "Oh, didn't I tell you? I *love* roller coasters. I guess *that* was one thing Samantha forgot to mention to you."

Her smile almost undid him. After that, it was a real effort to keep his hands off her. He wanted to make love with her again and again, mate with her, and stamp her as his.

It was crazy to get an acute stab of primal lust just because a woman liked speed, but there it was.

Fortunately, he knew his days of having to take cold showers were numbered. Soon, their remaining week and a half would be up and Kayla would announce she had enough to write her story.

"Really?" Noah said as casually as possible on Kayla's last day visiting Whittaker Enterprises on the following Tuesday.

"Yes," she said. "The article will be appearing in Thursday's paper. I want to thank you for your cooperation."

The way she said that last part had him focusing on her mouth. He wanted to kiss it. Now. He'd been patient, but his self-control had started to ebb.

"No problem," he murmured.

She shifted, seeming suddenly nervous. "Yes, everyone's been very helpful."

"Yeah." He strove to stay focused. "I hope you got enough about nanotechnology and its application to quantum computing."

She nodded. "I've got enough to know you're on the verge of some real breakthroughs here."

He nodded. "Yeah, it'll be great when we finally succeed in making a portable supercomputer."

He realized their conversation was becoming inane, but neither of them seemed able to stop talking. Suddenly struck with an idea, he said, "You know, the development team that just launched that new B-Smart PDA product on the market is going down to the Cayman Islands this coming weekend for a few days to celebrate at the firm's expense." At her raised eyebrows, he grinned. "Yeah, we treat our employees well. We have to. They're highly skilled, and our competition is stiff."

"Right," she said, looking like she was wondering where he was going with this.

"You should come down with us. It'll be a good postscript to the story you're writing and—who knows?—you may even get another story out of it."

He didn't have to add what they were both thinking: now that her story was about to be written and filed, her time was up and the gloves were off. If she came down to the Caymans, there was a good chance they'd wind up sleeping together. Pushing his luck where she was concerned had served him well so far, so he figured the tactic had a decent chance of working now.

"I don't know—"

"If it makes your journalistic soul feel better," he cajoled, "we've overbooked plane tickets. It'd be no different than journalists riding along on Air Force One when writing about the President."

She looked like she doubted it, so he changed tactics. "I've booked a hotel suite. It's got two bedrooms and two baths." He didn't have to state the obvious: he wouldn't pressure her to sleep with him, but if the opportunity arose…

"Traveling in style, huh?" she quipped.

He shrugged and said unapologetically, "One of the perks of the job."

She paused, then said, “Okay.”

As he looked into her upturned face, her golden-brown eyes wide and limpid, he knew, as she did, that there was a wealth of meaning behind that “okay,” and he planned to explore every nuance of it.

Eight

The Cayman Islands. They'd arrived at the airport on Grand Cayman just after lunchtime, having taken an early morning flight. From the moment Kayla had stepped off the plane, it had been warmth, sunshine and fun wherever she looked. Fun in the sun with Noah Whittaker. She still couldn't believe she'd agreed to come.

Noah had booked the penthouse hotel suite in one of the best island resorts, located right along the well-known Seven Mile Beach. The view from their hotel balcony was of endless ocean, which was bright and inviting in the daylight sun, and, Kayla supposed, dark and mysterious under the moon at night.

Looking down now at the bikini that she was wearing, she wondered whether it had seemed so small when she'd packed it—or whether it had just lost inches while airborne.

She spun in front of the mirror on the bathroom door. As she turned to the side, her gaze came to rest again on the king-size bed that dominated the hotel bedroom.

She'd known from the moment she'd accepted Noah's invitation that they'd wind up *there* together.

Yet, he hadn't pressured her. Instead, he'd taken over the other bedroom in the suite. But she knew, as surely as the sun rose in the morning, they would end up making love.

"Ready?" Noah called from the living room, causing her to jump a little.

She took a deep breath. "Just a minute."

She put on a sarong-like wrap that matched the tropical colors of her bikini, then grabbed her beach bag off the bed.

As soon as she exited the bedroom, any insecurities she had were erased.

"Wow," Noah said, taking her in with one glance.

Her laugh came out sounding nervous to her own ears. He was dressed only in swim trunks, and her pulse picked up.

His hands went to the sides of his head and moved it from side to side.

"What are you doing?"

He gave her a lopsided smile. "Wondering whether I'd come unglued."

She giggled, relaxing a little, and, realizing that was probably what he intended, relaxed even more.

"Let's go," he said, holding out his hand.

She took it—felt her hand encompassed by his bigger, sturdier one—and let herself be tugged out the door.

That afternoon they strolled the beach, taking in the disappearing rays of the sun before eating at one of the finer restaurants on the island.

She loved the local Caribbean cuisine with its emphasis on vibrant seasonings and regional staples such as coconut, plantain and yam. She had mahi-mahi encrusted with herbs and spices and also sampled some of Noah's beef tenderloin stuffed with lobster.

That night, exhausted from a long travel day, she fell onto her bed and was asleep before her head hit the pillow, saving her from making any awkward decision about sleeping with Noah.

The next morning, they woke early and Noah teased her about being out like a light the night before.

"What are we doing today?" she asked, dodging a direct reply to his comment as they ate breakfast at one of the resort's outdoor restaurants.

"Whatever you want. I'm all yours."

And *that* was what she was afraid of, she thought.

Still, she found herself having fun. In the morning, they went snorkeling in nearby reefs. Afterward, they took out a Wave Runner: she clung to his waist as the wind whipped her hair and they raced over the bluest water she'd ever seen.

She supposed she shouldn't have been surprised Noah enjoyed being active: he had the toned and well-muscled body of an athlete. The only surprise was that he combined physical pursuits with the career of a computer geek and the social life of a playboy.

As the day progressed, she found herself dwelling again and again on the contradiction at the heart of Noah Whittaker. Certainly, she'd done him a disservice by focusing on one aspect of his life in her column. She was coming to realize he was a complex, multifaceted man with layers beneath his easygoing facade.

Still, his go-go-go attitude soon had her calling him "Action Man," and teasingly asking whether he ever slept.

His response was to quirk a brow and joke, "According to your column, I spend most of my time in bed."

In response, she'd flushed and resolved not to give him another opening that led into dangerous territory.

Yet, despite having fun, she did find herself thinking back at a point or two during the day to what Ed had said about an illicit offshore company in the Cayman Islands possibly connected to Noah.

Of course, she'd come across no evidence of a connection, and the more she knew Noah, the more she believed a connection to be unlikely. Still, her mind skittered to the fact that she *was* in the Caymans, and if such a connection were to be found, now was the time to try to find it.

At the same time, she knew that finding out anything wouldn't be easy. Given how much secrecy was permitted to companies incorporated in the Caymans, she doubted she could get much information—at least without going down to the government records office herself and attempting to bribe, cajole or lie her way toward gaining access to information. And *that* would also entail lying to Noah so she could sneak away for a while.

No, she didn't have much of a shot. And, then again, there didn't seem much reason to try: Noah had given her a fantastic news story about Whittaker Enterprises. He'd lived up to his end of the bargain. With any luck, that story alone would shoot her career to a whole new level.

She should be relaxing and letting herself bask in the attention of a good-looking guy—just as Samantha had suggested. And, if she were honest with herself, she'd admit Noah was the most fascinating man she'd ever met. She was, in fact, having trouble keeping her hands off him, particularly since, for most of the day, he was dressed in nothing more than his swim trunks.

In the afternoon, they went scuba diving, jumping into the water from the back of a diving boat. They swam together and Noah waved to her, pointing out dazzlingly colored local fish, some swimming in schools. He'd brought along an underwater camera and snapped her picture.

Posing for a photo, she realized with some surprise that, over the past weeks, she'd become immersed in Noah's world and she kind of liked it. It really wasn't as bad as she'd built it up to be.

As their scuba boat approached shore, Noah glanced down at Kayla again. Even in a wet suit, with her hair plastered to her head, she looked great.

He'd done his best to keep his hands off her during

their time in the Caymans so far, not wanting to pressure her. Still, he was experiencing an odd, stir-crazy sensation that was increasing as evening approached.

Yet, while he was going mad with lust, she'd given him no sign that she was feeling similarly…pent up.

When they got back to shore, he asked, "What would you like to do with the rest of the day?"

He prayed she would say something energetic like parasailing, anything to take the edge off his mounting sexual frustration.

"What?" she asked in mock surprise. "No plans for windsurfing or waterskiing? There've got to be plenty of sports that we haven't tried yet."

Yeah, and he could name one that involved a bed, no clothing and plenty of sweaty exertion. Aloud, he said, "Nope. What do you want to do?"

He figured there was practically no chance she'd read his mind and exclaim, *Excellent! Just what I was thinking. Off to bed we go.*

She seemed to consider him, and he wondered for a second whether he'd spoken out loud or she'd picked up something in his expression.

She glanced away. "Hmm."

Was it his fevered imagination or did she seem uncomfortable?

She looked up at him. "Let's go into George Town and take in the shops."

"Great." He figured he did a passable job of looking enthusiastic about window shopping.

When they got into the convertible that he'd rented

at the airport on their arrival, he took the wheel for the short drive to George Town.

Stopped at an intersection, he glanced over at Kayla. She'd been quiet—subdued even—yet tense during the drive so far and, actually, since they'd gotten back from their scuba dive.

Puzzled, and because he was short on patience, he asked bluntly, "What?"

"I want to make love with you," she blurted, then clamped her mouth shut. She looked horrified at the words that had just come tumbling out of her mouth.

Noah felt as if he'd been hit over the head with a sledgehammer. Still, he struggled to appear casual…as if he hadn't been thirsting for this moment…as if, with parched throat, he hadn't just arrived at an oasis in the desert.

Then another thought intruded, and he groaned as he leaned forward and rested his forehead against the steering wheel.

"What?" she asked, sounding startled by his reaction.

"You just realized?" he said, his voice coming muffled to his own ears. "What about five minutes ago? When we were at the hotel and three steps away from a private room?"

She said nothing, and he sat up and hit the gas, turning right.

"What are you doing?"

"Making an illegal U-turn," he said. "Keep an eye out for the police."

A laugh escaped her.

Well, he thought, at least the tension between them had been broken. Now, if only he could get to the hotel room before the last of his self-control dissolved: her admission that she wanted him had already sent it plunging like a runaway elevator.

Out of the corner of his eye, he noticed she was tugging at the neckline of her top and the bikini beneath.

"What's wrong?" he asked, then he tossed her a wicked smile. "You know, I'd love for you to start stripping, but the island has a public-decency ordinance."

She gave an exasperated sigh. "Be serious! I'm just adjusting my bikini. The cups on this one sometimes shift out of place."

"That's right, talk dirty to me."

She laughed. "Hurry."

"What do you think I'm doing?" he asked with mock impatience.

Kayla was amazed at how aware she was of him. If she weren't feeling so desperate, she would have laughed.

Noah had looked thunderstruck at her blurted words. His unguarded reaction had erased any doubts about the response that her declaration would get.

Since their arrival in the Caymans, she'd been waiting for him to make a move, at moments so needy for him that she wanted to scream. Could she be blamed for coming out and saying what she wanted?

She chanced another glance at Noah behind the wheel of the car. He seemed to be driving with a single-minded urgency.

She couldn't believe she'd brought the mighty Noah Whittaker to the edge this way. Then again, not too long ago, she wouldn't have been able to imagine wanting to.

She stifled a nervous giggle.

He took his eyes off the road for a second. "What's so funny?" he demanded.

"You," she said. "Driving as if your life depended on it."

"Laugh while you can." He waggled his eyebrows. "Soon, very soon, baby, you'll be having a different reaction."

"Promises, promises," she retorted, even as she felt her face heat.

He looked at her again as they pulled up in front of the resort. "I can't remember the last time I was this desperate for someone."

Her heart lifted at his words. "Me, too."

They were like two teenagers as they strode across the lobby of the resort and into an elevator.

Once inside their hotel suite, Noah locked the door behind them, gave her a slow smile, backed her up against the wall and proceeded to claim possession of her mouth.

She sighed. He smelled of sand and surf and *male.*

Cupping her face with his hand, he pressed down on her chin with his thumb, opening her mouth wider and sinking more fully into their kiss.

She couldn't get enough of him. Their mouths met, angled, then feasted some more. He sipped at her bottom lip, sucking on its plump softness before his tongue slipped inside her mouth, lazily probing.

The kiss went on and on, gaining urgency as she molded herself to him. She moaned low in her throat, holding him close as the headiness of sensation swirled around them.

When he lifted his head, it was to place light, feathery kisses on her lips, her eyelids and along the curve of her jaw. "Do you know how hard it's been to keep my hands off you until now?" he muttered, his voice husky.

"Mmm," she said, her eyes closed, feeling him everywhere. "Then why did you?"

His laugh held a note of self-mockery. "Trying to prove to you that I wasn't untrustworthy."

She found it hard to think when his hand was kneading her breast through the material of her bikini and sleeveless blouse. "Hmm," she said, opening her eyes. "Seduce me, and I'll let you know whether you've lived up to my evil thoughts."

He laughed softly. "Are you inviting me to do my diabolic best?" he asked, his breath fanning her ear.

"Or worst," she heard herself say even as a voice in her head screamed, *Stop talking and take me!* "It depends on your perspective."

He stifled a laugh. "I don't think I've ever laughed so much while trying to get a woman into bed."

"Neither have I." She tried to clear her head. "I mean, while trying to get a man into bed."

Actually, she couldn't recall ever requesting before that a man make love to her—let alone seducing him into bed—but why quibble with details? Especially when she was concentrating on his hands at the buttons of her blouse, which hit the floor seconds before he disposed of his T-shirt.

She drank in the sight of him shirtless, a familiar sight from the past forty-eight hours, but one she could now openly admire instead of stealing surreptitious looks at. His chest was all hard planes and lean, sculpted muscle, his navel dusted with hair just a couple of shades darker than that on his head.

She let her hands trail over his smooth, tanned skin. "I've been wanting to do this since yesterday," she murmured.

"What?"

"Touch you."

"Yes." He said the word fervently, his hands tightening on her waist. "Touch me."

Below the waistband of his shorts, his arousal pressed against his zipper. She stroked upward.

"Ah, Kayla." The words were torn from him. "I want you so much."

He raked her with a hot gaze as he unsnapped his shorts and let them drop, so that only his swim trunks remained. A second later, he had her skirt pooled at her feet, so that only her bikini was left. "That bikini has been torturing me all day."

She'd never felt sexier than at that moment, knowing he wanted her with a keen need.

Before now, she'd never considered herself the type to make men weak. She knew she had some nice features, and, as a curvy blonde, was some guys' ideal, but she'd always been too straight-laced and serious to consider herself the bombshell type.

Noah, though, made her feel gloriously sexy.

His hands came up to cup her breasts and his thumbs stroked her distended nipples through the nylon of her bikini top.

A moan escaped her and her eyelids felt heavy. Hot, throbbing need coursed through her and settled like a dull ache at the juncture of her thighs.

"Look at me," he said, his voice deep with need. "Watch me make love to you."

She forced herself to focus on his face, which was tight with arousal. He bent his head and sipped from her lips, teasing her, as his hands began to explore her barely-clothed body.

His touch was light and fleeting, yet infinitely arousing. "Your skin is incredibly soft and smooth," he muttered.

"Moisturizer," she said inanely.

He chuckled, then kissed the side of her mouth. "All over?" His hand went to the juncture of her thighs and cupped her there. "Damp," he breathed in her ear.

Her eyes closed. She couldn't help herself. He was doing incredible things to her. His touch sure, deft…wicked.

"And it's got a lovely sun-kissed tone."

"Hmm?"

She heard his husky laugh. "Your skin. It's beautiful, like the rest of you."

Her eyes fluttered open again. "Cuban roots—thanks to my grandmother. I don't need a tan, but getting one will deepen the golden tone. It helps," she said, struggling to stay focused as he continued to rain kisses on unexpected places, "when you need to socialize with the summer-house set…and can't afford a real vacation…and fear sunlamps."

"Ah." His lips trailed across her jaw to her ear. His hand moved, cupped her rear end and brought her snug against him. "Remind me to thank your grandmother."

She moved against him and heard him groan, then gasped as he nibbled at her neck. "Noah…"

He lifted his head, his lips hovering above hers. "You called?" he breathed.

"Yes." Her eyes drifted closed as he bent closer. The kiss, when it came, was searing, deep and demanding.

She didn't know how much more she could stand. She couldn't remember ever wanting someone this much. And he was making sure she was brought to a fever pitch.

When he lifted his head, he looked down at her with hooded eyes, his face a mask of desire. "Now, baby?"

"Yes." She wanted to be joined to him, to know him in the most elemental way possible. "I need you."

"Yes," he muttered. "Oh, yeah." His hands went to her bikini top. He made short work of loosening it, then followed its descent with his mouth, sucking first on one breast, then the other.

She leaned against the wall behind her for support, but her relief was short-lived.

He straightened before her and slipped his hands beneath the band of her bikini panties, sliding her last piece of clothing off her in one fluid motion.

He got rid of his swim trunks then, and she allowed herself a moment to gaze at him. He was big, aroused and ready for her.

She licked dry lips and he half groaned, half laughed. She watched as he reached over to the entry table for the knapsack that he'd dropped there earlier. Reaching in, he pulled out a foil packet.

"Let me," she said, just because she itched to touch him.

He stopped in mid-motion and looked up.

"Let me," she repeated, taking the packet from him.

"Honey—"

She pressed a finger to his lips, not giving him a chance to say more. Then she slowly rolled the protection onto him.

He sucked in a breath.

"There," she said, looking up at him through her lashes, continuing to stroke him. "Done, but not done."

"Oh, we're not done, all right." He took a step toward her, backing her into the wall again. "Now where were we?"

A giggle escaped her and she took a step sideways, then another, inching away from him. "Don't you remember?"

He followed her progress. "It's coming back to me."

She laughed again before turning and making a run for it, dodging his arm as he tried to grab her.

He caught up with her at her bedroom, tumbling her backward onto the bed and coming down on top of her.

They sank onto the mattress together and she was blissfully aware of every inch of him.

"Oh, baby," he muttered, "I've got to have you."

"Yes," she said breathlessly.

And then he was there, probing, stretching her, causing them both to expel a breath when he was inside her. They began to move and set up a rhythm.

It was good, so good. She moaned. "Oh, yes."

"Kayla," he breathed, his face tense with pleasure. "Ah, honey."

She met his thrusts, riding the building pressure until their bodies were damp and sweaty, and still she clung to him.

And then, all at once, she went tumbling over the edge, calling his name as she spiraled into a universe of pure sensation.

He gave a hoarse groan, strained, thrust and seemed to follow her into a realm of exploding stars as he collapsed on top of her.

Nine

Kayla woke up the next morning feeling blissfully used, deliciously achy and thoroughly loved. Only the last gave her pause.

Love?

Sitting up, she looked over at Noah, still asleep, sprawled across most of the bed, the sheet riding low on his chest.

Yes, she *loved* Noah. Not because he'd just given her the best night of her life, though *that* element definitely couldn't be dismissed lightly. Rather, he'd scaled the ramparts even as she'd been manning the fortress of her heart. Underneath the surface of the carefree-playboy image was a guy who continued to surprise and challenge her. He was fantastically smart, teasingly funny and touchingly thoughtful.

That last quality had been on display when she'd run into Bentley Mathison. She'd been feeling vulnerable and weepy, and Noah had been right there to lend comfort and support.

She watched now as he stirred, his lashes flickering as he shifted.

"Hi," she said when he opened his eyes. It seemed like such an insignificant thing to say when her heart felt full to bursting with momentous news: *I love you.*

He smiled slowly and reached for her. "Hi yourself."

Laughing, she attempted to wiggle away even as he pulled her down next to him and proceeded to kiss her thoroughly.

Coming up for air, she glanced over at the alarm clock on the night table. Eleven. "We're sleeping the day away," she protested.

"Really?" he growled against her neck. "I can't think of a better way to spend it."

It wasn't until much later that they got out of bed.

While Noah showered and shaved, she padded into the living room area of the hotel suite in a bathrobe, intent on getting herself some orange juice from the small refrigerator there. She was feeling ravenously hungry.

Passing a console table on the way to the fridge, she glanced down and noticed a couple of legal-sized envelopes. Her eyes skimmed the writing on the top one: it was marked private and addressed to Noah from the registrar of companies in the Cayman Islands.

She paused, her pulse picking up. Despite herself, she inched aside the top-most envelope with her finger and read the writing on the one beneath it: it was addressed to Noah from a law firm on Grand Cayman.

Her mind raced back to what Ed had said to her about rumors of a mysterious offshore company connected to Noah. *A story like that could practically guarantee you the job you want.*

The private letters beckoned and mocked her.

She jumped when the phone rang. She picked it up from the console table next to her. "Hello?"

A tinkling laugh sounded at the other end. "Well, well. I'd heard the rumor but, I confess, I wasn't quite sure I believed it."

Kayla recognized the voice instantly. "What do you want, Sybil?"

She knew her voice sounded brusque, but she didn't care. The puffy little cloud she'd been walking on since waking up was suddenly seeming less buoyant and she couldn't help feeling annoyed at Sybil's intrusion.

"Now, now," Sybil responded, "no need to get touchy."

Kayla guessed that Sybil had called the front desk and asked for Noah Whittaker's room. What rotten luck that she just happened to be the one picking up.

"I called," Sybil continued, "only to confirm what I'd heard through the grapevine—you and our adorable Noah are having a romantic interlude in a tropical paradise. How delightful!" At Kayla's stony silence, Sybil laughed. "I don't want to intrude. I wish you only the best, Kayla dear." Her voice lowered confidingly. "But then I'm sure you're in good hands. Noah has a reputation as a fantastic lover."

Annoyed, Kayla responded, "Is there a purpose to this call, Sybil—other than to bandy about absurd conjectures, I mean?"

When Sybil's voice sounded again, it was cooler and overlaid with false hurt. "Kayla, darling, I'm just surprised, that's all, that you're in the Caymans with Noah. It was the last thing any of us expected, given what he let slip."

"Oh, and what would that be?" The minute the question was out of her mouth, she hated herself for asking.

"Why just that you're his latest fling, dear! You know, I'd said to myself, wouldn't it be delicious if Noah wound up promising a happily-ever-after to his old nemesis in the press? But, no—" Sybil sighed "—Noah corrected me right away. He just laughed and insisted that the day he got serious about you would be the day he'd call himself to feed me details about his private life." Sybil's tinkling laugh sounded again. "Can you believe what a naughty boy he is?"

Kayla felt numb. She wanted to laugh along with Sybil. She wanted to be blasé. *Yes, wasn't it all too funny?* she wanted to say. Instead, a dull ache was growing in the region of her heart. "I'm sorry, Sybil. I have to go," she said, then hung up.

When she'd replaced the receiver, she stood staring at the phone for a minute. She was a fool. A veritable paragon of naiveté.

She began to move around the room—opening the fridge, drinking some orange juice and looking out the window at the bright sunshine—but without taking anything in.

She'd been riding a wave of bliss this morning, spinning fantasies and imagining herself in love, when what she ought to have been doing was asking someone to smack some sense into her.

She and Noah had struck a bargain and, other than for fantastic sex, he hadn't strayed from that deal. Sure, she'd thought something more meaningful was developing between them, but hadn't she also learned that dreamers were losers in the game of love?

She'd heard the story of her mother's youthful indiscretion countless times, yet she'd gone ahead and more or less committed the same mistake herself: fooling herself into believing some wealthy and well-connected guy was interested in her for more than a fling. Her mother had gotten a hard lesson in rejection from Kayla's biological father, and she'd now set herself up for the same thing from Noah.

Hadn't she learned anything from her family history? From her biological father's failure even to acknowledge her?

It appeared not. She was a glutton for rejection.

Coming to a stop again next to the console table, she looked down at the correspondence she'd discovered minutes ago.

She was an even bigger fool for hesitating to read it. Didn't she want to be a hard-nosed journalist? What journalist worth her press pass would turn away from an opportunity like this?

Certainly not one who was going to be dumped after a casual affair. *Certainly not her.*

Drawing forth the sheets from the first envelope, she told herself that once she knew enough, she'd confront Noah.

The contents of the first envelope included copies of a memorandum and articles of association for a company called Medford. Noah Whittaker was listed as the sole shareholder.

She moved to the second envelope and scanned the contents of a cover letter addressed to Noah. The letter advised that an annual return had been filed for Medford and that disbursements to the tune of thousands of dollars had been funneled to the intended beneficiaries.

Perplexed, she scanned the correspondence again, trying to piece together more of the puzzle, when a low sound alerted her to the fact that she was no longer alone.

Raising her head, she found herself staring straight into Noah's frowning face.

Noah couldn't remember the last time he'd felt as good as this morning. Last night with Kayla had been great. No, more than great. They'd made love, fallen asleep and made love again…and again. It had been fantastic.

Which was why, as he emerged from the bedroom, he had a hard time processing the image that confronted him: namely, Kayla looking guilty as hell, holding a sheet of paper and standing next to the console table where, he now recalled, he'd absentmindedly left sensitive correspondence yesterday.

Damn. He felt his smile vanish.

"What are you doing?" he asked, having already formed an opinion but hoping to have it contradicted.

Kayla's chin came up. "Shouldn't I be asking *you* that question?" She held the paper out to him. "What is this?"

He felt his lips tighten as he moved toward her. "You went through my mail? You were snooping?"

How many times had he had to deal with invasions of his privacy? Photographers who'd put their high-powered lenses right up to the windshield of his car? Reporters who'd go into restaurants he'd just left and bribe other diners into divulging what he'd eaten and what he'd said?

"I'm a gossip columnist, remember?" she responded coolly. "Prying is my job."

What the heck was wrong with her? She was a far cry from the warm and willing woman that he'd held in his arms last night. In fact, she was acting like those colleagues of hers in the press who were the bane of his existence. *She'd* been the bane of his existence until recently.

"What the heck is that supposed to mean?" he asked, pulling the paper out of her hand. Glancing down and realizing it was the letter from his lawyer, he forced himself to tamp down on his temper. No one was supposed to know about Medford and his involvement with it. He'd gone to great lengths to ensure that.

"What do you think it means, Noah?" she demanded. "Did you expect me to set aside my journalist's instincts just because you arranged to have a little fun in the sun with me?"

He went stony. He'd had women slap him with less sting. "Right. Excuse me for thinking your career ambition might come second to loyalty to friends—or *lovers.*"

She laughed cynically. "Loyalty? And what would you know about that?"

He reached across her and grabbed the rest of the correspondence off the table. "Enough to think you'd be satisfied with our bargain and the news story that I'd fed you," he bit back. "Obviously, I was wrong."

She folded her arms. "And I suppose your concept of loyalty is flexible enough to encompass a love'em-and-leave'em philosophy?"

"What are you talking about?"

"Sybil LaBreck just called," she said, as if that explained everything.

"Yeah?" He thought for a second. "How the heck does she know we're down here?"

"We gossip columnists have our ways."

"You don't say."

She nodded. "Sybil seemed quite happy to have the rumors of our romantic idyll confirmed by my picking up the phone in the hotel suite that's booked under your name. She was just—how did she put it?—*surprised.*" She added, her voice dripping acid, "After all, you'd told her that the day you got serious about me would be the day that you called her yourself with a story for her column."

He had some vague recollection of running into Sybil at the Charlesbank Association charity event. She'd been irritating and had asked probing questions. She'd hinted that she suspected he and Kayla were really having an affair and not just attempting to bury the hatchet for appearance's sake. He recalled saying something dismissive in order to get rid of her. And now, it seemed, that *something* was coming back to haunt him.

Still, he wasn't going to try to explain to Kayla that the comment had been made half-jokingly in an attempt to make Sybil go away. Because what counted was that Kayla hadn't trusted him.

She hadn't trusted him enough to give him a chance to explain what he'd said to Sybil. If she'd trusted him, she wouldn't have sneaked into his private correspondence.

It was clear that she valued getting a story more than any feelings for him. And, given his experience with the press, he was ten kinds of sucker for ever thinking otherwise. Even if they'd made the earth move last night.

He held up the correspondence that he clutched in his hand and demanded, "You want to know what these papers are about?" When she made no reply, he continued, "I'll tell you—the worst ten seconds of my life."

She looked taken aback.

"That's right," he said. "The racing accident I'd give anything to undo."

She shook her head. "But those papers refer to a company called Medford."

"Right. The company that I formed for the sole purpose of supporting Jack's family since the accident."

"But that's a good thing..."

It gave him perverse satisfaction to see she seemed perplexed. "What? Are you disappointed you haven't discovered another scandal connected to me? Did you think I didn't know there'd been rumors—despite doing my best to keep Medford under wraps—that I was involved with a mysterious company in the Caymans?"

"But why create an offshore company? Why try to hide the fact that you're doing something good because...?"

He arched a brow. "Because, instead, people might believe I'm doing something bad? Is that what you were going to say?" He shrugged. "I didn't want Jack's family to know who was helping them."

"But why?"

She was pressing him for answers that he wasn't prepared to give. She had a journalist's doggedness all right and at the moment he was finding it damn irritating. "I just preferred it that way," he said, adding sarcastically, "is that okay with you?"

She unfolded her arms and looked shocked. "You still carry an enormous amount of guilt about the accident, don't you? Do you blame yourself?"

"What is this? Pop psychology 101?" he snapped.

He could swear a flash of hurt crossed her face. Well, that made two of them with open wounds.

"I was just asking."

"No, you were asking *and* snooping." The betrayal cut like a knife. She was prepared to sell him out for a moment's glory in the newspaper and a shot at a better job. Hell.

He turned his back on her abruptly.

"Where are you going?" she asked.

"To pack," he said curtly, not looking at her. Today was supposed to be their last day in the Caymans anyway. Might as well pack it in early. "It was fun while it lasted, honey, but now it's over."

Noah shoved his hands in his pockets and paced to the windows of his office, where he stared out unseeingly.

Surly. That described him to a T lately.

After the debacle with Kayla in the Caymans, he'd been mad as hell. He should have stayed mad as hell. Instead, he'd started to invent reasons to see her point of view. Had started to think maybe he was partly to blame.

Which was crazy. Just as crazy as the fact that he'd trusted a reporter to begin with. He needed his head examined.

To top it off, Sybil LaBreck was hot on their trail again. Her most recent headline, just after his return from the Caymans, had shouted: Is Noah Whittaker Finally Getting Paired Off? Sybil went on to detail his and Kayla's getaway in the Caymans despite his recent denials that anything romantic was going on.

He thought back to his face-off with Kayla in the Caymans. If he hadn't been so pissed off, he might have tried explaining to her about his comment to Sybil. At the time he'd tossed off the remark, all he'd wanted was to throw Sybil off the scent—because he'd already started lusting after Kayla intensely.

And the sex, when it had happened, *had* been incredible. Hotter and steamier than he'd fantasized. It had been good. *They'd* been good.

His mind went to the question that had been chewing at him more and more: was it fair of him to have expected Kayla to check her reporter's instincts at the door of their hotel suite?

That was precisely what he'd expected, he realized. Because of the sex, because he'd started wanting and needing her and because she'd gotten under his skin.

But, even if he had a right to be angry because she hadn't trusted him more, *he'd* been the one to leave the Medford correspondence lying around. And—he could now concede, putting himself in her shoes—Sybil's call had led her to believe he was an untrustworthy jerk.

"Troubles?"

He turned from the window and saw Matt standing in the open doorway to his office. "No more than usual."

Matt came in, shutting the door behind him. "Yeah, well you haven't been your usual self lately, and people have started to notice."

He shrugged as Matt sat on a corner of his desk. "We all have a bad week occasionally."

"Yeah, and yours happened to coincide with your return from the Caymans with Kayla Jones. Don't think people didn't notice."

"So, let people notice."

Matt shook his head resignedly. "Stashing a sexy reporter in your hotel room during a firm trip to the Caribbean?" Amusement darkened his brother's eyes. "Probably a first even for you."

"I'm usually not that stupid." Or gullible.

"Oh, I don't know about that," Matt drawled. "You've got a well-known weakness for hourglass blondes."

"Did you just come in here for a comedy break? Because, if that's the case, I don't have the time. I've got deadlines." Deadlines he didn't give a damn about at the moment and couldn't seem to get focused on trying to meet anyway. He walked over to his desk and started shuffling paper.

Matt hopped off and turned to face him. "Want to tell me about it?"

"In a word? No." Then he added, because he couldn't let it go at that, "She's all wrong for me."

Matt shook his head. "Doesn't matter."

Noah's head jerked up and he asked incredulously, *"Doesn't matter?"*

"Yup, you've got it bad, little brother. Resistance is futile."

"Yeah, right."

Matt sauntered toward the door, turning back when his hand was on the knob. "Call me when you're ready to acknowledge the power of the force—the *female* force, that is. In the meantime, stop trying to wipe the floor with everyone who crosses your path around here."

"Right, thanks," Noah grumbled.

Matt nodded his head. "Great. I'll consider the advice delivered then."

When his brother had gone, Noah dropped the papers he was holding. Matt knew nothing about it. Still, he'd give it another week. With any luck, he'd be able to get a grip for that long. Then he'd consider his options.

The weekend after their return from the Caymans, Kayla was moping. Ultimately, she and Noah had wound up taking different flights back to Boston because she was able to get on standby on an earlier flight. And, frankly, the urge to flee had won out over the impulse to stay and appear unmoved.

Because when Noah had said it was over, she knew he didn't just mean their mini-vacation in the Caymans. Their ill-advised affair was over, too.

On Saturday, Samantha called and asked if she could crash on Kayla's sofa bed that night because she'd be in Boston to catch a concert. The next morning, Kayla found her already awake in the living room, Samantha having let herself in late the night before with a spare key.

Samantha took one look at Kayla's face and guessed something was wrong. Though she got peppered with questions, Kayla dodged most of them. The confrontation with Noah was still too fresh and ugly.

Instead, she faced her computer screen and forced herself to edit a story for work. However, by lunchtime she'd given up. She'd edit a sentence and find her mind wandering, replaying and analyzing the argument with Noah and questioning her judgment.

She wondered now if she'd been too suspicious and had jumped to conclusions. Maybe she should have questioned him before opening the letter, instead of deciding to confront him afterward. And, given Noah's history with the press, she supposed she shouldn't have been surprised that he'd been annoyed when he'd caught her prying.

At that last thought, she stopped short. What was she doing? Maybe it had been wrong to look at his mail, but she was still a reporter—one who'd been doing a story on *him* and Whittaker Enterprises. Sure she'd been incensed by Sybil's phone call, but he hadn't denied treating her as no more than his latest blonde and letting everyone know it.

And, to add insult to injury, he'd had the nerve to make her fall in love with him.

She was an idiot.

She dropped her head against the computer monitor, then hit her forehead repeatedly.

"Kayla, what are you doing?" Samantha asked with a mixture of exasperation and amused alarm.

Before Kayla could answer, the apartment buzzer rang.

"I'll get it!" Samantha said. At the intercom, Kayla heard her say, "Who is it?"

"Allison Whittaker," came the reply.

Kayla raised her head and Samantha said, "It's—"

"I heard," Kayla responded, then sighed. "Tell her to come up."

Ten

When Allison entered the apartment, she said, "Sorry to drop in on you like this without warning."

"It's okay. It's a Whittaker trait that I'm already familiar with," Kayla said dryly.

Allison gave Kayla a knowing look as she shrugged out of her leather jacket. "My husband thinks I'm crazy for coming." Samantha reached for her jacket and Allison stuck out her hand. "Hi. I'm Allison, Noah Whittaker's younger sister."

"I'm Samantha, Kayla's little sister," Samantha replied, taking the outstretched hand. "Glad you're here. She's been in a funk all morning."

Allison broke into a toothy smile. "It's always the baby sister to the rescue. What would they do without us?"

"Dunno. I ask myself that all the time."

"Samantha!" Good grief, Kayla thought, did her sister have to tell the Whittakers everything? "And I was *not* in a funk."

"Yes, you were. I heard you. Under your breath, you were saying that word that's a one-letter difference from *funk.*"

Kayla rolled her eyes. Wasn't she entitled to feel a little blue every once in a while?

Noah's sister stifled a grin. "I wish I'd had a sister when I was growing up. Instead, I got the Marx Brothers—Chico, Harpo and Groucho."

"Which one's Noah?" Samantha asked as they went into the living room.

Allison cast them a sidelong look. "At the moment, he's definitely Groucho."

Kayla felt a strange thrill go through her. Covering the sudden feeling of discombobulation, she asked, "You stopped by because…?"

"I'm paying it forward."

At Kayla's confused look, Allison waved a hand. "It's a long story. Let's just say, we Whittakers like to assist each other, whether the help is wanted or not."

As Allison sank into the armchair, Samantha joined Kayla on the couch and said, "So, Groucho. Noah. Interesting."

Kayla shot her sister a wide-eyed quelling stare.

"Yup, Noah's been hard to live with," Allison said. "Or, I should say, hard to work with."

"Does he know you're here?" Kayla asked, then immediately wished she hadn't done so.

Allison shook her head. "No, and he hasn't confided in me either. Except, when I stopped by his office the other day, he got stony and monosyllabic when I mentioned Sybil's headline about the two of you in the Caymans together. He claimed nothing was going on, at least not anymore."

Kayla dropped her gaze.

"But," Allison continued, "I know *something* must be going on. Apparently, the word around the office is that Noah's been miserable to work with recently. Even Quentin and Matt have noticed it." She shrugged. "I put two and two together and came up with your address, but let me know if I'm wrong."

"Is that why you're here?" Kayla found herself asking, unwilling to give a direct reply.

Allison tilted her head and looked at her for a second. "Isn't it obvious why I'm here? I love my brother and he's miserable."

"And you think I'm the cause of it?"

"No, I think your leaving is the cause of it."

She wished Allison was right, but Allison didn't know how badly things had ended between her and Noah. She'd felt raw and weepy all week. And Allison and Samantha's understanding looks only made things worse. Suddenly emotional, she blinked rapidly.

"Want to tell us about it?" Allison asked sympathetically.

Kayla took a deep, uneven breath and waited for her

emotions to subside. Then an explanation of everything—well, almost everything—came tumbling out of her.

She detailed how she'd gone down to the Caymans, had answered Sybil's phone call and had wound up looking at Noah's private correspondence, following which she and Noah had argued.

She didn't go into the fact that she'd woken up all starry-eyed after a torrid night twisting the sheets with Noah. She'd replayed *those* scenes enough times in her mind.

When Kayla was done talking, Allison looked like she wanted to ask more questions about what Kayla had read in Noah's mail, but resisted the urge. Instead, she sighed. "My brothers. What they don't know about women I could write an encyclopedia about."

"What?" Kayla said, even though she'd heard perfectly well.

"I knew one of Noah's flippant comments would get him in trouble one day." Allison shook her head. "I mean, anyone can see he's hooked on you. Anything he's said to the contrary is just evidence that he's a fish realizing he's been caught on a hook."

Kayla tried to picture Noah as a fish caught on a line and failed.

"Well, I've always thought Kayla had an issue with trusting men," Samantha said, "and that it all went back to Bentley Mathison."

Now it was Allison's turn to say "What?"

Kayla shook her head. "Samantha's a psychology major. She's been reading one too many self-help books."

"Have not. Nobody in our family wants to listen to logic, that's all."

"What's any of this got to do with Bentley Mathison?" Allison put in.

Kayla shrugged in resignation. "He's my biological father."

"Wow," Allison said.

"I don't broadcast the fact," she said dryly, "and he doesn't know about our connection." She gave Allison a brief rundown on her mother's encounter with Bentley Mathison twenty-eight years ago.

Allison raised her eyebrows. "No wonder you looked shook up at the Charlesbank Association event."

"Was it that obvious?" Kayla said, startled.

"Well, you did look a little frazzled. That's the moment when I thought there was something going on between you and Noah. He acted all protective and concerned."

Kayla shook her head. "Maybe, but I wouldn't attach too much weight to it."

Allison gave her a shrewd look. "You know, Noah has plenty of faults. He can be too damn self-assured for his own good—"

"Yes, I know."

"But he's true to his word. He'd never have organized Whittaker Enterprises into a major force in the computer field if he hadn't been driven and good with the follow-through."

Kayla nodded. She knew that, of course.

She paused. Or did she?

Despite the fact that Noah had made sure to drive home to her that he wasn't like her biological father, when put to the test during their stay in the Caymans, had she fallen into the trap of thinking Noah was like Bentley Mathison?

Sure, there was a superficial resemblance to her biological father: both men were wealthy, possessed charm in spades, were successful with women, and had drive and ambition.

But Noah hadn't failed her. He'd kept to every single promise he'd made to her, including giving her unfettered access to Whittaker Enterprises.

In the past several weeks, she'd also come to realize he wasn't the pampered playboy she'd liked to portray him as in her column. He was way more complex than that.

And the truth was, if she'd been in his shoes and had had his history with the press, catching someone *she'd* just slept with snooping into *her* private correspondence would have made her crazy mad, too.

She looked at Samantha. "On second thought, maybe I ought to concede that you have a point."

"Of course I do!" her sister exclaimed.

She bit her lip. "What should I do?" she asked of no one in particular, the words just slipping out.

"That's up to you," Allison said.

"You know," Kayla said, uncertainty still gnawing at her, "he didn't even try to explain about his comment to Sybil."

"Typical," Allison responded. "He was probably so pissed off you'd jumped to the worst conclusion that he figured he shouldn't have to explain." She looked from Kayla's face to Samantha. "It's just the two of you? No other siblings?"

Kayla nodded.

"Right," Allison said briskly, leaning forward. "Listen, I grew up with three brothers, and I learned a few things. The male mind has two guiding principles—don't explain and don't ask for directions."

"You're kidding me," Samantha said laughingly.

Allison winked. "There's a self-help book waiting to be written there. Keep it in mind."

"Well, what do you think I should do?" Kayla asked. She wanted to believe Allison was right.

Allison stood up. "I'll leave that up to you. You'll think of something. Noah deserves a second chance, even though he's done nothing to explain himself. Trust me—I've seen the way he looks at you." She added, "It would be nice if life were smooth. The truth is, though, sometimes we come to a gap in the road and we just have to jump and hope for the best."

Trust, Kayla thought. Did she dare put it into play where Noah was concerned? But then, what choice did she have? She was in love with him. Who'd have thought?

When he got to work, Noah reached into the in-box on his desk and turned over a plain legal-sized envelope. There was no return address, yet suspicion curled within him. Later, he'd say it was an indefinable aura: the presence of *her.*

He slid his finger under the flap and, once he'd gotten the envelope open, two sheets came tumbling out.

It was the final draft of an article with Kayla's byline. The headline caught his eye immediately: Noah Whittaker's Secret Life Revealed. At the bottom of the first sheet, scrawled in ink, was a note that the article would be appearing in that day's edition of the *Sentinel.*

He froze.

She wouldn't. She hadn't.

Yet, his gut already told him otherwise.

Anger coursed through him. Hadn't she done enough to him? She'd wrung him out like a used washcloth and hung him out to dry.

Evidently, however, he was worth one more story, he fumed, and she was going to squeeze every bit of news that she could out of him.

He forced himself to read the article.

There was a description of his racing crash and its immediate repercussions. The article went on to discuss how Noah had gone back to the computer-technology field after leaving racing and had joined the family business, which he'd built into a major competitor in the computer field.

He read on, looking for and expecting an exposé of his secret involvement with Medford.

Instead, the article discussed how, contrary to his public image as a high-living playboy, Noah was a well-respected and hard-working entrepreneur who also had his eye on helping others—even if they didn't know that they were being helped.

That was it. No mention of Medford. No mention of the Cayman Islands. Nothing. The article concluded by saying that the author had discovered that Noah was much more complex and likable than his public image might have let on.

Noah put down the article and grasped his head in his hands. He knew without question who had sent the article to him. And now he knew why.

He'd believed Kayla to be treacherous. Now he found himself revisiting and revising that judgment.

He hadn't been able to forget her. In the past couple of weeks, he'd been in a foul mood, grousing to his brothers and cracking the whip with his subordinates. In general, he'd been a pain in the ass.

All because he'd been missing her. Wanting her.

Loving her.

He stopped.

Love. Was that what it was, this feeling of having his guts wrenched out of him, stomped on and shoved back into him upside down? This dull ache that he carried with him like an attaché case cuffed to his wrist?

Sure, he'd had the hots for a number of women in the past. He'd had crushes and, later on, serious cases of lust. He'd even had a couple of whirlwind affairs.

But none of those women had sucker-punched him, whipping the wind out of him the way that Kayla had. Certainly no one had gotten under his skin in the same way. No one had peeled away the layers and no one had kept on digging to get beneath the playboy facade.

He was glad it had been Kayla who'd finally done it and discovered the essence of him.

He raised his head, a wry smile tugging at his lips. With a sudden thought, he pulled open his desk drawer and found the photograph he'd tossed in there two weeks ago.

Kayla. She was smiling and happy and carefree in the Caymans—the best romantic idyll of his life. Her bikini molded the body that he'd come to know so well and that still made him ache at night.

Suddenly, he knew what he had to do. It was time for a call to Sybil LaBreck.

Out of habit, Kayla turned on her computer at work and clicked on the link on the *Boston World*'s Web site that brought her to Sybil LaBreck's column. Reading the headline, she nearly spewed her coffee. She set down her cup and dabbed at the hot liquid that had spilled when she'd jerked her arm away from her mouth.

Her eyes caught again on the headline: Ms. Rumor-Has-It Rumored to Have Gotten Noah Whittaker: Sweethearts to Walk Down the Aisle.

In all the times she'd read Sybil's column, she'd often been amused, sometimes annoyed, at being scooped, and occasionally disbelieving. This was the first time, however, that she'd been totally shocked.

It couldn't be! She'd never known Sybil to make things up out of whole cloth, but she supposed there was a first time for everything.

She forced herself to scroll down and read on: "Noah bought a four-carat sparkler for his honey."

She skimmed the article until her eyes came to rest on a quote purportedly from Noah himself: "'It's not an ark, but there's a twenty-foot yacht that I want to sail into all of our tomorrows with Kayla by my side.'"

Damn, damn, damn. She'd demand a retraction!

Sybil was in for one heck of a tough time. She'd be publicly embarrassed once it came out that what she'd printed wasn't true. And, of course, Noah could and probably would threaten to sue Sybil's socks off.

At the thought of Noah, she stopped.

She hadn't heard from him since she'd sent him a copy of her article. What was he thinking? He definitely wouldn't be happy about *this*—being linked in Sybil's column to her, a woman that he'd come to despise.

Unless, of course, he believed she was the source for Sybil's story? She dismissed the thought right away, then retrieved it. He wouldn't think so, would he?

She picked up the phone. There was only one way to answer that question. She dialed Whittaker Enterprises.

When she got through, Noah's secretary advised her that Noah was in a meeting. When Kayla asked when she could reach him, she was told he'd be out of his meeting within the hour, but then he'd be heading to the airport for an afternoon flight.

Not stopping to think, she grabbed her purse. She had to nip this story in the bud *today,* and that meant speaking with Noah *now.* They had to decide what to say when reporters inevitably started calling, not to mention how to curtail any more ridiculous stories from Sybil.

In addition, she promised herself, she was going to say her piece to Noah. Explain and apologize. Afterward, if he had her escorted off the premises by security guards, so be it.

Just as she slipped into her tailored jacket, however, she caught sight of Ed coming toward her, and groaned.

Ed slapped the copy of the *Boston World* that he was holding against his palm, his expression one of bemusement. "So," he boomed, his voice audible across the newsroom, "you've been holding out on us, Jones."

Kayla looked around. Because it wasn't even nine in the morning, the newsroom was mostly empty. Kayla sent up a prayer of thanks that her newsroom dramas seemed to occur before the office really got hopping.

To Ed, she said, not even pretending not to understand, "I know this will be hard to believe, Ed, but trust me. I'm not involved with Noah now, nor was I when I wrote that first story about Whittaker Enterprises."

She stopped to take a breath and Ed said, "Kid, one of these days I'm going to tell you how I met my wife while covering the biggest story of my career. Let's just say, a study in journalistic ethics it ain't."

She must have looked flummoxed, because Ed shrugged. "Hey, we're all human. Just keep your old newspaper friends in mind, will you, when you're schmoozing with the bigwigs?"

"Ed—" She stopped and shook her head. There were no bigwigs in her future, but she'd settle for keeping her job. All her explaining could come later, however, so instead she said, "Thanks, Ed," then took off down the hall.

She had a plane to beat.

Eleven

When Kayla got off the elevator at Whittaker Enterprises, she found Noah speaking with his secretary.

Just in time, she thought, then wondered whether what she felt was panic or relief. She barely had time to wipe clammy palms on her pants, however, before he looked up and caught sight of her.

"Hi," she said as she walked toward him. He looked delectable and she fought the urge to launch herself into his arms.

He turned to face her, shoving his hands in his pockets. "Hi."

"Can we talk?"

He nodded. To his secretary, he said, "Hold my calls."

"Right," the secretary replied, looking from Noah to Kayla speculatively.

When he'd ushered her into his office and closed the door, she took a deep breath and then plunged right in. "Have you seen Sybil's column today?"

He gave her an odd look. "Should I have?"

"Her headline claims the two of us are about to walk down the aisle!" Right away, she felt her face heat with embarrassment.

He arched an eyebrow.

"I just wanted to let you know that I had nothing to do with it."

"I didn't think you had," he said smoothly.

Relief seeped through her. "You didn't?"

"No." A wry smile curved his lips.

"I don't know who her source was, but—"

"I do."

"What?" *What?*

"I know who her source was."

He did? Well, no wonder he seemed so calm.

"Her source was very reliable," he went on. "He was totally trustworthy."

"Oh, right," she said crossly. "How reliable could he have been if he was totally mistaken?"

He cocked his head and gave her an inscrutable look. "How do you know he was wrong?"

"Because—" she spluttered. He was going to make her spell it out for him? "Because you…I…"

"Yes?"

"We're not getting married!" she exclaimed.

"Ah."

"Anyway," she said, changing the subject from a dangerous topic, "would you mind telling me who the source is?"

"A guy I know," he said enigmatically.

"A 'friend' of yours?" she asked disdainfully.

"He's a good guy," he countered. "Somewhat misunderstood and occasionally misguided, but well-intentioned."

"Uh-huh." He'd had the nerve to condemn her for being a gossip columnist, and yet he was all too ready to forgive a friend who'd run to the press with untruths. "Good guy, right!"

"Hey, you might hurt his feelings," he said, though he didn't look worried.

Far from it, actually. She paused as a touch of suspicion intruded. "How long have you known this friend?"

"Years. That's why I can vouch for his character."

Her suspicion grew and, with it, confusion. Was he playing with her? Did he believe he hadn't exacted enough retribution for her apparent betrayal in the Caymans? Was he angry about her news article and was this his way of punishing her? Or…?

She searched his face. He didn't look angry. If anything, he looked…expectant.

Her heart began to thud. "I'm surprised you're such good buddies with someone who'd run to the papers with details of your private life."

He held her gaze as he said, "Let's just say my friend's learned that society columns can serve a useful purpose."

"Really?" Well. "I didn't ask. Have I met this friend of yours?"

He took a step toward her. "You know him."

Her heart beat faster. "Is he good-looking?"

"Very." He took another step toward her.

"Oh." He was within touching distance of her now, and she was aware of every inch of him. "Smart?"

"I guess so."

"Funny?" Could that breathless voice be hers?

"Some say so."

"Oh."

"Why do you ask?" he asked, his voice low and husky.

She swept him a glance from beneath her lashes. "I may be in the market for a steady date."

A smile tugged at the corners of his lips. "Oh? That's too bad."

Her eyes opened wide. "Why?"

He shrugged. "Because I guess that means you won't be interested in this," he said, pulling something from his pocket.

He held it up, and the radiance of the diamond caught and reflected the light.

She gasped and lifted her gaze from the ring to his face.

"I was the source, Kayla. Because I love you, and I've been an ass."

He went down on one knee.

"Oh!" She felt tears threatening, then felt like an idiot for being able to manage only a half-coherent exclamation.

He took her hand, slipping the ring onto her third finger, as he gazed up at her. "Will you marry me?"

She looked at him through a sheen of tears. "I love you, too," she warbled.

His smile stayed in place. "I think the appropriate answer to that question is 'yes' or 'no.'"

He was joking, but his words were endearingly tinged with uncertainty.

"Yes!"

He rose then and folded her into his arms. The kiss that he gave her was soul-searchingly thorough, and she gave herself up to it.

She couldn't believe her luck, couldn't fathom how her dreams had come true. But, at this moment, she was content to revel in the fantasy turned reality.

Between kisses, she asked, "You planned this?"

"Mmm," he muttered before diving for her mouth again.

A moment later, she tried again, "I can't believe you planned this!"

He raised his head and smiled. A slow, intimate, caressing smile. "You know what they say, desperate times call for desperate measures. Sybil was only too happy to help."

Her eyes widened. "You mean you went to Sybil for help—"

He nodded, his smile widening. "She was quick to point out that I'd be eating crow." He added, his voice tinged with sheepishness, "You'll recall that I once said something to the effect that the day I got serious about you would be the day I'd call her myself with details about my personal life. Well, I can't imagine getting more serious about you than I am now."

"That's—" she began, then stopped as a thought intruded. "Your flight!" She looked around. "What time is it? You're going to miss it!"

He threw back his head and laughed.

Puzzled, she asked, "What's so funny?"

He managed to look sheepish and pleased with himself at the same time. "Er…"

Her eyes widened. "There is no flight, is there?"

She tried to slug him playfully but he caught her up in a bear hug. He kept laughing while she squirmed.

"All right," he admitted finally, "I convinced my secretary to say that I had a flight to catch. I was betting—no, hoping—you'd see the headline in Sybil's column and want to get to the bottom of the gossip right away. Just in case, though—" his guilty look deepened "—I decided to give you an extra reason to think you needed to come racing over here."

She looked at him. He'd gone to a fair amount of trouble. For her. She melted. "I suppose that explains why you were carrying an engagement ring in your pocket?"

"Yup."

"You move fast," she said laughingly. "Not that I'm complaining."

His mouth quirked up on one side. "I like speed, remember?"

She just gazed at him, this wonderful, funny, sweet

guy who'd taught her about trust, laughter and love. "I owe you an apology."

He loosened his hold and cocked his head. "For what?"

"For not trusting you more." She paused. "I thought you were just like Bentley Mathison because you have money and social status. I singled you out to be a favorite target of my column."

He rested his forehead against hers. "If it weren't for that column of yours, we would never have met." He gave her a quick kiss. "I'll always be grateful to Ms. Rumor-Has-It."

"You've done a major about-face," she teased.

"Well, I've learned a few lessons, too."

Now it was her turn to look interested and surprised.

He cleared his throat. "You were right that I've been a little rudderless since the accident." He shrugged. "I was torn up over Jack's death. The way I chose to cope was by turning to models and actresses and partying."

"And now you've turned to gossip columnists," she said impishly.

He cupped the side of her face, running his thumb over her lips. "I've discovered that gossip columnists have their charm, and that they have a difficult job, just like most other people."

"They're charming even when they dredge up the past?" she asked, unable to resist.

"Yeah," he said, holding her gaze. "Even then. Especially then."

Her heart lifted.

"I was wearing Jack's death like an old and familiar

shirt. I thought I had come to terms with it to some extent because I'd been rendered blameless by the official investigation and I was doing what I could to help his family." He paused for a few seconds. "I didn't realize how much I was still waiting for an absolution—until your article."

She nodded. "I was hoping you wouldn't be angry."

"I was when I first saw it, but then I actually took a look at what you'd written. Reading the article, I think I finally gave myself permission to forgive myself."

"I wanted to make amends," she said, "even though I thought I'd destroyed any chance of a relationship between us. And by the way, thanks to my story about Whittaker Enterprises, you're now looking at the newest business reporter at the *Sentinel*."

Noah laughed, then lifted her up and hugged her before setting her down again. "Fantastic!"

She knew she had a ridiculous grin on her face.

"So, who's taking over as Ms. Rumor-Has-It?"

"With any luck, Jody Donaldson and *not* my sister. Samantha has this ridiculous idea that the column is the way to meet guys."

"I like your sister. She's spunky."

"Well, don't worry, she's ready to welcome you into the family with open arms."

"Mine already thinks you're great for taking me down a peg or two," he teased, then got serious. "Speaking of family, what do you intend to do about Bentley Mathison?"

"Nothing." She thought a minute to figure out how

to express how she felt. "He obviously decided long ago not to have anything to do with my life, and, now that I've met him, I don't think I want to have anything to do with him either. And I've decided to stop beating up on myself for being genetically related to him. Genes are not destiny."

"Good," he said, appearing satisfied. "There's no use getting upset about things that you can't change, but realize there's a lot that you *can.*"

"I love you," she said. He knew her so well. This was what she'd yearned for…dreamed of. Noah understood her, so well, in fact, that she saw herself better.

A glint entered his eyes. "Want to demonstrate?"

Her eyes widened. *"Here?"*

He looked around the room. "Hmm," he said, "maybe you're right. We've only got the couch and the desk. It'd be better if we go to the firm's bedroom."

"The firm's bedroom?" she echoed, sure that whatever he was suggesting was scandalous.

His eyes crinkled. "Unofficially and euphemistically known around here as the *private* conference room." He winked. "It's a room for use by employees who are pulling a late night and don't have time to go home and catch some shuteye. But—" he leaned forward confidingly "—and I guess it's all right to share this with you since you're no longer Ms. Rumor-Has-It—it's been rumored to have been used for clandestine rendezvous."

Her gasp ended in a laugh. "No, we couldn't! People will see us!"

He waggled his brows. "Not if we're careful."

She started to protest again, but he grasped her hand, tugging her along.

Outside the office, she couldn't bring herself to look Noah's secretary in the eye as they passed her desk and Noah said, "I'll be out for a while, Maureen. Take messages, and ring me on my cell if the office is burning down."

They rode the elevator down a floor, anticipation and sexual energy crackling between them. When they exited and strode along the corridor below, Noah nodded to and acknowledged a couple of people as they passed. However, no one seemed to pay any particular attention to them.

When they turned a corner, Noah cast a quick look up and down the hallway before opening the nearest door and ushering her into a dimly lit room. He closed and locked the door behind him.

She looked around. The room was furnished with a double bed, a night table, a desk and a TV, and came equipped with its own bathroom.

She couldn't believe they were doing this! She nearly jumped when Noah slipped his arms around her from behind and nuzzled her neck. "Someone will hear," she said weakly.

"Don't worry," he said in a low voice. "This room has some soundproofing—an extra drywall to keep noise out—" he placed a kiss on her neck "—and in."

"Oh."

His hands stroked just below her breasts. "Though," he murmured, "we should probably try to keep down the decibel level."

"Think about your reputation in the office," she cajoled halfheartedly as his hands slid beneath her top and under her bra to cup her breasts. "If someone hears us…"

She trailed off as his hands caressed her.

Behind her, he was hard and hot. He blew into her ear. "Thanks to you, my *reputation* makes me the great seducer. I might as well try to live up to the title, don't you think? Where's the fun otherwise?"

Right. Of course.

The longer he kissed and caressed her, the more sense his logic made. In fact, he was starting to sound like a veritable genius…. She turned in his arms and pulled his head down to her for a hot kiss.

Soon his suit jacket hit the ground, followed by her top, and his shirt and tie.

He traced her cleavage along the contours of her lacy black bra. "Pretty," he murmured before divesting her of that item as well.

He slid his undershirt over his head and she trailed her fingertips over his flat, muscled chest and along the biceps of his arms.

Love had liberated her to admire him openly and desire him unabashedly. He was gorgeous and he was all hers.

The look in his eyes when her gaze connected with his again was filled with desire. "You're invited to touch me anywhere…and everywhere."

His words shivered over her skin, making her nipples tighten and the heaviness between her legs increase. She itched to be surrounded by him, consumed by him.

He bent and placed a kiss at the corner of her mouth. “Of course,” he said, “I expect reciprocal privileges.”

She heated at the thoughts that conjured.

He pulled her close then, and she gave herself up to a kiss that seared them both. The evidence of his need fueled her own.

When they broke apart, he said, “I’ve got to be with you,” and she could only think he’d given voice to her own need.

Quickly, they pulled off the rest of their clothes.

When he was gloriously naked, she reached out and stroked his erection, and he sucked in a breath. She watched as his eyes closed, his face a mask of need and desire and pleasure.

“You know we’re going to have a fantastic life together, don’t you?” he said hoarsely.

“Mmm-hmm,” she responded as she continued to stroke him, then added teasingly, “is this the fantastic part?”

Without waiting for a response, she dropped down and took him in her mouth, stroking and caressing him, hearing his hissed intake of breath.

“Oh, yeah,” he groaned. *“Kayla.”*

She took her time and, when she was done, she stood up and met his passion-clouded eyes.

“Wow,” he said hoarsely. Then he picked her up and tossed her on the bed. She let out a squeal but he cut it off with a swift kiss.

He trailed kisses down her body, blazing a trail of tingling sensation that caused her to shift restlessly. When he reached the juncture of her thighs, she whimpered.

"Shh," he whispered, his breath hot against her.

"Easy for you to say," she whispered back as his hands caressed her thighs.

"Trust me," he said soothingly.

And she did. In the deepest, truest sense, she realized, as he kissed her intimately, sending sparks shooting through her.

Her hands tangled in his hair. "Oh, Noah…"

When she thought she could stand no more, he lifted his head and reached for the pants that he'd discarded at the foot of the bed, then pulled out a small foil packet. He quickly donned protection, then stretched out next to her, gathering her into his arms.

She felt seductive, making love clandestinely with the man that she loved while wearing only the beautiful, sparkling engagement ring that he had given her.

He moved over her, seeking entry, and she shifted to accommodate him. She sighed as he slid inside her, and he expelled a breath that was half groan, half moan.

Then they moved together, loving each other and building to a crescendo that had her quivering and clinging to him.

"I love you," she gasped.

"Likewise," he replied on a groan.

She could feel the tension building within her, the world dimming. She knew she was close.

"So, is it enough?" he whispered in her ear, his breath coming heavily.

"More than I ever dreamed," she responded, and that was her last thought as she went tumbling over the edge along with him…and into their future.

Epilogue

"Who would have guessed Matt would be the last Whittaker standing," Noah said in disbelief. "The rest of us were running around trying to take each other out of the game while he just sat back and watched."

Allison nodded in agreement. "The fiend."

"Yeah," Noah joked. "To think he had the nerve to thwart your grand scheme to marry off all your annoying older brothers so you could rule the world."

He and Kayla, along with Elizabeth and Quentin and their baby, had shown up at Allison and Connor's townhouse in the Beacon Hill section of Boston to watch the New England Patriots take on the Pittsburgh Steelers in one of football's more heated rivalries. After his recent marriage to Allison, Connor had put his luxury condo on the market and moved into Allison's townhouse, though they had kept Connor's house in the Berkshires as their getaway home.

It was a blustery Sunday afternoon in November, and they were all sitting around Allison's family room, baby Nicholas asleep upstairs, waiting for the football game to start. Matt would have been there, too, but he'd begged off, citing an early dinner with some business associates.

"Matt plays his cards close to his chest," Quentin said. "We'll never know whether being the last unmarried Whittaker was his goal all along or whether things just happened that way. As we all know, Matt's always been sort of enigmatic."

"Well, I think it's time we got Matt to his happily-ever-after," Allison said. "After all, I tried to get you and Noah married off, and, Noah, you and Quentin helped me get married off. We practically owe it to Matt. I, for one, consider it almost my duty."

Noah and Quentin groaned in unison.

"What?" Allison demanded.

Noah and Quentin exchanged looks before Noah said, "Let's just say sometimes we wish you'd stop taking the sisterly loyalty thing to its illogical extreme."

"Ha, ha," Allison retorted. "The fact of the matter is, we have to do something—"

"And you're not above enlisting my help and Quent's," Noah finished.

Allison lifted her chin. "I'm not above making strategic alliances."

He snorted. "You're also not willing to concede defeat."

"The fact of the matter is," Allison said, ignoring him, "Matt doesn't stand a chance. I'm not above some scheming, and you and Quentin obviously know something about snagging a lifelong partner to head down the aisle with."

Noah cast her a skeptical look. "Just *how* are we supposed to get Matt shackled? He's notoriously private. I'm his brother, and I don't even know if he's seeing anyone."

Allison glanced over at Kayla. "Kayla would know. She gets the dirt on a lot of people."

Noah turned to gaze at Kayla, too. As usual, just looking at her made him feel good. Her hair was pulled back in a ponytail, and her ice-blue turtleneck contrasted nicely with the creaminess of her skin. He thought again about how much he loved her. "You know," he said, "you never did tell me who tipped you off about me for your column."

"Um." Kayla's eyes strayed to Allison.

Noah followed her gaze. "Don't tell me," he muttered.

Allison stopped with a glass raised halfway to her lips. "Don't flatter yourself."

Noah arched an eyebrow.

"Oh, all right." Allison made a dismissive gesture with her hand. "I may have said at a cocktail party or two, *There he goes! Go get 'im!* But only because I didn't want Kayla sniffing around *me* for a story."

"So you'd throw your own brother to the bloodhounds?" Noah asked in mock offense.

"No," Allison said archly, "but I'd feed him to the single women in the room." She looked from him to Kayla. "And I don't see you complaining."

He looked again at Kayla. He'd found love in the most unexpected place, but it worked for him. With her help, he'd put the past behind him instead of trying to forget it with an endless stream of women and parties. Though he and Kayla came from different backgrounds, it was like finding the other half of himself: *the better half.*

He dropped his arm onto Kayla's shoulders, pulling her to him. "Have I been complaining, Kayla?"

Kayla looked at the man who'd opened her eyes to a whole other level of closeness. Thanks to him, she'd learned that rejection and hurt and distrust weren't the inevitable consequence of loving someone who'd grown up in better circumstances than she had, just as she'd learned that those same circumstances of birth were the least important aspect of her relationship with Noah.

She looked now into Noah's green eyes, so happy that she was nearly giddy, and so secure in his love that she could tease right back. "Mmm, no complaints, but I'm spreading the word to Jody Donaldson and Sybil LaBreck that your title of Boston's most eligible bachelor should be passed on to Matt. As far as I know, he isn't seeing anyone."

Allison laughed.

Noah raised his eyebrows. "Honey," he pretended to plead, "don't tell me you're taking a cue from Allison and using the society pages for matchmaking."

Kayla smiled at him, while Quentin and Connor

joked about Noah joining the "married men's club," and Liz said, "Hear, hear!" in approval.

"You know what they say," Kayla said sweetly, just before Noah's lips claimed hers, "you can take the girl out of the gossip column, but you can't take the gossip columnist out of the girl."

* * * * *

EXPECTING LONERGAN'S BABY by Maureen Child

(Summer of Secrets)

Sam Lonergan was home only for one summer – until a night of explosive passion with the sexy housekeeper gave him a reason to stay.

THE SINS OF HIS PAST by Roxanne St Claire

Does paying for his sins mean leaving Kendra Locke, the only woman he'd ever wanted, for a second time? This time, would she walk away?

DYNASTIES: THE ELLIOTTS

CAUSE FOR SCANDAL by Anna DePalo

Sensible heiress Summer Elliott had posed as her flamboyant identical twin and bedded a rock star. Now the shocking truth is about to be revealed and she has some serious explaining to do!

THE FORBIDDEN TWIN by Susan Crosby

Seducing your twin sister's ex-fiancé by pretending to be her is not the best idea... Unless, like Scarlet Elliott, you've loved him for years and he willingly succumbs.

SEVEN-YEAR SEDUCTION by Heidi Betts

Would one week stranded together by a storm be enough to indulge in a seduction that's been seven years in the making?

THEIR MILLION-DOLLAR NIGHT by Katherine Garbera

(What Happens in Vegas...)

Businessman Max Williams has millions at stake, but one sexy, sinful ex-showgirl has him risking scandal – and proposing a merger.

On sale from 16th February 2007

Available at WHSmith, Tesco, ASDA, and all good bookshops

www.millsandboon.co.uk

INTRIGUE™

SECURITY MEASURES by Joanna Wayne

Vincent Magilenti had broken out of jail to find Candy Owens, the mother of his child and the woman whose testimony sent him away. But when their daughter disappeared, Vincent vowed to protect them both—even if it meant going back to prison.

THE MEDUSA PROJECT by Cindy Dees

Vanessa Blake was part of the first all-female Special Ops team in the US—the Medusa Project. Many wanted them to fail. But when their commander disappeared, the Medusas were the only ones the government could turn to to find him.

VOWS OF VENGEANCE by Rita Herron

Nighthawk Island

Stella Segall couldn't remember how she ended up in the seedy hotel room—or how the dead man got into her bed. Worse, she couldn't remember Luke Devlin, the sexy FBI agent who claimed to be her husband. Was she really a cold-blooded assassin?

DEVIL'S BARGAIN by Rachel Caine

Red Letter Days

Lucia Garza suspected she'd made a deal with the devil when she opened her detective agency. Every order came in a red envelope, and if she disobeyed, it could have meant someone's life or death. When she tried to get out, Lucia learned that the future of the world was at stake.

On sale from 16th February 2007

Available at WHSmith, Tesco, ASDA, and all good bookshops

www.millsandboon.co.uk